FREYDIS

A SAGA OF FREYDIS EIRIKSDATTER

DAUGHTERS OF FREYA, BOOK ONE

An imaginative interpretation based on historical fact

BY GUNHILD HAUGNES

The author can be reached at:

Email: gunhildhaugnes@msn.com

Website: gunhildhaugnes.no

Author page on Facebook: Gunhild Haugnes - Author

Series page on Facebook: Daughters of Freya - Series

English Edition, 2019

Translated by: Jennifer Kewley Draskau

Proofing/editing: Alexandra Lyngstad

Cover: Linn Tesli

Photo: Shutterstock/Valentina Zavgorodnyaya

Maps: Kjetil Waren Johnsen

ISBN: 978-82-999282-6-7 (ebook)

ISBN: 978-82-999282-5-0 (print-POD)

Norwegian Edition:

"Kvinnen ved jordas kant" 2017

Editor: Anne-Kristin Strøm

MAP
THE GREAT EXPLORERS

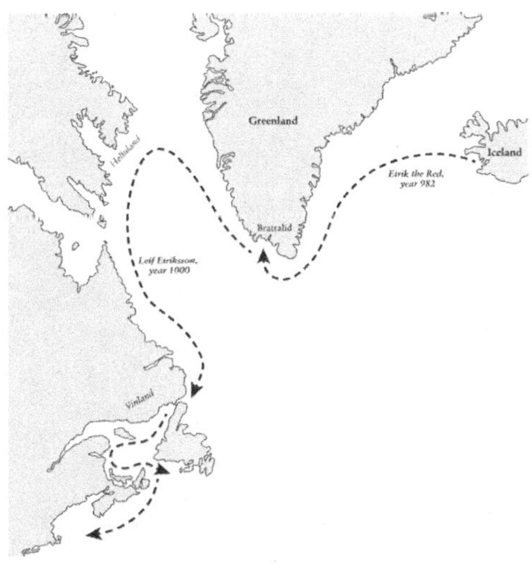

Eirik Raude discovered Greenland around the year 982 Leif Eiriksson discovered Vinland around the year 1000

QUOTES FROM NORWEGIAN BOOK BLOGS

The Norwegian title was "Kvinnen ved jordas kant" (The Woman on the Edge of the World).

Edge of a Word – Julie Karoline

> *"I loved this book. It brought me laughter and tears. It irritated me and delighted me. All in all, a very engaging book which I read very quickly. Recommended to all Vikings, especially those who wish to read more books featuring powerful women."* **DICE: 5**

My Criminal Mind – Ann Christin Berg

> *"I think Gunhild Haugnes is a fine writer. Her story draws the reader in. Despite the wealth of historical detail, the book is easy to read. It offers*

the reader new insights into the world of the Vikings, in an entertaining way." **DICE: 5**

Bok-Timmy

"Love thrills, strong female protagonists and the Viking age? Then look forward to the publication of this book. Also recommended to those who enjoy crime novels." **DICE : 5**

Tine sin blogg

"The book is based on historical fact and characters, brought to life by giving them thoughts and emotions."

Bokvrimmel

"The author's enthusiasm for her themes is evident, her feminism (if you will) and her main protagonist. Her Freydis won my heart..."

Min bok- og maleblogg – Åslaug

"I like reading historical novels, about the suffering and powerlessness experienced by both women and men, but also about their pleasures and their everyday lives. It is a long time since I had read anything about Norwegian history, and so this was a enjoyable read. I liked the tough, warlike red-head, Freydis."

Lukten av trykksverte

> *"The Woman on the Edge of the World was a book that caught my interest, possibly chiefly because of Freya, and the author's gift for description, so you almost feel you are present."*

More information at gunhildhaugnes.no

PROLOGUE

Greenland, the mouth of Eiriksfjord,
the year 1080

A GAUNT WOMAN stands alone on a rocky outcrop. She has stood there for a long time.

The woman has lowered her eyelids. She does not need to see the sea; She can sense it with all her being. That morning it had been shimmering blue. Now it is dark grey, almost black.

Her nostrils inhale the salty tang as she listens to the ever-increasing howling of the wind and its angry battle with the waves. She feels the dance as it grows ever wilder, whipping at her long white locks. The fair wind she has been waiting for is coming.

'I shall go out on the fjord today with young Eirik and the slaves,' she had informed her nephew Torgils that morning.

She found him on the sleeping bench in the heart of the longhouse as usual, wrapped up in seal and reindeer skins. He had been lying there for months.

Torgils had objected, of course, but without much conviction, only too aware that once her mind is made up, there is no dissuading her. Moreover, he had a good idea of her reason for wishing to sail with the men. Torgils often had such intuitions.

'A boat is no place for a woman. Besides, you are no spring chicken.'

'Neither are you,' she had retorted.

They had held each other's eyes in silence. A kindly gaze.

She gave him a silent nod, turned on her heel and strode out of his house with dignity.

She had always got on well with her brother's son. When she was widowed, he had given her leave to move into a house of her own on her childhood farm, Brattalid.

Torgils is an odd one. He came to Brattalid as a mere lad, sent there by his mother to live with his father, her eldest brother Leif. Torgils is Leif's only child, and he inherited the farm. He took no wife and has no offspring, but some years ago he gave Loke the slave permission to move into the longhouse. Now Loke has been dead for five years, and Torgils has never been the same.

A while later, the next master of Brattalid, young Eirik, and Unar, Arg and Hauk, the slaves, are making their way down to the beach and the ship.

There she stands, with wild flowing mane, her face deeply lined. The expression in her dark-green eyes is unfathomable. She is wearing an ankle-length robe of red wool. A thick black woollen cape is draped about her shoulders. In one hand she clutches a sturdy staff, decorated with brass, engraved with runes and studded with gems the same colour as her eyes.

Ignoring the men's loud complaints, who are reluctant to take her with them, she clambers aboard the *Dragon*. The ship that was once her father's pride and joy – Eirik the Red, Viking chieftain of Greenland. Now the ship is showing her age, the tooth of time has left its mark; She has been patched up again and again to repair damage incurred in incidents both great and small on her voyages on the high seas.

With the aid of her staff and her own stubbornness, she moves her frail body to the bow of the ship. She places one hand around the neck of the serpent, the carved wooden serpent whose head has reared above the waves on all the ship's voyages to Norway, Iceland and many other places.

The serpent remains as impressive as ever. She stays there as they sail out of the fjord to which her father gave his own name. Eiriksfjord – ever keeping her eyes on the open sea beyond.

They sail past a large iceberg that has been floating

in the fjord off Brattalid all summer long, melting. She does not hear the iceberg crack and then break with a loud crash into three pieces. She does not see that one of those pieces turns into a fox with a blue-green tail. The fox's head is turned towards the ship as it sails out of the fjord. Is it saying good-bye, or is it waiting for someone?

Not for an instant does she glance aside. She has seen it all before. The green meadows, the steep grey mountains, the rugged knolls, the fields, mauve, green and yellow, the streams, the beaches, the farms. Not least the beautiful shining blue and white blocks of ice drifting out of the ice fjord. Today there are not so many of them, so the ship slips past easily. Soon they are out of the fjord and the open sea lies ahead of them. Arg the slave is about to set a northerly course. Their destination is a farm a little further north where they will trade whale meat and blubber for mutton, fleeces and wool.

Abruptly the old woman turns around. She demands that they set her ashore on a small outcrop.

'No need to look for me on the way home,' she says, fixing her gaze on her great-grandson, young Eirik. He is a sprightly, enterprising fellow who will, she hopes, restore some order to Brattalid.

He makes no attempt to dissuade her from her purpose, but dutifully sets her ashore on the outcrop. Then he bows his head respectfully, turns and does not look back. Soon the ship disappears from view in the light sea mist.

But the woman takes no notice of it. Alone, she surrenders to the forces of nature. She is rigid as an iceberg – cold, hard, merciless.

At last, everything is ready. She opens her eyes. Far in the distance she glimpses the line, the line that separates the dark sea and the sky, a shade lighter. It is where she has always longed to go, to the far edge of the earth, where one world ends and another begins. The yawning abyss. Ginnungagap.

An ice floe drifts in from the left and gently floats to a halt right in front of her. Inviting her. She lets her woollen cape drop to the smooth rock. Discards her staff, too, and her sealskin mittens.

Her gnarled fingers grasp her skirts on either side. Her clothing is wet and heavy after the hours spent standing in seaspray. She raises her skirts. Then she raises her left foot.

LEIF'S FEAT

Greenland, Brattalid the year 1000

Day is breaking deep in Eiriksfjord. A heavy grey cloak has fallen over the mountains. Dew lies on the fresh green grass, studded with beautiful long-stemmed flowers, twinkling, yellow, blue, violet and white. It resembles a wonderful woven picture. And it smells so sweet.

Freydis thinks this is the best time of day. So quiet and peaceful. The murmur from the mountains sounds like harp music, the stream gurgles merrily and the wind sings along. The animals join in – the birds, the sheep, the cattle and all the others, each with their different sounds.

Today she has walked further than usual up over the meadows, unaware that this particular summer's day is going to mark a turning point in her life. Today, she will change from a child into an adult. She will become acquainted with sides of herself that she never knew she possessed. This day will also see the start of a new life for her whole family, for Brattalid, their family farm, indeed, for the whole of Greenland.

The seventeen-year-old has no fear of losing her way in the morning mist. She knows every hillock, every path, every hiding pace. She could walk here blindfolded.

Now she catches a glimpse of something she rarely sees so close to Brattalid: A herd of reindeer. Stately, noble creatures, calmly grazing or playfully testing one another with their antlers. They seem unaware that Freydis is staring at them; at any rate, it does not bother them.

Reindeer meat is the best meat there is. But the animals are so beautiful that she hardly likes to betray their presence to her father, although she knows it is her duty. They need all the food they can get – even their family, who live on the richest farm in the land.

Freydis takes her time before returning to Brattalid. She wants to relish the sight of the reindeer enjoying life as long as she can.

Suddenly she sees one reindeer standing on its own, a little away from the herd. Its head is bowed. It tries to walk, but it seems as though one of its forelegs is not working properly.

No doubt that one will be the first to lose its life when her father and his men begin the hunt.

A sudden depression overcomes her. They are the

same, she and that reindeer. She is not one of the herd either.

Although her father cares for her, she feels ostracised. Freydis is the youngest, the only girl, the only one born out of wedlock.

Her father's wife, Tjodhild, has always given Eirik's illegitimate child the cold shoulder. She treats her like a slave, at least whenever Eirik is not around.

Freydis has to do all the heavy work in the household and on the farm. She has to fetch water, wash, cook, light the fire in the hearth, take care of the livestock, gather moss and other winter fodder for them, weave. Weaving is the only part she likes and for which she has a talent. She hates all the other chores.

Freydis would really prefer to do the same work as the men on the farm. She is strong, and handles a sword well, better than her brothers. Had she been a man, and a Viking, these qualities would have been highly prized.

But she is a woman, and here in Greenland people are peaceful farmers. Eirik has promised Tjodhild that his Viking days with long voyages to new lands, plundering and killing, are a thing of the past.

Moreover, Freydis was born with a stormy temper. She has a very short fuse, something her two younger brothers have always known how to exploit.

The youngest, Torstein, with the big blue eyes and the golden curls, teases her the most. Hardly a day goes by without him putting a worm or some other disgusting object in her bed or hiding her hair clips or other things belonging to her. Freydis always rises to it, flying into a rage and running shrieking after the giggling Torstein.

Dark-haired Torvald, bow-legged and jug-eared, is more cunning. He lays traps for her. She might stumble over a rope he has stretched in her path, he might steal her milk buckets or piss on the clothes she has hung out to dry.

Freydis sighs. She can no longer put it off: the day's first meeting with Tjodhild. Her hateful glare and her sharp tongue. Again she will be bitterly reprimanded for failing to fulfil her morning duties. She has not lit the fire, and she has not milked the cows.

She is just about to turn and head for home when a figure slowly emerges from the mist. A short, crooked woman in a blue-green dress, wearing a worn brown apron. She wears catskin gloves and carries a stick in her hand. Her wispy greying hair is crowned with a pointed dark red hat. She says no word of greeting, but scurries past Freydis, then halts and stares into the paler mist that lies over the fjord.

Freydis is not taken aback by this, she has encountered this woman many times before on her morning rambles. She is somewhat strange, this Torbjorg Lillevolven, as they call her. She can see into the future. She is a wise woman, a soothsayer. Many seek her advice, about everything from illnesses and love affairs to weather and crops. She is reputed to have been one of nine sisters, all of whom possessed special gifts. Torbjorg appears to be the only one of them still alive. So they say. They say many things about Torbjorg.

She draws a deep breath, still without looking at Freydis.

'He is coming today', she says in a gruff voice.

'Who? Who is coming?' The girl asks, surprised. It is the first time Torbjorg has ever spoken to her.

'Your brother'.

For a moment Freydis stands stock-still, trying to take in Torbjorg's words. Then she sprints as fast as her legs will carry her, down across the green meadow to Brattalid. Her dark-blue skirt dances with joy and her long red hair flows in the gentle breeze.

Leif is coming home, Leif is coming home. Oh, how she has longed for this moment! He has been away so long, for two whole years. She has been so afraid she might never see him again.

Torbjorg stands looking after her, shaking her head. Her brow is deeply furrowed. The reunion with her brother will probably not be as joyful as Freydis hopes, she thinks to herself. The skeletal wise woman groans, wriggling a little, seeking a position which will ease the pains that rack her spine. She rests her hands heavily on her walking stick. She recalls the first time she ever saw Freydis Eiriksdatter. It was in Iceland, only fifteen years ago, though it feels much longer.

She was in Snaefellsnes near Breidafjord, on the west side of the island where there are volcanoes and glaciers. Eirik the Red and his crew were sailing homeward after three years' banishment as outlaws.

Eirik the Red, even as a young newcomer to Iceland, was a man of war. Once, his slaves accidentally caused an avalanche which damaged a neighbour's farm. The neighbour slew the slaves, and Eirik killed the neighbour.

The Red-haired Norwegian was also challenged to a sword fight with a man by the menacing name of Holmgang-Ravn. Holmgang-Ravn's body soon lay lifeless on the ground, while the arrogant Eirik the Red brandished his sword above his head and yelled in triumph.

These two events forced Eirik the Red and his family to move away. He built himself a new farm. But before long he was involved in a quarrel at the new place, this time with his neighbour Torgest. The cause of the dispute was some high chair pillars which Torgest had borrowed from Eirik and refused to return. They had been brought from Norway by Eirik's father, Torvald Asvaldsson.

It ended with a fight in which Eirik the Red and his men slew Torgest's two sons and some other men. Because of his part in this, the Ting sentenced Eirik the Red to stay away from Iceland for three years. He quickly decided that he would set sail and seek a land to the west, which his friend Gunnbjorn Ulvsson had once seen when he was blown off course.

Shortly afterwards, he sailed his ship out of Breidafjord with a crew of twenty. Hunters, farmers, fishermen, sailors – men who could build a farm. There were also slaves on board, two of them women.

Eirik's friends and enemies alike wondered if he would find that land, or make his way to some other land, or vanish at sea without trace. Most, no doubt, never expected him to return.

But Torbjorg knew they would see Eirik the Red

again. She knew it, but she told no-one. Nobody asked her anyway, not even Tjodhild, his wife. Perhaps she was afraid to.

People wanted to keep on the right side of Torbjorg to catch a glimpse of the future, which she saw at times with startling clarity. But they were afraid of her, too. They thought she was a sorceress, and perhaps she was. But she never used that power, certainly not for evil.

The years passed, and Eirik had paid his penalty. Then one day there was commotion in their little village. A smallholder from far up the fjord came riding into the yard of one of the large farms.

'Eirik the Red's back, he's sailing into the fjord right now!' he shouted, breathless, as he attempted to calm his excited steed. The people on the farm flocked around him, clamouring.

'Eirik the Red? Are you sure?' The landowner himself had come out on the stairs.

'Yes, it's the *Dragon*. I recognise that bow. There's no other like it.'

Then the messenger clapped his heels to his horse's flanks and galloped off. The rumour spread like wildfire, and people rushed down to the beaches. Some jumped into boats, others ran or rode along the fjord.

And soon they all saw it, the mighty ship sailing slowly into the fjord. It had a few gashes here and there but was otherwise in good shape. The forces of nature were smiling on Eirik that day. There was just enough wind that the crew did not have to take to their oars. The sun shone from an almost cloudless sky. Some of the men on board had stripped off their upper garments. They waved and shouted boisterously at the people watching.

But Eirik had kept all his clothes on – dark-blue trousers and a white linen shirt. Over the broad, blood-red cloak he wore at his wedding. His unruly locks and his beard were almost as red as his cloak. He stood tall in the bow of his ship with a broad grin on his face. He was holding something in his arms.

It was only when he stepped ashore that they saw what it was. A tiny girl, with a mane of flame-red hair. The child shrieked with laughter, and Eirik the Red laughed back at her.

The crew was greeted by a crowd of people who flocked around them. Family, neighbours, friends, and perhaps some inquisitive enemies. Tjodhild stood at their head, looking resplendent in a white gown. Her dark hair was severely bound in a bun at her neck. Her three sons took their places at her side.

The ship was laden with furs, meat and other wonderful things. But Tjodhild did not care. She stood there, arms crossed over her chest, and watched them disembark with eyes full of fire. Eirik strode up to his wife, leading the little girl with his right hand.

'Your beloved husband has returned to you,' he announced.

He went in for a warm embrace, but she turned away. Eirik then picked the little girl up and tried to hand her to Tjodhild, but she kept her arms firmly crossed.

'Who's this, then?' she demanded, tight-lipped.

'This is my daughter, Freydis,' her husband replied, staring firmly at his wife.

'So you have a daughter now. And where's the mother?'

'Ragni is her mother, as you might guess. She's dead,' Eirik said. There was a glint of pain in his sea-green eyes.

'Your concubine was with child? A bastard child, then. She will sleep with the slaves where she belongs.'

Tjodhild's voice was as hard and cold as Snaefell-sjoekul, the glacier at the mouth of Breidafjord. But her husband was undeterred.

'Freydis is my daughter, and she will be treated accordingly. You will take care of her and make sure she learns what she needs to know.'

He set the two year old child down at Tjodhild's feet. He then threw his arms up, grinned broadly and waved at the cheering crowd.

Eirik the Red was showing himself at his most endearing. Men and women alike were entranced by his gleaming smile, his silver tongue, his proud posture which made him seem taller than he really was. People buzzed about him. They all wanted to hear about his voyage. They had a thousand questions for him. Where had they been? What had they done? Had he discovered the land that Gunnbjorn had seen?

Eirik was only too happy to tell them about the fertile land they had discovered to the west. He was already enticing people to settle in the land he had called Greenland.

Torbjorg kept her distance from the events, as was her way. She had never fitted in with ordinary folk, destined as she was for a life on her own.

But she noticed the brief glares of hatred that Tjodhild sent her husband and his daughter.

Eirik's sons initially stood dumbstruck, overshadowed by the icy exchange between their mother and father. But the younger two, Torvald and Torstein, quickly set off after their father. Unlike their mother, they had every intention of basking in the glory of their father's magnificent discovery.

Leif, the eldest, clearly felt sympathy for his confused little sister, who did not know what to do when her father disappeared from view. He squatted so he could look her straight in the eye.

'Freydis, is that your name?' he asked, smiling.

'Yes, I'm Freydis Eiriksdatter.' She was on the verge of tears as she looked at him with her huge round eyes.

'That's a nice name. My name is Leif. I'm your big brother.'

'I want to go to Father.'

'Come on then, let's go and look for him,' Leif said. He lifted her up, held her close against his breast and set off after the others.

The next year, Eirik sailed for Greenland again, this time accompanied by his family and twenty-four more ships. The ships were laden to the gunwales with men, women, children, sheep, pigs, cattle, horses, household goods, timber, weapons, food, seed corn – almost everything they thought they would need. They had sold their farms and were leaving everything behind. The Icelanders were dreaming of starting a new and better life in Greenland. Torbjorg went along too.

On the day of their departure the air was buzzing with anticipation and the thrill of adventure. The ships needed to be in top condition, the sails, oars and everything else too. The discoverer of Greenland spoke with all of them, doling out encouragements and good advice.

Only fourteen ships reached Greenland. Some of them had been captained by unseasoned mariners. Their inexperience proved fatal on the tempestuous seas. Some foundered, others turned back before it was too late.

Those who made it all the way raised their arms to the sky and shouted with joy when they encountered seals, birds and a sea rich with fish and other marine life. Their excitement increased when they sailed into the south-western fjords. Eirik the Red had not lied to them. Here were good green pastures for their livestock. A land full of promise, they agreed.

The undisputed chieftain of Greenland, who had investigated the land thoroughly in advance, distributed the mild south-westerly fjords among his wealthy friends. He even named the fjords after them. In his own fjord, Eiriksfjord, he had already built the first house on his farm, Brattalid.

Smallholders and liberated slaves were given the land that was left over. There was room for all.

While Torbjorg is lost in her reverie, remembering

these bygone days, Freydis has reached Brattalid. She rushes into the yard, her long hair sticking to her sweaty face. She is immediately attacked by a furious Tjodhild.

Her stepmother is wearing her usual worn brown work skirt. She has bound a brown scarf tightly about her head. In her arms she carries a heavy trough.

'Where have you been, bastard girl? Get back to work at once!' she spits.

'None of your business!' Freydis shouts, running past her straight towards the horse. With an agile leap she springs on to its back and gallops off, followed by yells of fury from Tjodhild.

Freydis has no intention of informing Tjodhild that her eldest son is about to arrive. She has no intention of telling anyone. She wants to be the first to see him as he sails into the fjord. She does not doubt for a minute that Torbjorg is right. She knows with her whole being that Leif is on his way.

She drives the horse on at full gallop across the beach, wanting to reach the farthest point possible. Only her father's faithful Brosi follows her, barking, for part of the way, but then he gives up and trots back, ears drooping. Freydis does not pull up before she reaches a promontory which affords a full view of the bay.

The sun has risen high in the pale blue sky, its rays gilding the peaks of the little waves with silver.

Freydis quickly tears off her clothes and runs out into the sea. She must be clean and pure when Leif returns. The ice-cold water is so delicious. Afterwards she lies on the bare rock, arms and legs spread wide. The sun's rays dry and warm her naked body.

Then she gets dressed again and sits down on the very edge of the cliff, her legs drawn up to her chest. She is ready.

The waiting is long. She passes the time studying the closest icebergs, which have broken off from the great glacier in the heart of the ice fjord and floated down into Eiriksfjord this summer. One resembles a bear, another looks like a gaping mouth, a third, a reindeer in full flight. Reindeer. That's right. She must remember to tell her father about the reindeer.

She smiles to herself, thinking of her big brother. The only people she cares about in the whole world are her father and Leif, and she loves them fiercely.

Leif, with his cheerful nature and infectious laughter. He has always been kind to her. He is the handsomest of the brothers, with his manly stature, shining straight fair hair,

deep blue eyes and even features.

Her big brother resembles neither his father nor his mother, but Eirik always says there is much of his grandfather in Leif – the notorious Torvald Asvaldsson, who was forced to leave Jaeren and Norway and settle in Iceland. Like his son, he had been accused of murder. But Torvald had better control over his fiery temper than Eirik has. So has Leif.

It was Leif who taught her to ride, and they rode out together often in Greenland. This is how she had come to know her own country. She sits up and straightens her back at the thought that she was the first person to be born here.

Her eldest brother is also a master mariner. In that area, his skill even surpasses that of his father. It seems as though Leif has an innate understanding of the sea, the winds and waves, as though he were at one with them. He can foresee what is to come.

She remembers a time when she got to go fishing with him, far out at sea. The day was warm, with hardly a breath of wind. They just lay bobbing out there on the sea, hauling in fish, swapping stories.

Suddenly Leif barked out an order. They needed to move inshore as quickly as possible. None of the crew had sensed anything untoward, but they jumped to obey the chieftain's son's orders.

They had barely entered Eiriksfjord when a violent storm broke out. It would have been rough had they still been on the open sea.

'How did you know the storm was coming?' Freydis asked, once they were safely back at Brattalid.

'Something in the air, a tremor. And I looked at the birds, too.'

'What about the birds?'

'The way they were acting,' he replied airily.

But even though Leif is the greatest mariner in all Greenland, she has worried about him. He was not supposed to stay away for more than one winter, and now he had been away for two. But at last he is coming home. She is trembling with excitement.

Not until the late afternoon does she catch a glimpse of movement in the fjord. She gets to her feet and stands, staring out. Rearing its head skyward, a bow. A striped canvas, a sail. Something splashing in the shining bright mirror of the water, oars.

She has no doubt. It is a ship, and it is approaching. Now they have stopped rowing, the cool breeze drives the ship slowly forward.

She squeals with joy when she sees the familiar serpent's head carved on the bow.

Leif commands a ship that is twin to his father's old pride, the *Dragon*. Eirik ordered a serpent's head to be carved on the prow of his eldest son's ship, too. It would protect the ship's crew from the magic of the deep and from sea monsters. He got his way. Leif chose to call his ship the *Serpent*.

Soon the ship is so close that she can see people on board. It was not nearly so crowded when they left. Is Leif bringing guests? New settlers?

She stops speculating when she sees her brother – her wonderful big brother with his long blond hair. It has grown even longer, and he has grown a beard, too. He looks so much more grown-up than when he left. He is so handsome. Freydis waves her arms, jumps up and down, calling Leif's name, and he hears her, and waves back, grinning broadly.

Quickly she jumps back on the horse and pushes it as hard as she can. She needs to get back to Brattalid as fast as possible.

Leif watches her, his eyes smiling. He is glad to see his little sister again, and the familiar fjord opening before him. At last he is back in Greenland.

He lifts a hand to shield his eyes from the sun's glare. Now he can make out Brattalid in the distance, the farm he came to as a young lad and which he grew to love. It looks so small. But it is good to be coming home, nonetheless, especially from such a spectacular expedition.

He turns to his crew. Many of them are waving towards the shore, shouting with delight. Leif looks at his faithful helmsman, Hallvard.

'Can you make ready for landing one last time?'

'Ready. Shall I strike sail too?'

'Wait as long as you can before doing that, but give the order to the crew to start rowing.'

Then he turns to Turid, a sturdy slave woman who has been responsible for the victuals on board.

'How are the Icelanders faring?'

'As well as can be, but some of them are really feeling the cold. They need to get ashore and warm up by the fire,' she says.

'They soon will. We are nearly there,' Leif replies.

The longhouse fire. Tonight, when they are all gathered around it, he will warm their hearts with the tales of their voyage. He eyes the valuable cargo he has accumulated by honourable and lawful means.

Unlike his father, he has not won it by pillaging or murder. He has been given a noble mission. Things in Greenland are going to improve.

Eirik the Red will not appreciate his quest, but he will have to accept it.

Now he sees his mother and father. They are waiting for him on the beach, alongside everyone from Brattalid and those from the neighbouring farms who could make it.

The returning son gives his last orders before

swiftly swinging his legs over the gunwale and running with open arms towards his parents, laughing.

Eirik and Tjodhild fall upon him. His mother hugs him long and hard, while the chieftain emits a mighty roar and thumps him on the shoulder before lifting him up in the air.

They are surrounded by a chorus of happy voices. Brosi and the other sheepdogs bark for joy, running hither and thither between the legs of the excited people embracing each other after being apart for two whole years.

Freydis runs into the courtyard at Brattalid just as Leif's ship docks. She jumps off the horse, runs down to the beach and throws herself into her older brother's arms. He smells so fresh and unfamiliar.

'It's so good to see you. I have missed you so much,' she says, pressing her head to his breast.

'I have missed you too, sister,' he smiles, stroking her hair.

'Why did you stay away so long? You were only meant to be away for one winter?'

'We made a detour to unknown places. I have seen so much, experienced so many things.'

'Tell me, tell me!'

But now there are others clamouring for Leif's attention, others eager for a share of him. She has to release him.

His return is like an echo of Eirik's arrival in Iceland after three years as an outlaw. He returned in triumph, having discovered a new land. Now his son has done the same.

Eirik stands in the courtyard, brooding and weather-beaten, his hands at his sides. He scrutinises the sailors closely, his eyes narrowed. Grey strands streak his long red hair and his curly beard.

He is less quick on his feet than in his younger days. Nor does he talk any longer about setting off on Viking expeditions or embarking on walrus hunts in the north. But Eirik is still the chieftain in Greenland and the master of Brattalid – the land he discovered, the farm he built. Of that there can be no doubt.

Every single member of the crew Leif took with him when he left for Norway two years ago receives a pat on the shoulder and a friendly word from the chieftain. Excitedly, they talk about the many lands they have seen - Norway, the Hebrides, and another land. A completely new land. People crowd around them, their faces gleaming with curiosity. They want to hear all about it.

A group of people are standing in the background behind the joyful welcoming throng. They are patiently waiting, though shivering cold. They are Icelanders, fourteen souls whose ship was wrecked not far from the mouth of Eiriksfjord. Leif came sailing past not long after the shipwreck, discovered them, and brought them with him.

A beautiful young woman stands out among the others with her long plait of fair hair and straight back. Gudrid, like the others, is frozen to the marrow, but she conducts herself with impeccable dignity nonetheless. Calmly she waits until the chieftain of Greenland has time for them. When at last Eirik the Red approaches them, it is Gudrid who steps forward, says her name, and speaks on behalf of the group. She describes the shipwreck.

'My husband Torir was in command. But he was lost at sea. My father was, too,' Gudrid says.

Although she is clearly burdened by grief, her voice is clear and strong. She meets Eirik the Red's gaze without wavering.

'I am sorry to hear of your loss.'

'Thank you,' Gudrid says, bowing her head.

'What was your business in Greenland? Did your husband command a trading vessel?' Eirik asks.

'Yes. But there were some of us who wished to visit you and perhaps settle here in Greenland. One of them was my father, Torbjorn Vivilsson. He was a friend of yours,' she says.

A smile spreads across Eirik's face.

'Are you really Torbjorn Vivilsson's daughter? Gudrid, yes. I seem to remember you as a little girl.'

'I remember you, too. My father always regretted not accompanying you to Greenland. It was always his wish to come here before he was too old. Sadly, that did not happen.'

'That's too bad. Torbjorn was a fine man and a good friend,' Eirik says, and is silent for a moment.

Then he throws his arms around Gudrid and leads her towards the longhouse.

'You and your people are welcome to Greenland. You are my guests, for as long as you please.'

Eirik says that for the summer the guests can live in the small houses round the farm and up the mountainside. Later on, he promises to find them places to settle, should they wish to do so.

'And as for you, Gudrid, of course you will stay in the longhouse,' Eirik says.

Then he calls to the slave girls to heat up large quantities of water so the Icelanders can wash the sea salt off themselves.

Freydis brings clothing, furs and blankets for the guests, who gather round the hearth in the longhouse. Gudrid smiles in thanks, her expression friendly. Freydis acknowledges this with a brief nod, uncertain.

Eirik the Red is less enthusiastic about the two slender young men in long brown robes who also form part of Leif's entourage. They are Christian priests from Norway. Leif recounts how he met with Olav Tryggvason in Nidaros. As arranged, they had gone there to trade their wares from Greenland.

'The King of Norway wanted me, Leif Eiriksson, to be the one to bring Christianity to Greenland.'

His voice resounds with pride, and he dares to meet his father's thunderous glower. Two turbulent years under sail have made a man of him. Eirik the Red trembles with rage when he realises what his son is saying. Soon his face flares more scarlet than his red hair. No White Christ shall come to this place! Here Thor, Freya, Odin and the other Norse gods hold sway.

He is bitterly disappointed in his eldest son. The son for whom he built a splendid ship, the son who is to inherit Brattalid. But just for the moment he contents himself with firing off a curt response.

'We'll see about that. No White Christ is welcome on my land.'

Abruptly he turns away from Leif and the priests, throws out his arms and loudly welcomes all his guests to a feast in his longhouse. Tjodhild scurries up, promising the very best they have to offer of food and drink. She hastens to the larder, yanking the key off her belt. Then she orders the slaves to bring out butter, cheese and dried seal meat. The feast will be enhanced by the day's catch from the sea, not forgetting ale and mead.

Eirik is in charge of the mead. The barrel stands right beside his bed, and he guards it as though it were a pile of gold. But now the mead must flow. The return of his eldest son must be celebrated, and heartily so.

Soon the longhouse is heaving. Every bench is occupied. Some people have to sit on the floor, while others lean against the walls. The packed bodies and the hearth in the centre of the room soon create heat. The lamps send out a powerful aroma of fish oil. The steam rising from the warm food makes nostrils tingle. There is much laughter and shouting, many have great tales to tell. The din is deafening.

As the refreshments are passed around, Leif begins his tale of the voyage. After leaving Greenland's waters, they lost their course and ended up in the Hebrides. They spent the summer there before they had a fair wind and were able to continue their journey to Eirik's birthplace, Norway.

'The idea was to trade our goods and meet up with my father's old friend, Haakon, Earl of Nidaros. As you know, it was he who gave my father the nickname 'The Red.' The Red, because of the colour of his hair, and perhaps also on account of his fiery temper,' he says, smiling at his father.

But Earl Haakon was dead. Now Leif told them of a very different Norway from the land Eirik had known in his childhood. There had been life at Jaeren and later, Viking expeditions in the service of Earl Haakon.

'They want to stop the Viking raids; They want to live in peace. And it is a great honour that King Olav Tryggvason has sent with me Oddmund and Brynjulf to bring the true faith here to Greenland,' Leif says, allowing his gaze to sweep slowly round the room.

Eyes shining, he nods towards the two men in the brown robes. Leif and some of his crew have already converted to Christianity and been baptised, and now he hopes others will follow their example.

Eirik rises so abruptly that his mead goblet overturns. The alcoholic drink spills across the table. Sigrid hustles forward to clean it up. She peers fearfully at Tjodhild, but the woman of the house does not notice her plea.

But Freydis sees, and she knows why Sigrid is afraid. Sigrid, who is about her own age, is no ordinary slave. She is also the concubine of Eirik the Red.

A few months previously, when Freydis entered the longhouse carrying a bucket of water, she had stopped abruptly in front of the hangings that concealed her father's sleeping area. Through a gap between two hangings she had caught sight of her father's solid white rump. On his left buttock there was a large pimple. His hefty backside was pumping energetically back and forth. She heard her father emit a deep groan, then, with a grunt and a whistling fart, he rolled over on his side and lay there, relaxed, his eyes closed.

Freydis stood rooted to the spot. She had only a vague notion of what she had seen. She thought she had seen Tjodhild, right outside, with the livestock. Eirik the Red's two concubines were also at work. But suddenly she found herself staring into Sigrid's horrified eyes. They were imploring her, begging her not to reveal what she had witnessed.

And Freydis had no intention of saying anything, anyway. She could well understand that her father might desire someone other than that sour-faced block of ice, Tjodhild, and he had always had several concubines to disport himself with. But she was shocked that he should choose a concubine who was no older than herself.

She had run about the yard with Sigrid when they were both little, before she learned that slaves and the children of the master did not play together. Freydis liked Sigrid. But after seeing her with her father, she felt furious with her, even though she knew in her heart none of it was Sigrid's fault.

Did Tjodhild know about Eirik and Sigrid? If she did, she had shown no sign of it. Perhaps she was even pleased about it – it saved her the trouble. She had borne him three sons, she had certainly fulfilled her obligations.

The chieftain of Greenland is still standing at the table.

Sigrid has cleared up the spattered mead, and Freydis has had time to ponder these thoughts. The chieftain is silent. The room is so still they can hear the crackling of the fire in the hearth, and one of the guests is struggling to suppress a coughing fit. Everyone is waiting for the next move.

Eirik breathes hard; He is about to speak, but changes his mind. He sits down heavily in the high seat. Tjodhild glares at her husband. She listens to everything her eldest son says, and it appears she likes what she hears.

Leif says that already last summer they were on their way to Greenland. But rather than sailing up Eiriksfjord, they felt a desire to acquaint themselves with the northerly parts of West Greenland. They wanted to meet the people who had settled there, and maybe do some hunting both by sea and on land.

'The weather was good, there was a fair wind and we were in good spirits. We were all ready for new discoveries. But after a few great days hunting seal and walrus in the north, we decided we wanted to sail westward.'

The news of this bold move causes a murmur throughout the longhouse.

But this was no sudden ill-considered impulse. Leif confesses he had a dream. Bjarne Herjolvsson had seen a land in the west one time when he was far off course on a voyage between Iceland and Greenland.

Leif wanted his achievements to be no less than those of his father; He too wished to discover a new land and gain a glorious reputation. Perhaps find a land where he himself could be the chieftain, so he did not need to wrangle constantly with his father about everything.

He refrains from sharing the last part. Instead, he explains why he took the risk and embarked on a course with no idea of what lay in store.

'The weather and wind were favourable. Even the stars were with us. I knew we would find something.'

He would later be known as 'Leif the Lucky,' for luck was certainly on their side.

After sailing for a couple of days they caught sight of a land they called Helluland, because it was covered with shining glaciers and smooth, flat rocks. It did not look appealing, and they did not stop there.

They set a new course seaward, along the coast of Helluland. A few days later, a new land came into view – a flat area with forest and inviting white sandy beaches.

'We called it Markland. It looked more promising, but we could not see any pastures. We decided to sail on,' Leif explained, taking a deep gulp of mead.

Everyone is listening to the sturdy Viking son as he continues his tale.

Two days later, the explorers went ashore in a bay.

'There was fresh grass as far as the eye could see, and it smelled sweet, like honey. It seemed a good place to bring cattle, sheep and other livestock. The sea was deep and sloped gently to the shallow end by the beach. We saw forests and hills too,' Leif says.

His tone is almost singing as looks dreamily into space. His listeners imagined the scent of honey in their nostrils.

The explorers rushed about in high spirits, examining the place and deciding on a site for their camp.

Fortunately, Leif had brought men with him who knew all about felling trees and building houses. They were good men to have along, especially when they saw they could get all the timber they needed from the surrounding lush forests.

They were good times. But suddenly summer was drawing to a close, and the weather was growing more changeable. They decided to spend the winter there. In no time at all they had established a substantial longhouse and several smaller structures.

The winter was not so severe there as it was in Greenland at times, where you had to stay indoors for long periods, banking up the fire with turf.

It was mild, and there was little frost. There was no lack of food or drink. The sea teemed with trout, salmon, cod and other varieties of fish. There was also an abundance of fish in the freshwater streams and lakes, and the hunting was good also.

'There were plenty of animals there, species we knew as well as others we had not encountered before. But we saw no sign of any other human beings,' Leif says.

'Are you quite sure? Were there really no other people there, no signs of human life at all?' cried one of the smallholders.

Leif nods. Excited chatter breaks out in the longhouse. People shout, interrupting each other. Can Leif really have found a virgin territory, a land where life could be even better than in Greenland? What an achievement!

The next spring and summer the crew had explored the areas surrounding their little settlement – to the south, the north and inland. Everywhere was green and fertile. One day, Tyrke, who had been Leif's foster-father when he was growing up, disappeared. A few days later he turned up again, grinning and laughing, at first babbling away in German, which was his native tongue, and then switching to Norse.

'Look, I have found vines and grapes,' he cried, holding up juicy bunches of grapes, which they immediately gorged themselves on.

'And that's why we thought of calling this land Vinland,' Leif says. And then he tells them he wishes to settle there, but first he will fulfil his duty and Christianise Greenland. He avoids looking at his father when he makes this last announcement.

'We would of course need women and livestock if we are to live there.' Leif smiles, sits down and addresses his attention eagerly to the fresh fish that has been set before him.

They are all captivated by Leif's tale. Now that it is at an end, the gathering in Eirik the Red's longhouse is really buzzing. Many people have questions. How big is the new land? What animals lived there, what did they look like? Leif and his crew are only too happy to answer.

The atmosphere grows increasingly animated, and soon there are many who declare that they wish to settle in the new land. Toasts are drunk and songs are sung into the wee hours.

ODIN'S SWORD

BRATTALID, THE YEAR 1000

LEIF'S STORY fills Freydis with dreams and longing. A dream about living in a warm country, where grapes grow and the grass smells like honey. A longing to experience something different from the limitations of this Greenland fjord.

It was her father's accounts of his Viking voyages that first kindled the spark. Now it is her older brother who makes her yearn for a different life. Vinland, Vinland. That's where she wants to go. Every beat of her heart makes her think of it. Vinland, Vinland. Or perhaps she might even discover yet another new land – like her father and her brother.

But there is another reason Freydis sits there still and silent, with shining eyes and half-open mouth. She does not even notice that her brother Torstein is jostling her. He is in a mischievous mood.

For furthest down, close to the entrance, there stands a young man. He has a thick mane of dark hair, white teeth which he often shows, and full, berry-red lips. When she closes her eyes, she imagines she can taste their sweetness. His shoulders are almost as broad as the doorway. His arms are powerful, and he holds his head high. She has already guessed he is an Icelander, one of Gudrid's company. There is a gleam in his blue eyes as, smiling, his gaze meets her own across the room. He does not seem entirely indifferent.

He has borrowed the brown tunic and trousers he wears from Torstein. He also sports a wide black belt about his waist. Hanging from the belt is a sword, sheathed in a leather scabbard adorned with colourful stones and engraved with runes.

There is something special about that sword. Eirik the Red, too, has glanced at it more than once. Later in the evening, she hears the young man explain that he was given it by an Earl of Lade from Nidaros by way of thanks for saving his son's life during a campaign. Despite his youth, he is clearly a capable Viking.

The Earls of Lade believe they are descended from Odin and Skade themselves. Odin is the greatest of all the gods, while Skade is the goddess of skiing. Odin is said to possess a sword that can swing on its own.

'This is the sword of Odin. And my name is Sverre Sigurdsson,' the Icelander says to Eirik.

'It's a good sword. I'd be glad to buy it,' the chieftain says, scratching his beard.

'Sorry, it's not for sale.'

'Not even if I were to find you a fine plot of land

and build a farm for you here in Greenland?' Eirik proposes, cocking his head to the side.

'This is the one thing I will never part with,' the young man declares, gripping the sword hilt both hands.

Eirik the Red bursts out laughing and thumps Sverre hard on the shoulder.

'I quite understand. It is a treasure, and you must take good care of it,' he says, and pours a goblet of mead and then moves away to join his friends.

Freydis does not get to exchange a word with Sverre all evening. But that night she dreams about him. She breathes heavily, she sweats and writhes about in her bed.

She can't understand what is happening to her. She has never felt like this before. Never.

She is still glowing at daybreak next day when, yawning, she stumbles out into the daylight, sleepy after a night of hardly a wink of good sleep. She goes to the stream and splashes cold water on her face. Then she tries to tidy her dishevelled hair with the bone comb her father bought her last time a trading vessel put docked by Brattalid.

Then there's the job of clearing up after the previous day's feasting, and preparing the next meal. She and Sigrid go to milk the cows. As they trudge along in silence with their rattling buckets, the aftermath of the feast is all too evident.

Everywhere there are people sleeping it off – in the longhouse, the barns and cowshed. Some just lie stretched out on the grass. There are sounds of snoring, grunts and coughing. The skinny son of a smallholder wanders up and empties the contents of his belly right before the feet of Freydis. When he realises he has disrespected the chieftain's daughter, he is so embarrassed that he half runs, half crawls away from them.

One couple has found each other in the course of the night and lie closely entwined. Others are sleeping so soundly that they cannot be woken up for the meal which is being set out in the yard.

But Sverre is awake, and he takes a large helping of the food Freydis brings. To look her best she has dressed up in her blue homespun skirt and a white blouse as soft as silk. On her breast she wears a beautiful piece of silver jewellery engraved with magic runes.

Even in the cold light of day, Sverre is just as irresistible. She busies herself with small tasks that keep her near him. Tidying away cups and platters, washing up cooking pots, folding up rugs. She smiles and glances at him coquettishly, showing off.

She knows that when she behaves this way men find her attractive. Freydis is tall, strong and shapely – and when she lets her smile reach those great bright eyes of hers, she can look beautiful. Then it is easy to forget her sharp aquiline nose and her rough hands. She can feel the warmth of his gaze on her back when she turns away from him.

When the meal is finished, people go off to their various tasks. But luckily Sverre is in no hurry. Freydis wipes her trembling hands in her apron as she plucks up her courage. Her cheeks blushing scarlet, she goes over to him and holds out her hand.

'Freydis Eiriksdatter.'

'Sverre Sigurdsson,' he replies, loud and clear. He gets to his feet and takes her hand in his firm grasp.

'So, you were on the ship that got wrecked?' Freydis asks, even though she knows the answer.

'Yes,' he says, staring at her, cocking his head.

Just so as to have something to talk about, she interrogates him about the whole episode, and how he managed to save himself. She asks about his family, about where he comes from, whether he intends to settle in Greenland, and many other things.

His answers please her, and so does his deep, lilting voice.

'Would you like me to show you around?'

Before she has a chance to reflect, the words are out.

'Yes, please. Greenland seems welcoming and beautiful.'

'It is, indeed. We have a good life here, though it can be a bit monotonous at times.'

And off they go, up across the green meadows between the rocky knolls. Side by side. Later, Freydis has no recollection of what they talked about.

She knows exactly where she wants to take him; to one of her favourite hiding-places. It lies behind an odd-shaped rocky knoll that looks steeper than it really is. Because of this, not many people go there. But behind the knoll there is a flat green area offering a magnificent view of the fjord.

They sit down on the grass, close together, enjoying the warm breeze, the shining buttercups and the chirping birds. Freydis becomes aware how hard her heart is pounding, and not just because of the climb. She has lost the power of speech and when Sverre chats about the view and the grass, which is more fertile than that of Iceland, she is unable to reply.

'This must be good pastureland for the livestock,' he says, turning to Freydis with a smile.

She has removed her heavy jewellery and unbuttoned her blouse a little to cool off. She does not reply, but there is fire in the glance she sends him. Sverre catches sight of one pert breast beneath her blouse and averts his eyes in embarrassment. Freydis hides her face in her hands, but she cannot quench the fire that burns within her.

Two pairs of eyes, one sea-green, the other deep blue, meet again. Sverre runs a hand through her loose hair. He draws her to him and slips his other hand under her blouse. Freydis trembles and groans aloud, throws back her head and falls back on the grass. Then he is on her, and she welcomes him.

Awkwardly, they tear off their clothes, and soon they are both naked. Skin against skin. Mouth to mouth. Breath to breath.

Freydis only manages to catch a glimpse of his proud manhood within its wreath of bristly dark hair, before he plunges it into her hard, again and again. The tingling sensation radiates from her abdomen to her legs, her arms, her head. She feels she has almost stopped breathing.

Suddenly she feels as though a river in full flood is flowing through her body. As though at a distance she hears Sverre give a great roar. She is unaware that she too has yelled out just as loudly. She feels she is hovering in the air, like a bird with a massive wingspan, floating on the wind.

Then everything is silent. Side by side they lie in the grass. Exhausted.

When Freydis comes to her senses, she still finds the man lying sleeping at her side irresistible. She studies his handsome face, with its long eyelashes and straight nose. His breast, rising and falling. She lays her head on his soft belly and breathes in the titillating aroma of sunshine and fresh perspiration.

Now his member lies away from her, soft and flaccid. She toys with it with her fingers before she bends over him. He wakes up. They make love again.

The sun is high in the sky when, laughing, they make their way back down to Brattalid. They do not see the silent, grim-faced woman standing on the rock above them. Her hands, in their catskin gloves, grip her walking stick. Sombrely, she shakes her head from side to side.

Nobody has discovered their absence, except for Tjodhild. But she is quite used to Freydis shirking her duties, so she will just deliver the usual sharp telling-off. She does not notice that her stepdaughter is bathed in a strange and radiant light.

Tjodhild appears unusually pensive. Freydis suspects it may have something to do with Leif's conversion to the Christian god. She does not like it. What is this White Christ to do with them?

The farm is quiet. Some people have gone off to

hunt the reindeer Freydis saw the other day, while others have been set the task of unloading the timber and the rest of the ship's cargo Leif brought from Vinland.

The women already have plenty to do with the daily chores around the farm: Fetching water, milking cows, washing, and so on. Now they have even more people to take care of. Freydis quickly finishes her tasks so she can sit down to her weaving with a clear conscience. There, in the heart of the longhouse, she can indulge her fantasies in peace. Her head is filled with thoughts of that young Icelander. She feels elated that he is to spend the winter at Brattalid.

Her father is already busy organising accommodation and sleeping areas for the survivors of the wreck. He would gladly have sent the two priests packing back to Norway, but for once he does not get his way.

Leif insists that he intends to keep his promise to Olav Tryggvason. Not even a chieftain, not even the discoverer of Greenland, is above the king. Even though Greenland is not subject to Norway or any other country, Eirik the Red knows he would be ill advised to go against the wishes of the King of Norway.

Moreover, Tjodhild sides with her son on the matter of the White Christ. She has lengthy conversations with the priests, and the more she hears about Christianity, the more it appeals to her. She intends to be baptised and become a Christian.

'They speak of love for one's fellow man and tell us that we can be baptised. Jesus, the Son of God, will redeem us,' she tells Eirik, her eyes brimming with tears of emotion.

'What's the matter with our own gods? Tor has helped me out plenty of times when I have been in a tight spot. I'm not going to abandon him. I've never seen anything about this White Christ,' Eirik growls, turning on his heel and stomping away from his newly-converted wife.

'The Norse gods are bloodthirsty and malevolent,' howls Tjodhild.

But the words run off her husband's impervious back – hard as granite, smooth as wet ice.

It is as though a blanket of fog as heavy as lead has fallen over Brattalid. Everyone notices the chilly atmosphere. They all try to find jobs to do that will take them far away from the longhouse.

After a while, it gets so bad that Tjodhild refuses to share Eirik's bed. She wanders about with a needle-sharp knife in a sheath attached to her belt. She keeps it close at hand even when she sleeps. If he tries anything, she will be ready with her knife.

In the end she decides to build a house of her own, with the help of Leif and his slaves. After all, the timber that came from Vinland belongs to Leif. Eirik is frothing with rage but he has to swallow it if he wants his share of the valuable timber. There has not been a ship in Brattalid with timber available for sale for a very long time. And now he needs it to build several smaller dwellings for the guests from Iceland.

Tjodhild's house is soon finished. She dresses the walls with woven hangings and takes with her most of the pots and pans from the longhouse. She has hardly moved into her new house before she is making plans for another building project. A church.

This is almost more than Eirik can bear. A Christian church. At Brattalid! The place he discovered, the farm he built, where he is master.

The chieftain strides about aiming kicks at everything in his path until he hurts himself and starts to limp. His face is red as blood and he is panting like a mighty walrus bull. He roars at the slaves and clenches his fists. For days, every creature avoids his presence, both people and animals. Even his trusty Brosi whines pathetically and quickly creeps away with his tail between his legs when he sees his master.

The only one who does not care is his eldest son. He is busy cutting the timber and making everything else ready for the church. The Christian god has imbued Leif with a new confidence in himself. He has discovered a new country, one more welcoming than Greenland. He has no need to feel overawed by his father.

The church is built, but not on the farm yard. Eirik manages to put a stop to that. The lovely little church is built several stones' throws away from Brattalid.

The more personable of the two priests, Brynjulf, is already evangelising the true faith in Greenland. Oddmund stays at Brattalid, supporting Leif and Tjodhild. He has kept abreast of developments in the building of the new house of God.

Although the majority of Greenlanders remain true to Eirik the Red and the Norse gods, the White Christ gains a small group of faithful followers. The newly Christian Greenlanders meet in Tjodhild's church, each of them dressed in their best. Men and women, rich and poor, slaves and freemen. God's house is open to all; That is the church's message.

'They'll be dragging in the cattle and the pigs any day now,' Eirik the Red yells furiously one day as he rides past the holy building.

Afterwards, the church-goers are invited into Tjodhild's house to sing hymns. She serves good food and drink to all who come, even the slaves.

Her husband takes care to reward those who resist conversion and stay loyal to him, performing sacrifices to the old gods alongside him. Now Eirik wishes to build a new house of sacrifice, one that will be much larger and more splendid than Tjodhild's church. Excitedly he confides his intentions to Freydis. He is delighted that she has refused to be baptised.

He has already imagined how it will look. Inside, he wants a great table. This is where the sacrifices will be carried out. And his friend Torgrim Knutsson, the Norwegian carpenter, will make chairs for him. They will be the largest and most magnificent chairs in all of Greenland, with carved images of his gods. Chairs worthy of a king. Which is almost what he is, he reckons.

Torgrim is also an authority on runes and can write verses. He has been commissioned to compose a suitable verse which will be carved into the door of the sacrifice house. This door is to be the portal into a world where both gods and men can feel at home. Eirik wants the door and the long table to be made from the straightest, sturdiest piece of timber from Vinland. He has already selected it. But first he needs to speak to Leif.

He strides over to his son, who has embarked on the construction of the foundations for his own house on Brattalid, right next to Tjodhild's church. What is left of the timber from Vinland, lies there, stacked. The stack has quickly grown smaller; There has been much construction work of late.

'A fine plot, this. Not too far to the god's house, either!' Eirik says, trying to make a joke of it.

'Yes, it will be great,' Leif replies curtly, then shouts to one of his slaves telling him to roll a boulder over to the wall.

'So, now you have helped your mother with a new house and a church. Your father, who has taken care of you all your life, wants to build a house of sacrifice. This piece of timber here would be just right for the door and the table,' Eirik remarks, nodding towards the wood he has selected, with the air of a connoisseur.

Leif looks at him. His expression is inscrutable. He pauses before answering his father.

'I'll think about it.'

'How long will you need?' Eirik struggles to keep his tone cheery and unconcerned but fails. But his son does not reply. He just walks off.

It is no longer a secret that Sigrid is Eirik's concubine. She has even moved into his sleeping alcove. The girl no longer seems quite so terrified as before, although she usually lies still as a statue when Eirik demands his rights.

But it seems she stands taller, for it is better to be a concubine than a slave. She ignores Tjodhild completely, and refuses to take orders from her, even though Tjodhild is still the mistress of Brattalid. Eirik does not reprove her. On the contrary, he seems to find the whole thing funny. He has also given Sigrid the key to the larder where the choicest food is stored.

Freydis has little care for anything that is going on around her. She thinks only of Sverre. A glance, a nod exchanged, and they have arranged a tryst at their secret meeting place as soon as possible.

And when they are not physically together, he is inside her anyway. In her mind, in her heart, in her body.

She has no respite from him. Nor does she wish for it. For she has never felt so happy. The sun has never shone more warmly, the wind has never blown so softly, the meadows around Brattalid have never bloomed so fair as this summer.

Not even the cold sharp rain squalls that herald the arrival of a new season can depress her good spirits. She goes about her duties humming and singing to herself. She trots off cheerfully down to the stream to wash the clothes, a cold, unpleasant task, without even arguing with her stepmother.

Sometimes, holding hands, they chat and talk of their dreams. Then he tells her about Iceland, about his family and about the sword he takes with him everywhere, except when he sleeps. He grew up on a large farm in Iceland. But it was soon decided that his older brother would take over the farm, and that Sverre would go on Viking raids.

It was when he was on an expedition with the Norwegian earl's men that he performed the outstanding feat of saving the earl's son from an attack from the rear. He would often tell the story of how he came by the sword. His pride in it is so great he even calls his member 'Odin's sword.' This always makes Freydis giggle.

But there were to be no more Viking voyages.

'I've made my mind up that I want to engage in trading instead. Perhaps I can settle in Greenland and build a ship of my own. Few people are going on raids these days. It's because of this White Christ,' he says, looking at Freydis.

'What do you think of him? Are you thinking of getting baptised?' she asks.

Sverre shrugs.

'Not sure. I like our old gods, and I'd rather stick with them, but it might not be possible much longer,' he says pensively.

Personally, she has little time for these men in long robes who wander about the place seeking to convert everyone. She fully supports her father, but it hurts that the brother she loves so much has become a Christian.

One day, when she is sitting dreaming over her weaving as usual, Leif appears.

'So this is what you get up to all day, sister. Do you fancy coming out with me? Maybe we can walk to the rock where we used to have our chats,' he says softly.

'Yes, let's do that,' she says happily, putting on her outdoor shoes.

They have not had a real conversation since he returned from his voyage of discovery, but he has finally made time for her. He has tamed the unruly hair and beard he had when he returned from his expedition, and his expression has grown more austere and serious.

They chat about this and that until they reach the rock. From here they can see far across the white glacier. The siblings sit down side by side, as they have done so many times before. For a while they sit there in silence while the wind ruffles their hair and cools their perspiring bodies. Then Leif turns to look at her. There is something he wants to say.

'Freydis. As you know, I have been entrusted with the task of converting Greenland to Christianity. Many have already embraced the faith.'

Freydis nods. She knows where this is going.

'Look around you. All this was created by our almighty God. Look at the heavens. That is His abode, the Christian God. I want the best for you, Freydis, and you will have a better life if you hearken to God's word and let yourself be baptised.'

'I've been to church, and I have listened to the priests. But I never felt what I feel when I think of Freya, Tor and the others, and when father speaks about them. How will getting baptised change anything for the better?'

Leif is silent for a moment or two, his gaze fixed on the distant mountains.

'The Norse gods are ruthless. So is our father. The

Christian God is goodness itself. To Him, all are worthy. He saves everyone.'

'You shouldn't talk about father like that when he's done so much for us. I don't want to be baptised,' she says sharply and glares at her brother.

'Well, it's your decision,' he says, getting up quickly.

He stares at her with his ice-blue eyes and then turns and strides purposefully off down to Brattalid. Freydis gives a great sigh and is nearly in tears as she stumbles after him. She can't keep up with her brother; Her long skirt is slowing her down. Besides, it does not seem like he wants to speak to her anymore.

They no longer have the happy confiding relationship they once had. There is so much that separates them. Not only Christianity. Leif is unrecognisable. No longer the caring brother who taught her everything, was always on her side, always had a funny anecdote up his sleeve. He rarely smiles anymore, and when he does, it is mainly for the priests and the other Christians.

At times she misses the old Leif so much that she feels she has lost an anchor in her life and is simply drifting. But these bouts of depression are short-lived, because luckily, she has Sverre. The very thought of him makes her blood surge through every vein. How did she ever manage to live without him? The truth is, before she met him, she was not really alive, she merely existed.

Rumours about them spread. They reach the ears of Oddmund the priest. He asks to speak to her. She refuses, but she is commanded by Tjodhild to meet with him in the new church. Tjodhild insists, in her capacity as mistress of the house, with Leif's support. Eirik refrains from making any comment. He is still hoping to obtain that special piece of timber he selected, and he does not want to antagonise Leif.

Oddmund is a young man, perhaps five-and-twenty, but he looks closer to sixty. Bowed head, bony body, hollow cheeks, thin, colourless hair, and surprisingly big brown eyes as round as cartwheels.

He has two robes which he wears in rotation. The thin white one with the cross embroidered on the breast is the one he wears for mass and holy days. The other is a dirty brown, thick and ankle-length, with a hood and a rope girdle round the waist. He is wearing the brown one now. He is sitting by the altar, and he asks Freydis to sit down on the bench to his right.

She is wearing a worn blue skirt and an everyday blouse. She has not even bothered to change her dirty apron, which was once white. She can see no reason why she should dress up for the priest and his White Christ.

Without beating about the bush, he asks her what is going on between her and Sverre. Freydis stares at him insolently and tells him it is none of his business.

'We are doing no more than what your priest friend Brynjulf is doing. I've lost count of the number of women he's been enjoying on his trips around Greenland.'

'You lie. You should be aware that God knows all things, sees all things. The day will come when you will have to stand to account for your misdeeds,' he says sharply, his eyes boring into her. 'And remember, you are a woman. You cannot go around behaving like a man.'

Freydis is seething with rage; She rolls her eyes and glowers towards the doorway. She can't get away quickly enough. But Oddmund wants her to hear God's word first.

He begins with the Christmas Gospel, which he thinks the most wonderful story in all of the Holy Book. He clasps his hands and lets them rest in his lap and closes his eyes. In a chanting singsong, he tells how the Virgin Mary conceives by the Holy Ghost.

'The Holy Prick, more like,' scoffs Freydis.

She immediately feels ashamed. She has uttered a word she has only heard the roughest of sailors use. Sometimes her father's cronies have shouted that word late at night hours when the ale goblets have been raised many times. Such disgusting language ill befits the daughter of a chieftain.

But there is something about this priest that provokes in her a desire to do something disgraceful. Had it only been Brynjulf. At least he is easy on the eye, and he does not seem so severe.

Oddmund's eyes blaze and there is thunder in his voice when he scolds her, then he draws a deep breath and continues his story. Freydis hears how Mary and Joseph sought a place to spend the night when they were on the way to complete the census. She hears about the birth of Jesus in the stable, about the angels and the wise men. Oddmund declares that Jesus is born of David's line, and recites the whole of Joseph's pedigree. He knows it by heart.

'But Joseph isn't his father. Didn't you just say it

was the Holy Pr— eh, the Holy Ghost that was the father? Then how can he be of David's line? And why don't you mention Mary's pedigree? Is he not her son, when she has just given birth to him? Does the family history of the mother mean nothing at all in the Bible?'

She fires a hail of questions at the priest, who struggles to respond.

Freydis has trenchant opinions about what is said in the Bible and the things Oddmund has learned by rote. The priest sighs dejectedly and asks her to come again next day.

Perhaps his message will be more successful when she has mulled over all she has learned, he thinks. They are like sharp-clawed wild cats, these Viking women. He had been prepared for it, but it seems worse than he had anticipated.

No matter what Biblical stories he comes up with, Freydis has more questions, and she is never content with the answers she gets.

She meets up with him in the church every day for a whole week, until Oddmund gives up on her. He would so have liked to instil the Christian faith in her, but it was not meant to be. He dare not insist. She is, after all, the daughter of Eirik the Red, and Eirik the Red is still the chieftain of Brattalid. It is by his grace that Brynjulf and Oddmund are there at all.

Of course, this one is the child of a concubine, conceived in sin. Small wonder she is the way she is. But the day will come when she will regret her sharp tongue and her quarrelsome spirit. Of this, Oddmund is sure.

And now it is Eirik who wishes to hold a serious

conversation with his only daughter. He is seated in the longhouse in one of the chieftain's high chairs and he bids her take a seat in the other one, which is intended for Leif. It is rare for him to bestow upon her such an honour.

They are alone in the house; everyone else has been sent out. His lower arms rest on the arms of the chair, he sits straight and tall, and he is not smiling. What is on her father's mind? Does he suspect her and Sverre? She is aware of the rumours circulating, but she doubts that anyone has found the courage to run to her father with gossip.

She braces herself.

'Well, now Leif has come home, and we have arranged accommodation for our ship-wrecked guests. It is time for us to start planning your wedding to Torvard Einarsson. It would be best to hold the wedding before the winter sets in in earnest.'

Freydis freezes. She had completely forgotten about this. Or rather, she had striven to repress the thought.

'Oh, surely he can manage to wait another winter,' she says hastily.

She is not ready to tell her father about Sverre. Not yet.

Eirik wrinkles his bushy eyebrows and stares at her with surprise. He seems to have no idea about Sverre; He had thought she would be looking forward to her wedding.

But she senses a hint of relief, too. Perhaps he is not in the mood for feasting and celebrations. All the fuss about the White Christ has caused unrest in his land

and it has hit him hard. Besides, both Tjodhild and Leif have turned against him.

As chieftain, it is also up to him to cater for all the people who will spend the winter at Brattalid. He must ensure there is sufficient food, and the matter grows pressing. He seems ill at ease, and over the past few weeks he has lost weight and looks much older. Poor father. Freydis throws her arms round him. She, for one, is on his side.

It is almost two years since Eirik agreed with Einar Torvardsson of Gardar that Einar's son Torvard should marry Freydis.

Torvard himself had requested the alliance after a feast at Brattalid. There she had caught his eye, the well-developed red-haired girl, rushing about serving reindeer meat and mead. He had spent most of the evening sitting in his chair gazing at her. He had paid little mind to all the grinning people pushing him about in an attempt to make him join in on the singing and foot-stamping. Even his goblet of mead stood before him untouched.

Freydis had not opposed the match. She knew Gardar was the second largest farm in Greenland after Brattalid. It was the best offer of marriage she could hope for in the land. Becoming mistress of her own household and getting away from Tjodhild was also a pleasant prospect. Pleasing, too, were the many pieces of jewellery Torvard gave her.

But Torvard himself aroused no feelings in her. He was rather an insignificant man. He was short, shorter than Freydis herself. He was also thin, and his left leg gave him a slight limp. He wore his straight, light brown hair cut short, had hollow cheeks, large blue eyes and surprisingly long, slender fingers for a man of the soil.

Torvard had a reputation as a good farmer. He was a gifted hunter, too, they said. None could stalk so close to the game as Torvard Einarsson. But none of this impressed Eirik the Red's daughter. He was really too old for her anyway, certainly over thirty. The heir to Gardar was for his part completely obsessed by Freydis and wanted the wedding to take place at the first opportunity. He had been talking about it ever since their first meeting, but Eirik the Red wanted to wait until his eldest son returned.

Eirik understood Torvard's urgency and took pity on his plight. He sent his daughter to visit Gardar as a guest.

'A man has his desires,' he muttered gruffly, although she hardly understood the deeper meaning behind his words.

Torvard certainly had his desires, and Freydis allowed him to satisfy them. It didn't hurt. She thought it was just something men liked and women accepted in silence. She had known no different, not until now.

And now she can think of no other man than Sverre, even though he is not as rich as Torvard, even though he has never given her jewellery, even though he is not going to inherit a farm. What is she to do? Now, luckily, she has managed to win herself another winter to work out how she is going to get out of this mess.

The autumn is long this year. A heavy grey blanket lies over southern Greenland. Sometimes the clouds release a downpour. On its way down, the wind seizes it, making the rain blow in horizontal gusts. It is bitter weather, and they have already begun to light the fire as though it were winter already. Day and night, plumes of smoke rise from the houses – both Tjodhild's new dwelling and Eirik's longhouse.

The people of Brattalid have almost forgotten what the sun looks like when it suddenly beams down one morning. The whole landscape is covered with sparkling frost. It is so cold the frost sticks.

A few days later it snows big white flakes that melt as soon as they touch the people of Brattalid, warm from their day's labours, and the livestock, which have not yet been put in the barns. But most of it lies on the ground, the roofs and the fjord, which soon freezes over. Soon it is not only the eternal glacier that is white. The whole of Greenland is covered with its white shield – mountains, meadows, waters, and parts of the fjords.

Freydis likes this season. Now she can walk on the water as much as she likes, just like the White Christ man, Jesus. She can enjoy the sight of the stars and the moonlight that floods the glittering white landscape, touching it with magic. Sometimes a green flare lights up the sky. She likes the cold, the way it bites her cheeks, and the fresh wind, clean and invigorating.

But the daily work is harder now, especially for the womenfolk. The stream is frozen; They have to melt snow over the fire in the hearth. Large quantities of water are needed in a household as large as that of

Brattalid this winter. Drinking water, water for cooking. Water for the farm animals in the stable and the barn. Water for washing the pots, the floors and the ceiling. And once a week, for bathing. For that, they have to bring out their biggest cauldron.

Clothing has to be washed now and again, too, although less frequently in wintertime. Mostly, they wear various kinds of fur or wadmal. The smell of wet wool permeates each house, mingling with the odour of human sweat and the nauseating stink of fish oil from the oil lamps which usually remain lit throughout the day.

There are only a few hours of daylight, and people are generally inside by the time it gets dark, except for 'necessary errands.' Then one has to bare one's backside, squat over one of the logs set up for this purpose, and let nature take its course.

Freydis is fully occupied with her weaving; She has a new assignment. Her father wants her to weave carpets, cloths, chair cushions and other items required for the house of sacrifice he intends to build. Eirik has given her a free hand, since he knows how skilled she is with the loom.

Alongside Sigrid and the other slave girls she works the wool, spinning large amounts of yarn. The women sit in a circle and do their work in silence. Here they are all equally important. An egalitarian co-operative. Even though Freydis is wearing a beautiful new dress of blue wool, a snowy white linen apron and a heavy bracelet of brass engraved with runes.

Even though Sigrid has been given a new red skirt by Eirik. Even though the other three are wearing the same colourless skirts, blouses, aprons and shoes they have been wearing for years.

They sit close together. As they work, Freydis reflects on that the other girls are real people, just like herself. She too is descended from slaves. Her mother was a slave. She was Eirik the Red's concubine, just like Sigrid.

Freydis peers at her where she sits, bent over her work. Her fingers run swiftly through the wool in her hands. Her pretty young face is hidden from view, but Freydis peeks at her hair, the colour of wheat, and the long plait that hangs down her back.

Maybe she should have a little talk with Sigrid. Find out what it is like to be her father's concubine. Perhaps she could learn more about her own mother. What was she like? What were her thoughts? Where did she come from? How did she end up a slave? Freydis has asked herself these questions a thousand times. She longs to know more.

But no, she will not ask Sigrid. Ragni and Sigrid have nothing in common. Her father told Freydis that he loved Ragni. She does not think he loves Sigrid the same way. And Sigrid just accepts it – after all, she is better off as a concubine than as a mere slave. What happens between them bears no relation to what happens between Freydis and Sverre, or what there once was between Eirik and Ragni.

Freydis sits up straight and stretches her arms up in the air, takes a deep breath and pushes her thoughts away. After all, she is the only daughter of Eirik the Red – the man who founded a realm in Greenland, a land without kings or earls, a land he could build up from nothing himself.

And he did so. And as far as she is aware, people are happy to have Eirik the Red as their chieftain. He is no ruthless tyrant. He allows others to speak their mind – at least if they are his friends. He has held many meetings at Brattalid where people have come together to discuss all manner of things, such as land boundaries or how best to deal with trading vessels so they can obtain the best possible exchange for their own trade goods.

During these meetings, a market is usually held at Brattalid. People from other farms come, set up booths and display their merchandise – food, clothing, shoes, iron work, tools, troughs and other items. They bring gossip, too, and slaves to be sold.

Often enough, the smallholders bring along cows and ewes to be covered. Only Eirik the Red, the master of Gardar and another couple of men own bulls and rams.

'Who wants to purchase the seed of my finest stud?' her father will shout.

And the smallholders come flocking. They are happy to trade fleeces and reindeer skins for bull semen. Sometimes, Eirik the Red wants something else.

'Have you got a pretty daughter or a hard-working son?' he asks them, and often the small-holders are glad to oblige and to have one less mouth to feed.

'Yes, but then I want both my cows served by the bull,' the smallholder often replies. 'Agreed, if I may borrow both your son and your daughter too,' Eirik says, slapping the farmer cheerfully on the back.

'But then I'll have nobody to look after mother; She's old and sick.'

Often the negotiations are prolonged, and in many cases, they are not resolved until a large quantity of ale has been consumed long into the night. The chieftain always gets his way.

Eirik and the other major landowners see to it that the number of livestock on the smallholdings does not rise more than is desirable. They alone have the right to keep male animals. The class system must be preserved, or fighting would break out in this green land where they live such a good life.

On market days there is a feast in the evening. Fresh fish is cooked in cooking pots down by the beach, seal and reindeer meat is roasted over the fire. There is laughter, singing, dancing. People telling wild stories and children running about and squealing. It is the best time of year. Freydis's father agrees. He roars and swaggers about the place, towering over everyone with his chest thrust out, wearing a broad grin on his face, thumping people on the shoulder in manly fellowship.

The women have finally finished their work with the great heaps of wool. The circle of co-operation is broken, but there is enough yarn now to furnish the house of sacrifice and more.

Eirik procures for Freydis all the dyes she wants from the trading ships, and she creates her own, too, from Greenland's plants. She knows the art of blending colours. She learned this skill from a man who had come on a rare visiting ship from southern

Europe. His name was Giuseppe and he came from Rome. A man of refinement, with pale soft hands and a mincing walk like a woman. With a single touch he could create a rainbow.

Now she can do that, too. Red like her own hair against the snow, orange like the sun at daybreak, gold like the buttercups, green like the pasture in spring, blue like sea ice, dark-blue like the waves of the ocean in the moonlight, and violet like the stones in the jewellery her mother left her.

She starts to weave, letting the shuttle run between the threads almost of its own accord. A picture is emerging. A naked woman. She sits on the ground in a colourful meadow studded with flowers, one leg crossed over the other. She is shapely, full-breasted, with a narrow waist and soft white thighs.

The red-haired woman is looking to the side towards an equally naked man squatting beside her. He meets her eyes and holds one hand over his lower body, the other hand reposing on the woman's naked knee. The man is young, dark-haired. The couple are bathed in sunlight.

Eirik's eyes go wide when he sees what Freydis is weaving. He scratches his beard thoughtfully with his strong gnarled fingers.

'She looks like you. Have you woven a picture of yourself?' he says, studying his daughter's face. Freydis blushes furiously.

'No, it's just some random woman,' she whispers, and pretends to be engrossed in her work. Eirik chuckles.

'She could just as well be Freya. It would be a fine

thing to have a picture of the goddess of love herself hanging in the house of sacrifice,' he says mildly.

The woman must be Freydis herself, he thinks to himself. And the fellow must be none other than her future husband, Torvard Einarsson. Torvard must have awakened some feeling in Freydis. He had not thought Einarsson capable of it. In truth, he had never seemed the right man to kindle the fires in his hot-blooded daughter.

They were so different, the future couple, the thoughtful Torvard and the fiery Freydis. He had been wondering if they were suited to one another. But he must have been mistaken. Freydis seemed so happy these days.

'Maybe the man was one of Freya's lovers,' he says, trying to keep the conversation going. These days his daughter is a woman of few words.

'Yes, let's say that,' Freydis replies, turning a beaming smile on her father.

Eirik smiles too. He sees so much of himself in his daughter. If only she had been born a boy, what a Viking she would have made! He had personally taught his daughter to wield a sword, to set traps and hunt reindeer. She had even been along on whale hunts. You never know what skills she might have need of, even if she is to be mistress of Gardar.

Tjodhild had refused to allow him to teach his sons the skills of the Viking. Her sons were not going to be robbers and murderers, she said. Leif had become an explorer, just like Eirik himself. If only his son had not got involved with this awful White Christ. The blood rushes to Eirik's head, and he clenches his fists.

But he chokes down his anger and continues to study the picture his daughter is creating, as if by magic. It will look splendid in the house of sacrifice, he thinks. Then he senses that he is growing hard and warm, and he hurries out to find Sigrid.

Eirik the Red's mind is at rest. They are ready for winter. There is enough food and all the guests have a place to sleep. They will even be able to keep warm, he thinks, no matter how cold it gets. They have enough dried turf, branches of mountain birch, driftwood and the off-cuts of planks left over from the summer's construction activities. Now the roof is on the house of sacrifice, which stands tall on a small hill behind Brattalid.

The Icelanders have proved hard workers, both the men and the women. They have made a huge contribution towards preparing Brattalid for the cold season. They know just what to do.

Gudrid is in charge. Young as she is, she exudes an aura of natural leadership which causes the Icelanders to follow her. She never raises her voice but issues her orders with quiet dignity. The work gets done. Before long, Eirik feels the same respect for her as he had for her father.

The days are short and cold, and they spend many hours inside the houses. The Christians live with the mistress, and pass their time singing hymns with solemn faces. One of the priests reads aloud from the Holy Book. All is peaceful and quiet.

There is singing in Eirik's household too. But here

they sing the old songs of Iceland and Norway, which tell of the Viking raids of yesteryear and lusty tales of love.

Now and again Eirik's friends will sing a new song composed by Bjarte Torsson from the stranded Icelandic ship. His songs often celebrate Eirik's many successful expeditions all over the world, including his triumphant discovery of Greenland. These songs gladden the heart of the ageing chieftain. And when he is in a particularly jovial mood, the ale are rolled out.

The ambience grows increasingly convivial as the goblets around the long table are replenished. Toasts are drunk, and many a tongue is loosened. The old sagas of Norway and Iceland are told again and again, until they are barely recognisable. They tell of kings, earls and chieftains, of women hungry for love, of Viking raids, of Tor and Freya.

The longhouse rings with laughter as the warmth increases and the smell of the oil lamps becomes stifling. The hour grows late, and the women and children long for bed, while the men often go over to the house of sacrifice to continue. Often, it is far into the night before it is quiet after these parties. Next morning, most people are not lying in their own beds. The household often does not awaken before the ominous bawling of cattle from the barn reaches their ears.

Freydis is starting to lose patience with these nights of carousing, not least because it is she and the slave girls who are tasked with clearing up after them.

One morning she wakes up after one such occasion and goes up to the house of sacrifice. The table is in a terrible state. It is clear that the menfolk have brought in an ewe this time. Brown flecks of dried blood from the sacrificial beast, pieces of bone, plates and dishes all in a heap, overturned drinking cups, stinking vomit mingled with sour warm ale. One guest is snoring in a chair, another on the floor. Seething with rage, Freydis sets the slave girls to the task of tidying up.

Throughout the autumn and winter, a power struggle has been developing over the slave girls. It comes to a head on the day Tjodhild wants to use the Icelandic slaves to do a full scale clean, washing her house. Gudrid strenuously objects.

'I need them for the milking and other work with the livestock. Besides, they are busy sewing clothes. You know most of their clothing got ruined in the shipwreck,' Gudrid says.

'You know that I am the mistress of Brattalid. It is I who shall decide what work the slaves shall do,' Tjodhild thunders.

But Gudrid refuses to give in. Calmly she returns Tjodhild's gaze.

'They were my father's slaves. He is dead, and I have inherited them. And so long as we remain here in Greenland as guests of Eirik the Red, they will be employed in his service.'

'Oh ... Eirik, that bullheaded oaf,' Tjodhild huffs.

Freydis has overheard the whole heated exchange between the two women and now stands grinning at its outcome. Just then, Gudrid turns and looks at her. Their eyes meet, and they both smile.

The chieftain's daughter is becoming increasingly impressed by Gudrid Torbjornsdatter. She had been quite suspicious of her at the start. She seemed rather full of herself. Also, Freydis has to confess that she was jealous of the other girl's beauty. But there is no doubt that there is more to Gudrid than a pretty face.

Later, Gudrid admits to Freydis that she found it difficult to decide whose house to stay in – whether to lodge with Tjodhild or with Eirik.

'I was baptised along with my husband before we set sail for Greenland. So I should probably have moved in with Tjodhild. But I am still not sure that getting baptised was the right thing to do.'

'No, I understand. I'll certainly never become a Christian. The White Christ appeals to me less and less. He has caused trouble here at Brattalid and elsewhere in Greenland,' says Freydis.

Gudrid nods, silent and pensive.

'I prefer Eirik to Tjodhild, even though I'm not much fond of his parties.'

'Luckily we'll soon run out of ale and mead. And there's hardly any grain left.' They laugh.

'Men get so handsy when in their cups. They think themselves irresistible when they lean over me and I get the sour stench of ale right in my face,' says Gudrid.

But the men soon remember their manners when she puts them in their place. She is the head of the Icelanders, after all. They leave Freydis in peace, too; nobody dares lay a finger on the daughter of Eirik the Red. Or do they?

Is something going on between her and Sverre Sigurdsson? They never touch each other when everyone is gathered together in the longhouse, but Gudrid thinks she has seen them exchanging hot glances.

She does not know Sverre all that well. But her father and Sverre's father were good friends. They had arranged for Sverre to go on the Greenland expedition. The idea was for him to learn more about trading. She wonders whether perhaps she ought to warn Sverre not to get involved with Freydis; after all, she is betrothed to the heir of Gardar. Is it her duty, as leader of the Icelanders? So far she has let it pass – they are both free people, after all.

Freydis is only a couple of years younger than Gudrid, and she feels she would like to get to know her better. But they hardly ever talk about anything except day-to-day matters. The chieftain's daughter is certainly nothing like the description of her that Gudrid had heard – quick-tempered, stubborn and conceited.

She almost looks as though she were in the heaven the adherents of the White Christ talk about as she sits in the middle of the longhouse, weaving. But the pictures she weaves have very little to do with heaven.

During the winter months, Freydis and Sverre hold theirs trysts in a cave. There they are sheltered from the teeth of the gale. The cave is lined with reindeer skins and woollen rugs to keep out the frost. Otherwise, they manage very well with the warmth they generate themselves. The fire of love is sustained despite the winter's cold, and blazes even more strongly when the spring sun returns, bringing everything back to life.

But now Freydis is full of dread, too, for soon there

is talk of the wedding again. She has made up her mind that it is Sverre she wants. The thought of marrying Torvard Einarsson is repugnant to her. If she is to avoid it, she must persuade her father to cancel the agreement with the master of Gardar. It will certainly throw him into one of his rages.

And perhaps that is the only thing she fears in the whole world: her father's wrath. She has seen him at his worst, terrorising other people, his face blood-red. He would scream and beat at them with his fists, or run after them with an axe. So far she has been spared being the object of his rage.

This spring something else occupies the minds of the people of Brattalid. Eirik's youngest son, Torstein, has decided he wants to go to Vinland, the land Leif discovered the year before.

Torstein has grown into a man, tall and broad, yet he has kept his boyish freckles. He swaggers about with his broad stance, chatting and joking and laughing with everybody. In this, he is like his father. But it is not the most intelligent, and he is not the best worker, either. He is definitely the least able of them when it comes to commanding a ship.

Despite frequent voyages made with Eirik and others of the Greenlanders who are skilled mariners, Torstein has never really got to grips with the intricacies of navigation. That is why Eirik is extremely reluctant to lend his son his precious *Dragon*.

Torstein's forte is his infectious laughter and his ability to charm people. Now he exercises these gifts for all they are worth to convince his father, and at last

Eirik gives in. Torstein even tries to persuade his father to join him on the trip.

'I could really use somebody who's taken part in a voyage of discovery before. What do you say to coming to along to a new land? It'll make you feel young again!' he entreats.

'I'm probably too old for that; I'm not as strong as I was. I don't have the energy to build something up from nothing once more.'

'You wouldn't have to build your own farm in Vinland. We'll live in Leif's house, and then we'll sail home again at the end of the summer with the ship laden with timber, furs and dried meat.'

'Good. I'd get away from the White Christ for a bit. And we do need more timber. There's at least one son here in this place who has nothing against his father!' Eirik booms, hoping his voice will be heard in Leif's house.

The chieftain feels bitter towards his eldest son, who has decided he will not let him have the fine piece of timber from Vinland which Eirik had been planning to use for the construction of a long table in his house of sacrifice. Leif has his own plans for the unusually long, straight timber from an unfamiliar but sturdy variety of tree. Now Eirik wants to go to Vinland and fetch a piece of timber just like this for himself.

To make sure neither Leif, Tjodhild or those priests manage to get their hands on his treasure while he is away, Eirik buries an iron casket full of gold and silver in a secret place close to the house of sacrifice.

Sigrid packs a chest with what he needs by way of clothing, shoes and other necessities for his voyage to

Vinland. She works as swiftly as ever despite her swollen belly. It seems she has no care for the child she is carrying. Nor does she display any emotion about Eirik's departure. She does not even watch as he waddles out of the door behind the slave carrying his sea chest.

It is not a long walk from the longhouse to the beach where the *Dragon* is ready to set sail, but Eirik wishes to arrive on horseback, as is proper for a chieftain.

The horse only takes a few steps before Eirik tumbles off its back and crashes to the ground. He gives a howl, partly of pain, but mainly over the shame. All of Brattalid and many from the nearby farms have gathered at the beach to bid them farewell. Tjodhild and some of her Christian friends cover their mouths to stifle a laugh at his expense.

People crowd round Eirik, wanting to help him; He cannot get up on his own. His chest and a foot are too painful. Synne, a slave from a neighbouring farm who is skilled at healing, comes over and begins to examine him. She thinks he has broken a few ribs and injured his ankle.

The chieftain is carried back into the longhouse so Synne can bandage his ankle. His ribs will have to heal by themselves, but Synne cooks up an herbal brew to help with the pain. Eirik takes this incident as a sign. He is not to travel to Vinland; It is not his destiny. He also thinks his fall is a punishment because he buried his treasure. It is quickly dug up again and hidden under his bed.

The ship's departure has been delayed because of

the chieftain's fall, but at last they are ready. Torstein and his twenty-strong crew sail out of Eiriksfjord. They have sworn to return with the *Dragon* laden with treasure.

Freydis is among the many people who wave them off. Freydis has never seen her brother look so fine or so happy. In anticipation of his voyage to Vinland he has also let his beard grow. Already it is bushy and strong.

It is high summer. Freydis and Sverre lie dozing side by side in the grass after their lovemaking. Sverre has seemed somewhat taciturn all day. But Freydis hardly notices, for she has taken a bold decision. She takes a few deep breaths before she reveals what is on her mind. She intends to cancel her wedding to Torvard and marry him, Sverre. She will brave her father's wrath.

'If we can't build ourselves a farm here in Greenland, I'll travel the world with you on trading voyages. I long to see new places, new people,' she says dreamily.

She cocks her head, smiling, and snuggles close to her beloved. Her bright eyes shine like silver. But he does not meet her eyes; He just lies there, silent, staring into nothing. He looks wistful. Is he not thrilled that they can be together?

When he finally speaks, he does not give her the answer she had been hoping for.

'I have something to tell you, too. Yesterday I learned that my father and my brother have been lost at sea. I have to go home to Iceland and take over the farm. I'm leaving tomorrow,' he says, sitting up suddenly.

Freydis feels as though someone has struck her on the head with something hard. She leaps up.

'Why didn't you say that right away? I'll go to Iceland with you,' she cried.

Then comes the unbelievable reply. Sverre doesn't want her. He says he has long had his eye on a girl at home in Iceland whom he intends to marry. He rises to his feet and gets ready to walk away.

Freydis shrieks. Sverre turns and sees her standing there, hair blowing in all directions, her blouse open, her breasts bare, with an expression that draws him in. Never has she been so desirable. The young Icelander quickly walks back to her.

'So, you want one last encounter with the sword of Odin?' he says bitterly.

Freydis throws herself upon him, spitting like a wild cat, tears off his clothes and hurls him down on his back. She throws her legs over him and rides him fast and hard, scratching his chest with her sharp nails.

'You're a madwoman,' Sverre groans in horror.

Freydis presses on until they are both sated, then rolls over onto her side and lies still.

Suddenly it is as though her whole body is filled with a strong, warm, tingling light. She knows what is happening right away. A soul has flown inside and taken residence deep in her belly. She is with child.

For a moment she feels tender-hearted and tells the future father. Surely now he will take her with him to Iceland. But the notion is brutally repressed.

'That doesn't change anything,' says Sverre, quickly pulling on his clothes.

He leaves her without a backward glance. Half-naked, helpless, Freydis goes on sitting there in the grass. She doesn't notice the dark cloud suddenly covering the sky. Angry tears rain down upon her. She is under water. Her loose locks stick to her skin, as do the few pieces of clothing she is still wearing.

She catches sight of her skirt, carelessly discarded further up the meadow, and crawls over to grab it. She presses the soaked wool skirt close to her chest. Then Freydis turns her eyes to the heavens and howls as loudly as she can. Her mouth fills with water, enough that it eventually quenches her screams. But within her rages a terrible fury, ready to burst out.

Unwittingly, she has summoned her goddess – the dark-haired woman from the other world who has appeared to her before. The first time was when Freydis was only a young girl, and she was lost. The goddess helped her find her way home.

Now and again the goddess has comforted Freydis when she was sad, and sometimes she has demanded something of her.

The goddess is probably a dead woman from her own family whose task it is to take care of her. That is Eirik's take on it. He is the only person Freydis has ever told about the goddess. But neither she nor her father know just who the woman is. She does not resemble any of the women in his family, according to the description Freydis gives him.

Freydis decides to ask a favour of her.

'Is this what you want? It will cost you in the end, the debt demands a sacrifice,' the misty woman hisses.

'Yes, I am sure!' Freydis cries frantically. The goddess dissolves and vanishes.

A crooked woman in a dark red pointed hat stands concealed behind a rock. She has observed the entire incident. She gives a deep sigh. She had known this was going to happen, known it since the first time Freydis and Sverre came to this place. But she had hoped, nonetheless, that she had been mistaken.

Freydis, Freydis, what have you done? How can you ruin so much for yourself because of a man? Torbjorg tugs off her catskin gloves. They have become wet and stiff in the downpour. But they can be saved. The question is whether Freydis can be saved.

She draws a deep breath into the depths of her stomach and staggers back to the cave where she has been spending the summer. Indeed, where she has lived every summer since coming to Greenland. The wisewoman takes a long look at the iron casket she has hidden in the deepest recesses of the cave. Suddenly she feels heavier than a block of stone. Her wicked roots emerge.

That afternoon there is uproar at Brattalid. Odin's sword is lost, and its owner is beside himself. He will never return to Iceland without that sword, and the ship he is due to sail with leaves the next day. Everyone takes part in the search, indoors, outdoors, in the mountain caves, in the sea. No-one can find it.

When dusk falls, Freydis is in her usual spot, weaving calmly in the flickering light of the oil lamps.

Sverre peers in and glowers at her furiously, but she does not look up.

'You of course have no idea where my sword is, isn't that so?' he snarls.

Freydis pretends she did not hear him, just carries on with her weaving, unperturbed, as though nothing had disturbed her. But the left corner of her mouth twitches in a little smile.

Early the next day, the household is awakened by loud cries from one of the slaves. They all throw on their clothes and meet down on the beach. Then, they all see it: the sword, sticking out of a huge iceberg.

The morning sun gleams on the steel, and the sword lights up the icy blue iceberg. There is a clamour of voices, excited, cheerful. Everyone is wondering how it came to be there. The smallfolk speculate wildly, and some people cast curious glances at Freydis, standing there at the back of the crowd. But her expression gives nothing away.

A row boat is set out on the water and a slave is ordered to climb up the slippery iceberg. It is no easy task, and the slave falls twice, on one occasion into the water. Someone fetches ropes and ice picks. The third attempt to retrieve the sword is successful.

Sverre gets his Odin's sword back. But the beautifully decorated scabbard has disappeared, and to the owner the sword seems to have lost much of its magnificence.

Since that day, he was never able to satisfy a woman.

MARRIAGE AND BIRTH

Greenland, Brattalid, the year 1001

The ship had gone off course early on. They drifted aimlessly without direction on the ocean for a long time, and the crew had no idea where they were until at last they caught sight of Iceland in the far distance. They had been sailing eastward instead of west.

In late summer, before the autumnal storm gods began their furious gusts, the ship slips quietly into Eiriksfjord with Torstein and his crew aboard. Even from a distance, the people of Brattalid can see this is no voyage of triumph.

Eirik is not surprised. He stands outside the door of the Brattalid longhouse, legs firmly apart, arms crossed over his impressive paunch. Torstein was never much of a sailor.

'You were more cheerful when you waved them

off,' he remarked drily. With a wry grin, he watches the crew unload the ship.

'Now you must do your duty as chieftain and take care of exhausted seafarers,' Torstein replies sullenly, without looking at his father.

Later, Torstein states that he wants to build his own farm in Greenland and propose to Gudrid. He has had his eye on her for a long time. Eirik thinks it's a good idea. He has grown increasingly fond of Gudrid, and the fact that she has the blood of slaves in her veins makes no difference. She is good enough for his son. Gudrid also claims that her slave grandfather Vivil was in fact a member of the Irish nobility. She will be happy to marry Torstein.

Freydis does not, as a rule, get on well with other girls and women; She is too fierce and too uninterested in household tasks. But she likes Gudrid, whose independence reflects her own; She has her own opinions. Freydis is delighted for her to be her brother's wife.

The two young women, so different yet so alike, become closer after Sverre leaves. Freydis senses that Gudrid suspects what was going on between herself and Sverre, as do many other people. But Gudrid never asks, and Freydis is glad about that. Nor does she ask why Freydis is always running behind the barn to throw up.

There are plenty of other things for them to talk about. And Freydis enjoys hearing the stories Gudrid tells. She is a gifted storyteller.

One of the stories she tells is about the wisewoman Torbjorg. Freydis has a feeling that Torbjorg follows her every action closely, although the crone rarely allows herself to be seen.

Gudrid tells her that they had been staying with some hospitable folk at Herjolvsnes on the southernmost tip of Greenland the winter before they were shipwrecked at the mouth of Eiriksfjord. It was a lean year and the hunting was poor. People had been lost at sea, too.

While they were there, Torbjorg Lillevolven suddenly appeared. She was kindly received. They prepared a high seat for her, covered in a rug made of hen's down.

Torbjorg was wearing a blue cape with ribbons edged with stones at the corners. The neckline was adorned with glass beads, and on her head, she wore a cap of black lambskin lined with white catskin. Her staff was decorated with jewels and brass.

From her belt there hung a large bag containing all the items she needed for her prophecies. On her feet she wore shoes of calfskin suede, and they had long, strong straps with big brass buttons on the ends. Her hands she kept warm in white catskin mittens.

'She always wears catskin gloves,' Freydis says.

She is surprised that Torbjorg should have got as far as Herjolvsnes in winter. Where does she actually live, this mysterious woman?

Gudrid continues her story.

'Torbjorg waited for them to set before her their finest fare. They did so, goat's milk gruel and meat from all kinds of animals. She ate with a brass spoon and a knife with a handle made from a walrus tooth.

But she refused to answer any of their questions before she had slept there one night. They agreed.'

Next day, the soothsayer told them someone must sing the song to summon the spirits for her. Without this, she would be unable to exercise her mysterious skill, revealing by sorcery and magic the secrets of the future. The song to summon the spirits is an incantation that opens the portal to the other world, Gudrid explains. Freydis nods.

'In the end, I had to sing the incantation for her, even though I did not want to do it. I was the only person there that knew it. I learned it from my foster mother. I felt all the spirits flying through the air while I was doing it. They made it possible for Torbjorg to see that which was hidden. But I felt terrible about it, because I had already decided I wanted to place my trust in Jesus.'

'The White Christ means nothing to me. Those who follow him say that women must be subordinate and obedient to men,' Freydis says.

'We already have to do that. It's men who are the kings and the chieftains and the masters of the farms.'

'Well, maybe. But it's worse with this new religion. Women have no role at all. They have just the one god, and he is a man hovering in the sky. He has a son who is the Saviour. And the Holy Ghost, and he's a man, too. So are all the disciples, the prophets – everybody of any importance at all. At least we have the Valkyries, the Norns, Freya, Frigg, Siv, Sol and lots of other females.' Freydis smiles. It is so good to talk about the gods she loves, about whom her father has told her so much.

'You may very well be right,' Gudrid sighs, and continues to talk about what else the soothsayer said, that time at Herjolvsnes.

Torbjorg foretold that the bad times would only last that winter. Next year the harvest would be better, and there would be less sickness.

She had also seen Gudrid's destiny clearly. According to Torbjorg, Gudrid would marry the most eligible man in Greenland, but she was not to expect it to last long. Then she would marry a rich man and go on a long journey. In the end she would return to Iceland, and her descendants would be many, worthy and highly regarded.

'We'll have to see whether she was right. Marrying your brother has to be a suitable marriage, but it is not going to last long,' she says sadly.

'Don't go thinking that way. There's little enough you can do about it, anyway. It's by no means sure she was right, even though she has been right many times in the past,' Freydis says thoughtfully, and she tells Gudrid about the day Torbjorg foretold Leif's return.

'But she never mentioned that you would be aboard his ship,' she says, smiling.

The nausea comes in powerful waves, sometimes so sudden and violent that Freydis does not have time to run and hide. Anything can set her off. The tang of salt sea air, the smell of the oil lamp, or a cow bellowing without warning and startling her.

Her bleedings have stopped. She is always

exhausted. She can no longer work with the same speed, and often has to sit down and rest. Even her weaving progresses more slowly, but she has almost completed the hangings which are to furnish her father's house of sacrifice.

These last pictures have no traces of light. They portray dark, gloomy clouds. Impenetrable banks of fog and mist. Stormy waves on the ocean. Melancholy countenances. Defeated warriors lying on the field of battle, with red-haired Valkyries, spirits of death, hovering over them.

One late afternoon, as she sits alone in the long-house weaving, she is interrupted. Sigrid staggers in, bent double, her face contorted with agony. She flops down on one of the benches and curls up. It seems the pain subsides for a moment, but before long she is again grimacing horribly. She is about to give birth. But surely it is too soon.

One of the slaves is despatched to fetch Synne, the skilled herbalist. Meanwhile, Freydis prepares the water and towels.

But before the midwife they have summoned appears, another woman enters the room like a vessel in full sail. Erect, her nose in the air, the mistress of the house herself strides over to where Sigrid is lying.

Tjodhild gazes scornfully at the woman in child-birth. In a tone reminiscent of cold snow crackling, she states her errand.

'So, the master whoremonger Eirik the Red is about to sire yet another bastard.'

She turns to Freydis.

'Yes, whore's child, no doubt you are gloating, now you are getting a brother or sister of your own ilk.'

Her words make the walls ring. That thought had never occurred to Freydis – that the child about to be born is her sibling. But the thought is pushed from her mind by her blazing anger against her stepmother. What is she doing here? Both Freydis and Sigrid glare at her fiercely.

Tjodhild thinks it best to make herself scarce, now she has said her piece. Head high, she marches out of the room, her skirts billowing behind her.

Shortly afterwards, Synne storms into the longhouse, and things start to happen fast. She undresses Sigrid's lower half and feels her opening.

'The birth is well advanced. This is going to be quick,' she says tensely.

She asks Freydis to sit behind Sigrid and support her back so that she is almost sitting upright.

Soon afterwards, Synne shouts to Sigrid and tells her to push. Sigrid obeys, with all her remaining strength. She does not need to push more than a couple of times before the child slips out of her and into Synne's great soft arms.

There is a feeble cry, then Synne's rough voice, announcing that the baby is a boy. Freydis is still registering that she has a new half-brother when Synne tells her to go and fetch Eirik.

He is not far away, he has heard the rumours that the birth is imminent. He shuffles quietly into the longhouse. He glances at Sigrid, still lying spread out on the bench, and then clumsily turns to Synne. Wringing his hands, the chieftain meets her gaze.

They whisper, but Freydis overhears.

'Is it a boy?' Eirik asks.

'Yes, and he is alive, but he is very small and weak. He may not make it,' Synne replies.

'Then there's no other way. He must be set out.'

Eirik's voice sounds firm and determined, but Freydis catches a slight tremor in his tone.

Without a glance at his newborn son he picks him up and walks quickly to the door.

Sigrid is coming to her senses and realises what is happening. Her screams pierce through the air.

'What are you doing? I want my baby! Let me hold my baby!'

But Eirik does not turn back and he does not answer. He keeps walking with the baby boy in his arms. It is Synne who has to explain to Sigrid what is going on.

'He was premature. Even if he did survive, he would always be weak and sickly. He would not be able to survive here in Greenland,' she says as she gets Sigrid cleaned up.

The young slave girl breaks down in paroxysms of tears. She lies on the bench, shaking all over. Then she suddenly stands up and rushes out into the yard wearing only a long white blouse. She paces to and fro, restless, wild-eyed. She implores Eirik to tell her where her baby is, but the master refuses to answer.

She goes on, round and round, calling out to Harald, which is what she has named the boy. The same name as her father's, the smallholder who slaved all his life to keep his family, only to have his two daughters seized by the Vikings. Then Sigrid was sold to Eirik the Red. What happened to her sister Gudrun nobody knows.

Sigrid refuses to let Eirik touch her, she howls and strikes out violently when he approaches. She refuses to eat, takes only a sip of water from the stream. At last Eirik takes pity on her and tells her where the child lies – in a cave in the mountains behind Brattalid.

Sigrid sets off at a run. She does not come back.

The next day they find her body, lying beside her son, holding his hand in hers. Both look peaceful. Harald has a bunch of buttercups and bluebells on his frail breast.

This incident affects Freydis deeply. She has lost a brother, and also a slave girl who, in spite of everything, she had felt a liking for. What if someone set her own child out? What if they thought it had few chances of survival? Still, she cannot understand how the quiet, soft-spoken Sigrid could go mad the way she did.

Some time after this sad occurrence, Brattalid is getting ready to celebrate. They are preparing for a double wedding. Torstein Eiriksson and Gudrid Torbjornsdatter will be married in a Christian ceremony, while Freydis Eiriksdatter and Torvard Einarsson will be wed according to the Norse Viking custom.

This was Freydis's decision. Torvard is converting to Christianity, but he falls in with the wishes of his bride and his powerful future father-in-law.

It was also Freydis who suggested they could combine the two weddings. After lying awake night after night pondering her wretched fate, she has found a solution.

She needs to marry Torvard as soon as possible, so he would never doubt that he had fathered the child she was expecting. Already her skirts are beginning to grow tight. If she does not marry Torvard, she would have to hang around at Brattalid, dishonoured, with a bastard brat in tow. Even Eirik would hate that. Besides, it would ruin his friendship with the master of Gardar.

Her wedding day starts with a warm bath. The slave girls have been up early to heat the water. Sweet-scented herbs from southern lands are scattered in the water. She bathes, head back, eyes closed, relishing her last bath as an unmarried woman.

Then she steps into a new, beautiful, deep-blue gown made of soft material purchased from a trading vessel the previous summer. The dress is embellished with colourful stones. Freydis puts on the costly bracelets and rings her future husband has given her. But what means the most to her is a heavy brass necklace with red stones. This belonged to her Norwegian grandmother, her father's mother, whom her father has always spoken highly of.

Now for her hair. Toril combs it and sets it up in an intricate knot. Toril is a lively, dark-haired girl who has taken over Sigrid's role. She is competent, but rather too talkative, Freydis thinks.

'Oh, you are lucky, getting married. I hope I'll get married one day,' she says dreamily, winding a sparkling string into her hair.

'That's not very likely,' snaps Freydis.

'Oh, you look gorgeous. You smell so good, too. Why aren't you smiling?'

'Mind your own business,' says the chieftain's daughter sharply.

After that, the slave girl says no more. She quickly finishes her task.

Freydis is ready. With heavy steps she makes her way to the ring of stones set up outside the house of sacrifice. Torvard is already in his place inside the ring. Everyone is waiting for the bride. Freydis goes in and takes her place at Torvard's side. He smiles, taking her arm.

Eirik is in his element. He fills the entrance to his house of sacrifice, standing on a large flat boulder. With a broad smile he advances towards the bridal couple. He has something in his arms; a wonderfully carved staff engraved with runes to bring good fortune. He presents it to the bridal couple.

The wedding guests raise their voices in a newly composed song in honour of the bridal couple. Freydis surveys all the familiar smiling faces from somewhere outside herself. For some reason her eyes rest on her future mother-in-law, her almost toothless smile, her hard eyes. Freydis will certainly need to watch her step there. The loud singing ends with rowdy stomping and clapping.

Then the chieftain throws his arms wide and summons everyone to a feast, a feast which will last for several days. Everything is ready in the new house of sacrifice.

A massive long table occupies most of the room in the house. Eirik had to obtain the timber at high cost because Leif refused to hand over the timber from Vinland that he had so desired.

Both the walls and the solid door are decorated with engraved verses. The room is hung with the bride's woven furnishings. Eirik likes the pictures of Freya and her lover best of all, and they hang in the place of honour. The dark pictures Freydis wove more recently are not on display.

There is much laughter and the atmosphere grows more lively as the wedding guests take their seats. Eirik occupies the high seat, as is his right. The bridal couple sit on his left, while the parents of the groom sit on his right.

At last the time has come to wield the knife and sacrifice the animals in honour of the gods.

'Silence!' roars Eirik, raising the slaughtering knife. The chieftain wears a shirt of violet silk with a gleaming breastplate over the top. He wears black homespun trousers and newly sewn leather shoes. His hair is combed back, and it seems the sun has sent some of its beams into his green eyes.

Freydis shines only with the jewellery she wears and the stones on her dress. But she does not reveal what she is feeling. The way her life has turned out, her only option is to marry Torvard Einarsson. She glances at her husband and he smiles back. It seems he can hardly wait to get her back to Gardar.

'You look so lovely today. Is all well with you?' he asks, stroking her arm gently.

'Yes, I'm fine,' she lies.

Torvard turns, laughing towards Eirik, who is

carving up flesh and splashing the whole table with blood.

Torvard actually has nice hands and lovely eyes, she thinks. Otherwise he is insignificant. He does not kindle the slightest spark in her, he is nothing like Sverre. Despite her condition, every fibre of her being trembles when she thinks of her lover. But alongside her desire her rage simmers.

She is not angry with Torvard. How could she be angry with a person who is so obsessed with her? And he does not seem a bad person. She will be able to put up with him. I shall have to find some fun once I am settled at Gardar, she thinks, and raises the brimming mead goblet. The guests follow suit, and then burst out into loud singing.

A reindeer, two sheep and several hares are sacrificed in the house of sacrifice. No expense is spared; This is, after all, the chieftain's only known daughter who is to be wed. The blood of the newly slaughtered beasts is sprinkled over the guests, those of them who remain true to the Norse religion, and on the walls and benches.

The gods are summoned to acknowledge the marriage. The loudest cries implore Freyr and Freya, the fertility gods; The guests hope they will ensure that Freydis and Torvard have many children.

The meat is cooked and roasted, and in the house of sacrifice the mood grows increasingly animated as the mead goes down their gullets. Suddenly the door is flung open. On the doorstep are the other two newlyweds.

'Anyone object to a new groom?' Torstein roars.

His smile is so broad it almost wraps around his head. He stands rock-solid, hands at his side, his chest jutting out, rejoicing in having won the most beautiful woman in Greenland.

Gudrid is as splendidly attired as Freydis in a long white linen gown. She too wears magnificent jewellery, and her hair has been splendidly arranged on the top of her head and adorned with pale blue glass beads which sparkle like her eyes.

'Yes, come in, come in!'

Eirik the Red is well content. He knows neither Gudrid nor Torstein frequent Tjodhild's church, although they have both been baptised. In spite of it all, he is the chief among the people of this land, and today he is marrying off two of his children. He cries out a hearty toast for both married couples. Today belongs to everyone.

One by one, guests from the Christian marriage in Tjodhild's church mingle with the Norse. But Tjodhild and Leif remain outside. They both congratulate Freydis, but she feels their good wishes are lukewarm. She had expected nothing better from Tjodhild, but she shrinks when she looks into Leif's cold eyes. Why is he being like this? Does he know about Sverre? Can he not at least forgive her, isn't that what the Christian god says he should do?

There is eating and drinking, singing and dancing, both inside and outdoors. The evening is fine, with a fresh but gentle breeze. Freydis joins in enthusiastically; It is better than sitting about moping.

Torvard stays in his seat, happily watching his wife swinging around with one man after the next.

Gudrid dances too, but only with Torstein. They make an odd couple, but seem happy enough. Later in the evening, Freydis takes her sister-in-law's arm and leads her outside. Laughing, they sit down on the ground with their backs against the house wall.

'That's some feast,' Gudrid exclaims, leaning back and shaking off her shoes.

'I imagine things are livelier here than over at Tjodhild's,' Freydis says, tugging at her red hair so it flows free.

'You better believe it! I thought Oddmund the priest was never going to stop his chanting! But we got wed, anyway!'

'Yes, how about that? Torstein was a pain in the neck as a child. And he's hardly the best worker. Would you not have been better off marrying Leif? He is good-looking, he's been on explorations, and he is going to inherit Brattalid.'

'That's true, but Leif never showed the slightest interest in me. Torstein makes me laugh, and he's easy company. That's enough for me. You can't find everything you want in one single man,' Gudrid sighs.

'No, you are right about that,' Freydis sighs too.

They fall silent. Gudrid looks as if a question is burning her tongue but something keeps her back.

Suddenly the chieftain comes swaying past them. He has thrown off his jacket and bursts out laughing when he catches sight of the two of them.

'So, this is where the brides of the night are hiding! Lucky me, I'm the father of Greenland's fairest maidens! Yes, you're my daughter too, now. And I'm glad of it,' he says to Gudrid, suppressing a belch.

'But now you'll have to come inside, so your husbands don't think you've run away,' he quips jovially, helping them to their feet.

Then he places his right arm round Freydis's waist and his left round Gudrid and escorts them proudly into the house of sacrifice.

There are guests from every corner of the land. The population of the Greenland settlements is small enough that they all know one another. During the night, the crew of an Icelandic trading vessel which has happened to put in at Brattalid join the feast, which will be famed for many years to come.

When day breaks, there are people lying about everywhere. Some splayed out on the grass. Luckily it was a warm autumn night, so nobody froze to death. A handful of hardy souls are still sitting singing inside the house of sacrifice. They are ready to go on feasting for the next few days. Others who overdid the mead have to stand behind the barn and relieve themselves.

The Icelandic captain does not make it that far. He throws up the remains of the wedding banquet right at the feet of Freydis, who is on her way to the stream to throw some cold water on her face. As he tries, deeply embarrassed, to throw some soil over his vomit, he stammers an apology.

'It's all right. I didn't get any on me,' says Freydis, walking on.

She's known this sort of thing before. But this is the last time – certainly at Brattalid.

The powerful nausea she has been fighting over the past few months has started to recede. But the sight of the hung-over ship's captain makes her belly writhe again.

She and Torvard spent their wedding night in Eirik and Tjodhild's old marriage bed. Torvard had his way with her and seemed well content when he rolled onto his side to sleep. She herself slept little, not only because of Torvard's droning snores.

The bridal chest with her dowry was packed long ago and now stands ready down on the shore. It is loaded onto a ship. The grey-blue clouds in the sky grow closer together as the newly-weds go aboard.

Eirik has come to wave them good-bye. He is in a cheerful mood after the great feast.

And now they are on their way to Gardar. It doesn't take long. They could have sailed out of Eiriksfjord and then turned into the next fjord to the south, Einarsfjord. But it is easier to sail a little further up Eiriksfjord and over to the other side of the fjord. From there it is not far to Gardar.

When they are halfway, the clouds release their heavy burden. Rain pours down on the newly-weds. That's all we needed, Freydis thinks gloomily – and then makes her mind up to make the best of things. She begins to laugh and prance. Torvard quickly joins in the game, running after her, and so, wet to the skin and giggling, they arrive at Gardar.

But they soon calm down when they see the whole household has gathered under one roof to welcome them, headed by Torvard's parents, Einar, the master of Gardar, and his wife Bjarghild.

'Welcome. What weather you brought with you!

We must see to it that you get warm and into dry clothes so that you don't get ill.'

'Yes, thank you, that will be lovely,' says Freydis, taking the hand Einar holds out. It is big, rough and warm.

Bjarghild is not smiling. Now she speaks.

'I was going to show you round the farm. But now we shall have to wait for the rain to stop. You'd better go with Torvard to the house you are going to live in,' she says.

Nevertheless, her mother-in-law begins to talk about the barn, the stable, the outhouses, the byres, and finally the enormous larder.

'But if you need to go in there, you'll have to come to me first,' she says, rattling the bunch of keys hanging from her belt, which is buckled too tightly about her considerable frame.

Freydis groans silently as she meets Bjarghild's hostile gaze. She had expected to be the mistress of Gardar herself, with responsibility for the keys. But she cheers up when Torvard shows her the longhouse he has built for them – the house the newly-weds will have to themselves.

From the outside it looks like any other house, with outer walls of turf and stone, a hefty door and a pipe on the roof. The grass on the roof is fresh and green. The house is supported by long pale timbers. It smells of fresh wood. No smoke has yet had a chance to stain the wooden walls. There is no sickly aroma of oil nor the smell of wet woollen clothing.

The loom from Brattalid stands waiting for her in the

middle of the room. Next to it there is a little alcove where Freydis can keep her clothes, jewellery and private possessions. There is a sleeping bench there too, but no doubt the expectation is that she will sleep in the marriage bed with Torvard, which abuts on her own room.

Behind the loom she finds the kitchen equipment: kettles, troughs, ladles, spoons, bowls and much more. There is a chest there too. It contains cloths and table linen and other items. On either side of the central passageway there is a small elevated wooden platform. Here they can sit and eat, and in the winter the slaves can sleep here. These low platforms are covered in reindeer pelts.

Skins hang on the walls, too. They seem to be the skins of seals and other marine animals. A brand-new cauldron hangs over the hearth in the centre of the house. It is attached to a wooden bar in the ceiling. In the outer corridor there are buckets, scythes, axes and knives.

Torvard has laid it all to rights in hopes of pleasing her. Now he studies her face tensely.

'Well, what do you think? Does it look good?'

'Yes, it's great. '

'I want you to be happy. You need only say it if there's anything else you need,' he says, looking at her with eyes full of desire.

Her soaking dress sticks to her body, revealing her figure. Hastily they tug off their wet clothing and initiate their marriage bed. Afterwards, she lies warm and dry beneath the furs, staring at the ceiling.

She is content. She is safe and she has all she

needs. But there is nothing here that sets her pulses racing, nothing that kindles her fire.

Already now, on her first day at Gardar, she wonders if she will be stuck here forever. Slaving away day after day, the same tasks again and again, at the beck and call of Torvard's parents. Work. Sleep. Eat. Work, Sleep. Eat. What must she do to feel alive?

She represses the thought. The dreams of another life must wait. Wait until she is established at Gardar. Wait until the child is born, and she is mistress of her own body again.

Freydis refuses to be bossed about by Bjarghild. One of the first things she does after she arrives at Gardar is to establish a larder where she can make her own food. She has no intention of asking her mother-in-law every time she needs something.

Bjarghild stamps about the yard, wrathful that this newcomer of a daughter-in-law is doing as she pleases. But the mistress does not dare provoke her too much, for she is, after all, the daughter of the chieftain of Greenland.

Freydis and Torvard get two slaves of their own. They are siblings, about the same age as Freydis, and belong to an Irish family defeated by the Vikings. The master of Gardar bought them some time ago.

The slender blonde girl with the deep brown eyes bears the name Bjadok. Her job is to tend the fire, fetch water, do the milking of the cows that have been given to the newly-weds, gather moss, heather and other winter fodder for the animals, cook and do the washing.

Once a week she heats water all day so that Freydis

and Torvard can have their bath. Then the great tub is brought in and filled with water and scented soap. When the couple have finished bathing, Bjadok and her brother Brian can climb into the tub.

The girl does the tasks assigned to her without complaint, but she says no more than she has to. It is only when she is arranging Freydis's unruly locks that she opens up, and lively songs in a language Freydis doesn't understand come pouring out. But Freydis likes the sound of her voice; It is like going on a voyage.

'That's a lovely song. Where does it come from, and what's it about?' she asks one morning. Bjadok draws the comb through her hair and forms a thick plait.

'It's a song from my own homeland. From Ireland. It's about always keeping up your hopes and your love, no matter how dark things look,' she stammers.

Freydis is silent, thinking about her words. She is not the only one here at Gardar who longs for something. But Bjadok is only a slave; Freydis is the daughter of a chieftain, after all.

'What's Ireland like? Is it like Greenland?

'It's a funny thing this country should be called Greenland, for it's much greener in Ireland. It's warmer, too, and we don't have all this snow. It is so beautiful,' Bjadok says, staring into the distance.

'I should like to go there,' Freydis eagerly.

'So would I,' the slave girl murmurs, staring at the floor.

Freydis takes charge of spinning, weaving and sewing. She likes to see her work bearing results, to feel like she is making something. Now she has started making clothes for the baby she is expecting. Trousers, shirts, leather shoes, nappies, a hat and a thick wool-lined sleeping bag to keep him warm in the cold season.

She thinks about the child. What will he look like? She knows she is expecting a boy. Smiling, head awry, she strokes the small but rapidly increasing bulge in her belly.

Just as she did back at Brattalid, she rises with the dawn and embarks on long hikes in the surrounding area to acquaint herself with nature as it wakes after its nocturnal inactivity. This is when she day-dreams. She dreams of travelling, seeing other countries, other people, experiencing new things. She dreams that people will like her and look up to her as they do her father and brother.

But most of all she thinks about Sverre. She is furious that he deserted her. Furious at the humiliation. Furious with herself than she cannot seem to forget him.

And she is sad, too. Sad about the love that died. Regret for the passion she no longer feels. Regret at the life she has to live now. As Sverre's child grows within her, so her sorrows seem heavier and heavier to bear. At times she feels she is carrying a stone that continues to get heavier – a stone that kicks. She is expecting a real man.

In the late winter months these lonely rambles come to

a halt. Freydis begins to feel so heavy that she has difficulty making her way through the snow.

This year the winter is hard and rich. The snow lies about them like a mighty shield as far as the eye can see. On the fields, on the hills, on the fjord. Everything is white. Silent, cold, unrelentingly white. It feels as though the eternal glacier has thrown its arms around the poor people who have chosen to make this land their home. Many of the animals have turned white too. All that can be seen of them is their tracks.

Freydis can hardly remember a time when it was this cold. When she goes out with a kettle full of steaming water, the steam turns to snow and falls gently to the ground.

But it is also incredibly beautiful. When the sun comes out and changes the whiteness into flashing crystals. When the whiteness is tinged with blue as day turns to night. When the moon casts its light on the whiteness while the wolves howl in the distance.

She prefers to spend the evenings inside. It is cosy and safe when she hears the gusts of wind roar against the walls of the house. Anything strong or hard falls victim to the wind.

When she is in good spirits, she occasionally casts a grateful glance at her husband, sitting by the oil lamp carving a wooden horse for the child. The flickering light makes him look peaceful.

But even the gales must rest now and then from the fury that has driven them for weeks and months. And when Tor's servants, the eight lords of the winds, finally decide on a truce, the wind gradually abates, until it is no more than a breath. The air grows milder, the snow melts and flows down in the streams and then into the sea. Spring is on its way. Nature awakens.

One grey rainy afternoon as Freydis sits at her weaving, she feels a sharp pain in the small of her back. Then it comes again. She is about to give birth. Two of the slaves are sent to fetch Gerd, the midwife.

They do not return before late in the evening. Freydis is lying in bed, doubled up with agony; The pains are almost constant. They go on and on, giving her no respite. Gerd, a strong, well-developed woman, strides authoritatively into the longhouse. She deposits her sack on the bench. It contains everything she will need for the birth.

She tells Freydis to lie on her back. Then she removes her clothing and performs a quick examination of her lower body. Bjadok is told to make sure Gerd has access to water and cloths. Then Gerd walks firmly over to Torvard, who is pacing restlessly about the yard, his hair and clothing saturated. He has not noticed the pouring rain. He looks anxiously at Gerd, whose brow is furrowed with concern.

'This is going to be long and difficult birth,' she says.

'But they will be well – both Freydis and the child?' quavers Torvard.

'We must pray to all the gods we believe in. Here on this farm there seem to be all sorts of gods about, as far as I can see,' says the newly christened midwife in mild mockery, but loud and clear so her words reach the ears of everyone. She calms down when she sees she is frightening Torvard.

'I'll do the best I can. It will all work out. But you

had better come inside now and get some warm clothes on. It'll be no help to anyone if you go and make yourself ill.'

'Thank you,' the husband says, and does as she suggests.

Although Gerd has just been baptised, she brews up a strong herbal remedy which she hopes will speed up the birth process. The recipe has been used by the wise women of Gerd's family for generations. She scatters herbs round the house to chase away evil spirits, demons and other undesirables. Then she takes a small jug containing sheep's blood which serves a similar purpose. While she does it, she hums Christian hymns, just to bc on the safe side.

Next morning the brew is ready. Freydis is exhausted after a sleepless right, racked with pain. The herbs speed up the pains, and now it hurts so much she screams aloud. Late in the evening of the second day, her waters break. But only when the sun is rising behind a small bank of cloud does Gerd tell Freydis to squat and push.

Gerd tries to grasp the head when it appears. Freydis musters the last of her strength. Something loosens and slides out of her. Freydis faints and drops to the floor.

When she comes to, Gerd is standing there smiling, holding a small bundle wrapped in a blanket. She knew it all along. A boy. She takes him in her arms. She is delighted to see that the child looks like his grandfather, Eirik. He has the same bright red hair, which she has also inherited.

His eyes are just two narrow slits, he seems to be

sleeping. But when she lays him to the breast, he latches on and sucks strongly at once. She feels calm now and allows herself to breathe out after the rigours of the birth.

Then he opens his eyes. She peers at him, and a shudder runs through her. The boy child has Sverre's eyes. She sighs deeply, throws back her head and feels the tears well up. Will she never be free of him? Is she to be reminded of the man who betrayed her every single day for the rest of her life?

Those eyes mean she cannot delight in her son as much as she should. She feels like packing him off on the first boat to his treacherous father in Iceland. She nurses him. All the rest of his care she leaves to Bjadok.

But Torvard is enchanted. Proudly he struts about with the infant on his arm, smiling and laughing at him. Does he not even suspect the child may not be his?

He cannot fail to have heard the rumours, but he never questions her. Perhaps he is afraid to hear the answer. And so long as he doesn't ask, she has no intention of saying anything.

But Bjarghild has no such qualms.

'Amazing how big he was, for a premature baby,' she says, narrowing her eyes as she scrutinises Freydis.

'Well, as you know, in our family we are big and well-nourished. Anyhow, it might have happened when I was visiting here in August to plan my wedding. Your son couldn't manage to wait for the wedding night.'

She stares back boldly at her mother-in-law. Bjarghild is the first to blink. She says no more about the matter. Torvard wants to call the child Einar after his own father, the master of the house. Freydis raises no objections. The name is as good as any other. And in fact, she is quite fond of Torvard's father, at least he is preferable to his wife.

The other marriage that was celebrated at the legendary feast in Eirik the Red's house of sacrifice was of short duration. Torstein and Gudrid took up residence on a farm in the far south of Greenland, with Torstein the Black and his wife Sigrid.

But in the depths of winter, a terrible sickness came to the farm. Sigrid was the first to succumb. Then Gudrid's Torstein became ill. He lay long in bed, twisting and turning in fevered dreams.

Suddenly he sat bolt upright. He stared at Gudrid with round imploring eyes. He had had a vision about her future.

'It will be good. You will marry a rich man, but he is not from Greenland. And you will have children you can be proud of,' he said to Gudrid, who held his hand, weeping.

'Don't worry about me. You must lie down and rest and get well again.'

But Torstein wanted to use his last minutes telling her how he wished his funeral to be.

'I want to be buried at Brattalid according to the Christian rites,' he said as he drew his last breath, at almost the same time as his sister delivered her first child.

His body lay long at the farm. They wanted to make sure the sickness had left the place for good. They did not want to carry disease to Eirik the Red and his people.

While they waited, they comforted one another, Gudrid and Torstein the Black. Perhaps they took the comforting too far, in some people's view. The rumours spread like wildfire.

At last Torstein was transported to Brattalid. A sorrowful group stand waiting on the beach. Tjodhild, deathly pale and dressed all in black, throws herself tearfully on the coffin containing the body of the son she had married off only a few months prior.

He is buried in Tjodhild's church. The priest drives a stake down to his breast and then pulls it up. The priest pours holy water into the hole, and they celebrate mass.

Freydis has not recovered fully from the birth. But nonetheless she crosses the fjord to bid farewell to Torstein. Although they had not got on well in their childhood, she had begun to like him.

She hugs her father for a long time, breathing in the familiar smell of fresh sweat, warm, dry wadmal and sunshine. The chieftain's hair is going grey, and the lines in his face are deeper than ever.

Despite his grief for his son, Eirik manages to be delighted with the newborn grandchild who has come to the funeral with his mother. Einar waves his arms about and smiles at his grandfather.

'He looks like me,' Eirik grins, rushing round the yard with the baby boy in his arms.

'Yes, he does indeed,' Freydis agrees, smiling.

She turns to Gudrid, who is standing by Torstein's grave with bowed head. She is wearing a sober grey homespun gown. She has made no effort to dress up. Even her long fair plait looks dishevelled. She is almost unrecognisable as the bride she was.

Freydis goes up to her and places an arm round her shoulder and draws her close. Gudrid bends her head and leans into the embrace. The two young women are so alike, yet so dissimilar. One red-haired, quick-tempered, hot-blooded. The other fair, erect, dignified. Both independent, both strong.

'Torbjorg Lillevolven was right. Our marriage was not to last long,' Gudrid says dolefully.

'She is usually right. Unfortunately. It is frightening, talking to her.'

'Now I just have to go and wait for the rich man who is my destiny.'

Freydis doesn't say anything to that. They stand there a long time in silence, until Gudrid says she wants to rest. At the age of twenty she has been widowed for the second time. She has also borne two still-born babies – one by her first husband, Torir, the other by Torstein. She can hardly bear to look at little Einar.

The young widow is received at Brattalid with open arms. She is given her own alcove where she can be on her own and reflect on her future course of action.

For Freydis, everyday life soon resumes its rhythm. Morning rambles, nursing her son, weaving, sewing. Einar grows and he is a good little boy, but she is still unable to love him as a mother should.

To get away from the farm, she sometimes goes hunting and fishing with the men. And here she sees a different side to her husband. Torvard, the born hunter, has the gift of creeping right up to the quarry, as though he were invisible to it. His prey discovers his presence too late, just before he delivers the coup de grâce. Swiftly and accurately, he thrusts his spear in so the blood spurts.

He shows all his teeth in a smile when he pulls the spear out again and lifts up his kill. And then Freydis returns his smile. She had thought of him as feeble and weak, someone who just wanted to potter about a farm and live in peace and quiet. She would not have believed that Torvard would take satisfaction in killing an animal.

But most of the time she feels trapped. At night she dreams that a serpent has coiled itself about her throat and intends to kill her. Often she wakes with her hands clutching her throat, sweat pouring off her body.

Torvard's parents show little desire to hand over the farm to their son and daughter-in-law. Bjarghild is not very pleased with Freydis. Not that she says much. But the glares, the heavy sighs, and her expression when she looks at Freydis betray her feelings. She does not think Freydis is suited to being mistress of a household. And, her daughter-in-law reflects, she may be right.

Is this all life has to offer? She asks herself this more and more often. She has tried several times to conjure up the dark-haired goddess, to ask her advice. But the goddess has not appeared since that wretched day when Sverre left her.

VINLAND

Eiriksfjord and Vinland, the year 1003

One summer's day two ships come sailing into Eiriksfjord. The sun is high in the sky; its beams make the sea and the green meadows sparkle cheerfully. A white hawk has spread its wings wide and hovers casually over the stately ships making their way towards Brattalid.

Already from a distance the people on land can see that these are no ordinary trading vessels. There is something magnificent about them, especially the leading ship. It lies well in the water, is large, long and broad, and fully laden. It has blue sails, the largest sails they have ever seen.

The bow is adorned with a carved head that closely resembles the ship's master and chieftain, who, they soon learn, bears the name of Torfinn Karlsevne and hails from Iceland. He stands squarely just behind his own carved likeness. He is a wealthy and well-born man. Torfinn is tall and powerfully built, broad-shouldered with a large square face. His hair is cut short and is dark brown, like the large eyes which bore into anyone who dares to meet their gaze.

As helmsman he has Snorre Torbrandsson, who sits further astern and issues commands to the crew who will have to row the last little distance, because there is no wind in the heart of Eiriksfjord. Altogether there are thirty free men and women on board, and about ten slaves.

The smaller ship also holds some forty people. It is a vessel of more average size, older, and seems to have seen many hours at sea. Nor is it decorated up to the same standard.

The ship is commanded by two Icelandic master mariners, Bjarne Grimolvsson and Torhall Gamlesson. Torhall, nick-named Fisher, is an old friend of Eirik's. He is tall of stature, dark-haired, troll-like and taciturn. Like Eirik, he has remained true to the old Norse gods and refused to be baptised.

'Torhall!'

A loud yell of delight is heard long before the ships reach land. Eirik stands waving his arms at the second ship. Torhall waves back.

But Karlsevne lands first. The elderly chieftain goes forward to greet him.

'My name is Eirik the Red. Welcome to Greenland,' he says, holding out his hand.

'I have heard a lot about you. I'm Torfinn Karlsevne, and we are from Iceland,' the ship's captain says, holding out his hand to Erik the Red.

'Excellent. What brings Karlsevne to Greenland?'

'I was curious to see what you have made of this land, but we bring trade goods, too.'

The two men fall silent, measuring one another up. Then Torhall's boat comes in and Eirik hurries towards it. Torhall springs ashore. And soon the two old friends are leaping joyfully about the yard, slapping each other on the shoulder. Suddenly they lose their footing and tumble to the ground.

Eirik pretends to take a stranglehold on Torhall, roaring with mirth. Torhall feigns dead, then hauls himself free and rolls away from Eirik the Red. They lie there, then sit up panting side by side on the grass.

'So here you are, at last. What took you so long?' Eirik demands, wiping the sweat off his brow.

'I know, I know. I did mean to come here sooner, but it didn't happen till now. I've been on Viking raids,' Torhall says.

Eirik's eyes are shining.

'Let's hear!'

And Torhall tells of Ireland, the Hebrides, Norway. Of gold, silk, iron and other riches. And of beautiful women, too.

'But you haven't got yourself a wife?' Eirik asks.

'No, that's not for me.'

'I understand. There's always trouble with women-folk. My own wife's gone completely crazy. She's become a Christian and built a church here at Brattalid.'

Torhall's eyes widen in horror. The two old friends have so much to talk about, they get lost in their reminiscences. But now Tjodhild appears and asks Eirik whether he is thinking of attending to his guests. They are still standing waiting by the ships.

As is the custom, the crew are invited to a feast by Eirik the Red. A sheep is slaughtered and roasted. Fresh fish from the fjord, dried meat of seal and reindeer, cheese and butter are served. There are great quantities of ale. And, of course, the mead barrels are rolled out. Guests and hosts tuck into the offerings of food and drink.

The evening and the night are warm, and spirits are high. There is singing, and many toasts. The tone between the Icelanders and the Greenlanders is cordial. There are several reasons the Icelanders have come to Brattalid. Some are thinking of settling in this green land of which they have heard so many good things.

The tales of Eirik the Red's land in the west are doing the rounds in Iceland. Some tales tell of a rich and fertile land where people live at peace with one another. Other tales, doubtless started by Eirik's numerous detractors, speak of a barren land with towering icebergs and steep grey cliffs, and one tyrannical chieftain who rules over all.

Most of those on board believe the first account rather than the second. They want something more than volcanoes, glaciers and hard, stormy weather. They cherish the dream of a green, temperate southern Greenland.

No doubt they also long to get away from the many powerful chieftains on Iceland who make life difficult for everyone else. They have heard that Eirik the Red is a hard man but a fair one, a chieftain who cares about his subjects.

Others are keen to trade with the Greenlanders and then return to Iceland as quickly as possible. Torfinn Karlsevne is among the latter, but is also open to any opportunities that may present themselves.

The Icelandic guests will have more time than they anticipated to make up their minds. A huge crack in the glacier at the heart of the ice fjord on the other side of Eiriksfjord sends a massive fleet of icebergs out into the fjord.

It would be impossible to try to sail past the icebergs without the ship being trapped. Besides, the summer is nearly over. The fjord begins to freeze over unusually early. The weather keeps Karlsevne and his company stranded at Brattalid. There is no other option but for Eirik the Red in his hospitable way to offer winter accommodation to everyone.

The chieftain quickly sees that it will be crowded, even if he takes all the dwelling-houses on the farm into use. The Icelanders cannot sleep aboard ship when the winter storms set in. A more pressing concern is whether there will be enough food for everyone. Restlessly he paces about, peering into the larders, tugging at his beard. There are not enough provisions and the situation is becoming desperate. He sends both the Icelanders and the Greenlanders out hunting and fishing, as it is still possible to get down to the fjord.

But even if all the men went hunting throughout the winter, there would not be enough food. When the snow and ice lie heavy and impenetrable, the results of the hunt are much more sparse than in summer.

He wonders whether he should ask Freydis if Gardar can help. But that is not Eirik's way. The chieftain of Greenland does not ask others for help. Besides, he knows that most of the other farms have enough trouble getting food for themselves. Karlsevne senses his unease.

'It seems there is something on your mind, Eirik the Red. Can I be of any help?' he asks one day when they bump into each other in the yard.

The chieftain frowns and shifts his weight from one foot to the other. He does not want to confide in Karlsevne. He is still not sure he likes him. But this is a matter of survival.

'There will be many of us here at Brattalid this winter. I am not sure we shall have enough food,' he says shamefacedly.

'Why didn't you say so before? I have honey, malt, corn, dried fish and meat and large amounts of other food aboard my ship. Torhall certainly has supplies, too. There should be enough for everyone,' he smiles, and goes down to the ships with Eirik the Red so he can see for himself.

The Icelandic leader is in no hurry to leave Greenland. The beautiful widow, Gudrid, had soon caught his eye. Now he has the whole winter to court her. He showers her with gifts and promises of a splendid future. He wants to marry her, slave blood or no slave blood, even though she has been married twice before, with tragic consequences.

Gudrid, for her part, has little liking for this braggart of an Icelander. There is nothing about him that appeals to her or make her heart beat faster. He does not have Torir's boyish adventurous spirit nor Torstein Eiriksson's seductive attractiveness and good humour. Nor is he to be compared to Torstein the Black. She melts when she remembers that second Torstein who comforted her after the death of her husband.

Even so, Gudrid is giving a lot of thought to her future. She is happy at Brattalid, and they are kind to her there. But she cannot stay here for ever as a burden on Eirik the Red and his family. There is something she has been dreaming of, too. And the dreams do not come to her in Greenland, even though she enjoys the mild summer evenings here. There is nothing so lovely and peaceful as the sun's rays touching the landscape with a warm red glow, and when the spring stream chuckles merrily as it meanders across the meadow. The only disturber of the peace is the tiresome mosquito.

Karlsevne, she realises with a heavy heart, is her best way out of her situation. She has not forgotten, either, that Torbjorg Lillevolven foretold that she would marry a rich man and found an honourable dynasty. Torstein Eiriksson, too, had babbled about a rich husband who was not a Greenlander while on his death bed. She cannot deny her destiny. And her destiny is Torfinn Karlsevne, like it or not.

On one of the darkest days of the year a wedding is celebrated at Brattalid. For the second time in a twelvemonth, Gudrid enters Tjodhild's church as a bride. This time, too, she wears a newly sewn dress of white silk with silver jewellery about her neck, her soft wrists and in her elegantly arranged hair. About her shoulders she wears a white woollen cape embroidered with small beads whose glitter rivals that of the snowflakes that sparkle in the few hours of sunshine. An ice queen. But her smiles are few and far between.

Torfinn Karlsevne, on the other hand, is grinning from ear to ear. He too is dressed in his best. Trousers and long jacket in dark blue wadmal and a silver waistcoat with brass buttons. The fine-looking couple get wed by Oddmund the priest, who is still striving to Christianise Greenland. Slowly but surely, things are beginning to go his way.

Then everyone is invited to the wedding feast at Brattalid. Dried meat, dried fish and cheese are served. The evening is full of song. Both hymns and newly composed verses are sung in the bridal couple's honour. The verses are short and easy to learn. Soon all the guests are singing along. Then there are competitions in the snow – races, wrestling and throwing of snowballs and stones.

And of course, there is storytelling. The ancient stories of the Norse kings, the new settlers in Iceland, grand Viking voyages, brave men and strong-minded women, and the life and times of the Norse gods. There are many good storytellers who catch the attention of the wedding guests. Other stories make the room shake with laughter and leave the walls ringing.

Freydis has heard most of it before. But every time the story is slightly different, especially the accounts of her father's voyages, which become wilder with each retelling. She does not like hearing tales about all the women they took by force and enslaved.

Freydis is the only representative of Gardar at the wedding. Torvard has a fever and has been in bed for a few days. And she thinks Einar is too small to be transported so far in the biting winter weather. Freydis arrives on horseback, riding across the snowy fjord currently covered in a thick sheet of ice.

Freydis sees how the Icelanders eagerly swallow Leif's tales about Vinland, and she overhears some of them saying they would like to travel there in the spring. This kindles a hope in her. It is what she has been longing for. To leave everything behind, experience something new. Vinland sounds increasingly appealing. She starts to pay closer attention to her brother's tales than she did when he had just returned from Vinland.

Karlsevne moves into Gudrid's little house. It is a humble dwelling compared to what he is accustomed to, but he fills it with the goods and gold he has brought with him from Iceland. The slave girl who shared Gudrid's dwelling has to leave. Now Gudrid must light the fire herself, melt the water and carry out the rest of the preparations for the day. Karlsevne will certainly not be doing it. He snores loudly and does not usually wake up before the house has begun to get warm.

'You'll have a better life when we get to Iceland. I have a big farm and plenty of slaves,' he says one evening as they lie naked side by side on the bunk.

'I am sure it will all be fine,' Gudrid replies listlessly. She is tired, and she aches all over. She feels like all she does is fetch and carry.

'Or maybe we should go Vinland first,' he says pensively. Gudrid pricks up her ears.

'Yes, can we do that? It sounds like a fertile land,' she says, seeing a chance to leave all the misery behind and start a new life in a new land.

Several of the guests who were stranded by the weather are growing increasingly keen to travel to the alluring land in the west. When spring comes, almost all of them intend to go.

Leif had said earlier that he wanted to return, but now he is fully occupied helping the priests spread the Christian gospel. He is afraid Eirik will send the priests back to Norway on the first ship if he is not careful. But Eirik's middle son, Torvald, wants to go.

Freydis hears of the plans, and now her mind is made up. She wants to go to Vinland too. This is what she has been waiting for. She would really prefer to travel alone, but she realises that she can't go without her husband.

As expected, Torvard is not overly enthusiastic; He likes living at Gardar. He has all he needs there. He enjoys his work on the land and with the livestock. He has a wife and a son. He gets enough excitement from hunting and fishing with the other Greenland farmers. Last year they travelled to northern Greenland to hunt walrus – wonderful days which he often talks about in the evenings while he is sitting carving a piece of wood into a trough.

They had fair weather the whole time, and the hunt was successful. Twenty men had stood shirtless on the beaches slaughtering the animals until late into the evening. There had been laughter and singing.

They had laden the ship to the gunwales with meat, skins and walrus teeth, which were much sought after as trading goods. Freydis listens absent-mindedly. She never has such stories to tell about her own adventures.

Torvard buys silks and other costly items for Freydis. The last time a ship came, he traded and acquired a beautiful shining gold ornament with emeralds that gleamed like her eyes. It was said the ornament had belonged to Queen Gunnhild. He hopes it may soothe his wife's restless spirit.

'What do I want with more jewellery? I'm not going to go on slaving away for your parents here year after year,' Freydis snaps.

'We don't exactly slave away. We have our own household. Remember, we have a child. It's not at all sure a one-year-old would able to take such a journey.'

'He is strong and healthy. Don't forget he is of Eirik the Red's line. He can take it,' she replied confidently.

She entices him with the warm climate and the enormous wealth to be found in Vinland, everything Leif has been talking about. At last, Torvard is convinced.

Their plans are not well received by Einar and Bjarghild. They cannot comprehend that their son and daughter-in-law wish to undertake a voyage to Vinland, with all the terrible risks it entails. First, they must sail north along the coast of Greenland to the land of the white bear: treacherous waters with lethal ice floes.

Then they must set a westerly course and sail across the ocean. What if they fail to find the land on the other side, get blown off course, or overtaken by storms? Are they not well off at Gardar? Here they have everything they need. They lack for nothing, is that not so? The barrage of questions is never-ending.

Freydis gives the best answers she can but she does not expect them to understand. They can have no idea what it is like to long, to yearn for something else so hard that it could almost make a person ill. Nor do they know how depression can take hold of every part of a person's body and gradually extinguish all joy and love of life.

Then a thought strikes her. Perhaps they do understand. After all, they left all they had in Iceland and followed when her father told of the green land to the west. That enterprise had not been without its dangers, either. Several of the ships never made it to Greenland.

'You have been on a similar voyage yourselves. Didn't you leave Iceland to go with my father? Did you not have a spirit of adventure then?' Freydis asks craftily.

That was just what was needed. The mood changes. The master of Gardar and his wife exchange smiles, and suddenly the years drop away and they seem much younger.

'Our farm in Iceland was barren and open to all weathers. We were ruled by a greedy chieftain. We wanted to get away,' the husband, Einar, says.

'When your father came and told us of the fair lands to the west, we saw a chance. We sold the farm and bought a ship along with some of our neighbours,' says Bjarghild, turning to Einar, who is nodding.

'Remember how pleased we were when we saw that Eirik the Red had not been lying? The first years, when we were building up the farm, were hard, but they were happy.'

They say that they had never regretted following him here, and they realise that Freydis is her father's daughter. Although she is a woman, she has inherited both her father's good qualities as well as his less desirable ones, they think. A love of adventure and natural leadership. Ungovernable rages and indomitable will.

Gradually they come around to the idea of the voyage to Vinland. The young couple can go, so long as they leave Einar at Gardar.

'We must have an heir who can take over Gardar if you don't come back,' the master of the house says with authority.

Freydis is easily convinced. She will no longer have to be responsible for the boy or gaze every day into Sverre's eyes.

Torvard collapses; He adores the child more than anything in the world. They are always together. Already he has been teaching Einar how to run a farm, although the boy has hardly learned to walk. But Torvard concedes defeat. He agrees with his parents that it is vital the farm stays in the family's hands. Bjadok, the slave girl, is tasked with taking care of little Einar.

The couple from Gardar are to sail with her brother Torvald and his crew. The siblings have been allowed to borrow Leif's ship, the *Serpent*, which has been to Norway and to Vinland. Now they hope Leif's luck will be in their boat with them.

There will be thirty of them in all aboard Leif's ship. There are farmers, hunters, experienced mariners and men skilled in woodworking. A handful of them were on Leif's voyage, too. They hope to load the ship with timber. There is reputed to be an abundance of trees in Vinland. Now they can obtain timber for themselves without having to pay through the nose for it to Norwegian traders.

Eight male slaves are with them for the rough work. There are also nine women on board. As well as Freydis and her assistant Binna there are Torvald's two concubines, and Maja, who is skilled with herbs and has warm hands. Four of the men have brought their wives along, too.

Large quantities of dried meat and fish are loaded on board. And drinking water, of course. They are not guaranteed to find any on their voyage.

Some of the areas they will pass through are treacherous. The unpredictable ice floes and ice bergs in the sea can join up and crush a ship to pieces. That would be the end of them. Then there are the white bears.

Weapons, tools, household equipment, clothes and everything else imaginable that they might need in the new country are loaded aboard.

Freydis is disappointed there will not be room for her loom. But she is promised that a new loom will be built for her as soon as they reach the new land. One of the men on board knows how to do it.

There will be good grazing in Vinland. And they will need dairy products and wool, so two cows and six sheep travel with them. The cows are tethered to the mast, but a little enclosure is made for the sheep in the stern of the boat, close to the slaves' sleeping area. They are charged with taking care of the animals –

feeding them and throwing their dung into the sea. The people on board have to use buckets for their necessities and empty them overboard themselves.

Great efforts are required to lift the animals into the ship and tether them. The animals protest. One ewe kicks so hard that one of the slaves breaks a couple of ribs and has to be left behind in Greenland. But at last they are all in place.

Torvald has agreed with his brother Leif that they may use his accommodation in Vinland. It is called Leifsbudir. Freydis and her eldest brother have still not made peace after their quarrel, but now she has a job for him. She finds him with the horses and breaks the ice by thanking him for allowing them to use Leifsbudir. Since it is Freydis who will be in charge of the housekeeping, she has some questions.

'Right. Come inside for a minute,' he says curtly, leading the way into the longhouse.

Inside, he offers her refreshment, but she shakes her head. A slave girl is tidying up. Leif dismisses her.

Freydis asks about springs, about where berries and other plants can be found, what equipment they will need and many other things. As he responds she studies him. Leif the Fortunate, Leif the Lucky, he is called, because he has been lucky with the weather for sailing and with finding a new, promising land. But is he really lucky? He smiles much less frequently than before. Freydis remembers how he used to play with her when she was a child and he a young man.

But then perhaps the Christian god is no joke. They do not laugh much, the newly converted Greenlanders. Have they little cause for joy? Or does the

Bible forbid people to have fun? Well, what does she know? Oddmund never mentioned anything like that the times she went to the church.

'What about you, wouldn't you like to go back to Vinland?

'Yes, but I gave my word to the King of Norway that I would make Greenland Christian. I must do my duty. Some people have no concept of duty. Some people think nothing of leaving a farm and a little child,' he says brutally.

Freydis seethes inside. No reconciliation there, then.

Her son has grandparents and slaves to take care of him, she tells him.

'When have you thought about getting a wife and children of your own, then? You should have done that ages ago,' she says sharply. Leif is the most eligible bachelor in Greenland and could have anyone he wanted. She cannot fathom why he has never married.

'That is none of your affair. You have no right to comment on my life. I wish to serve God and behave decently, unlike you. I know Torvard is not the father of your son,' Leif says bluntly.

'You ought at least to get yourself a concubine or two, then you might be less bad-tempered. I've hardly seen a smile on your face since you came home with your precious White Christ,' says Freydis.

She stands up abruptly and leaves without saying good-bye. The ship is almost ready to leave, and Freydis climbs aboard to make sure all is in order. She touches the new sail. She wove it herself, with Binna's help. Leif's sail from his great voyage to Norway and Vinland is worn and badly torn.

Freydis is thrilled that she will experience something new at last. She can hardly wait. She has secured a sleeping place for herself, all the way at the front of the ship. She has arranged her furs and blankets there. This way she will be able to sit in the bows and look ahead, while the crew behind her row and man the sail.

She goes ashore again and walks towards the house of sacrifice. Her father has asked to speak with her before she leaves. It seems he wants to tell her everything he can about the art of oceanic seamanship. As though he hastily wants to pass on to her all he has learned from his own father and other old sea dogs, and what he has learned on his own. He begins with the story of the winds, which she has heard many times before.

'There are eight winds; eight chieftains. You need to understand them. From October onwards you must not set sail or go to sea,' Eirik says, closing his eyes and continuing:

'The east wind is mourning the loss of his rank. The golden crown which once belonged to him has been blown away. When the south-east wind sees his neighbour's distress, he splashes and splutters violently. The south wind wraps himself in a warm cloudy cloak which conceals riches and warm treasures. He is afraid and blows hard to defend himself.'

'When the south-westerly wind notices that peace and friendship have disappeared, he responds with dramatic rainbows. He screws up his eyes over his beard, wet with tears, blows hard under his heavily clouded helmet and blows out rain squalls. Then he arrives with great waves and huge breakers that will sink a ship and incite all the tempests of the ocean to wrathful raging.'

'The west wind sees that from the east there come miserable gales and sorrowful sighs from the very direction whence he was formerly accustomed to receive gleaming sun beams and noble gifts of friendship. Then he understands that the agreement is in tatters, all the peace the chieftains once enjoyed together has evaporated. He dons a black garment of mourning and pulls over it a grey cloudy cloak. Then he exhales sadly and sits there with wrinkled nose and tight lips.'

'When the blue lightning north-westerly sees how wretched his neighbours are and sees his own misfortune in no longer having the evening's pleasure he is used to, he displays his wrath and his savage temper. Angrily he furrows his brows and hurls forth rattling out hail, accompanied by crashes of thunder and terrible lightning.'

'But when the north wind misses the kindness and the lovely gifts he once received from the south wind, then he rummages in his secret hiding places and adorns himself with his greatest riches. He dons a dark fur with glittering frost, sets on his head an ice-cold helmet over his frozen beard and blows hard, and the cloud banks grow heavy with hailstones.'

'The north-easterly sits in a fury with his snow-cracked beard and blows cold through his wind-blown nostrils, opens his eyes wide beneath his frost-bitten brows, draws in his cheeks, touches his jaws with his ice-cold tongue and blows out strongly through the all-enveloping snowstorm.'

'When there is no peace between these eight chieftains, then that is not the time for men to be travelling over the ocean between one land and the next. The days grow shorter, the nights darker, the sea is restless, the waves grow greater, the surf is colder, the rain heavier, and the storm comes.'

'The ships are close to foundering, the cargo shifts, and the crew can easily be swallowed up in the foaming open mouth of the sea.'

'But from March onwards the days grow longer. The north wind scours the heavens with cool light gusts, sweeping away all the storm clouds, and asks the other seven chieftains for a new agreement, a new peace treaty.'

'The winds make peace. They are all longing for a rest. Now the rain showers almost cease, the waves calm down, the waves grow smaller and the rough swell on the sea disappears. The storms ease off. The sea is calm, calm again after so long.'

Her father must have memorised the story of the winds so that he can retell it when the occasion demands. Then he starts to talk about ice.

He says there is a great deal of ice round the coast of Greenland – less around here where they live than to the north and east. In some places the sea is frozen a far way out. Ships that run into it usually founder. Great ships have sunk to the bottom but sometimes the crew have escaped by dragging small boats ashore over the ice.

Many have stayed on the ice for days before they

were able to get back to land. The ice can also be strange and unpredictable. Sometimes it is quiet, and there are passages through it where sailing is possible. At other times it moves, sometimes as fast as a ship before a fair wind.

In addition to the flat floes there are also blue icebergs, which are much larger under the surface than above. They come from the glacier tongues that slide down the valleys and then break up and tumble out into the fjords and the sea. They exist in all shapes and sizes and have a life of their own; They go their own way. Slowly but surely, they melt in the warm summer sun and the sea.

'But father, I know about the ice. You don't need to tell me about it. Here it lies thick out on the fjords every winter. And I see the new icebergs that the glacier spawns every summer. We have even walked on the glacier.'

'Yes, but the ice is capricious. We can't predict how it is going to behave. You must never, ever imagine you understand the ice. It is superior to us human folk. Do you hear me?' he demands sharply, looking at her with narrowed eyes.

Freydis agrees, but her thoughts are elsewhere. Then someone calls her name; The ships are ready to sail.

'There is so much more I wanted to tell you,' Eirik sighs.

All at once her strong, impressive father looks like an ancient old wreck. He has lost weight, his face has acquired new lines. There is not a single red hair left either in his beard or in his hair. It is all as grey now as the wadmal he is clad in. His white arthritic hands shake, and the blue veins look about to leap out from his skin.

But worse than this is his downcast spirit. Where is the laughter, the joy, the boyish joie de vivre? He who played with her, tossed her in the air, invited her to great parties and feasts, he who was the natural centre of things? She has lost sight of him, he has gone. She shakes off the melancholy thought.

'You can tell me when we return with the ship laden with timber and furs. Then we can arrange and decorate this house of sacrifice of yours,' she smiles, puts an arm round him and pats his shoulder before she hurries away.

And now they are all ready, the three ships which are sailing to the west this summer.

'We'll be back. And we'll bring timber and all kinds of treasure,' shouts Torvald Eiriksson encouragingly to all the people who have gathered on the shore at Brattalid. Eirik is not the only one who feels sad.

Freydis stands, chin up and chest out, one hand resting on the side of the ship. Her long hair is flowing, and she is smiling. Her eyes are shining. She has longed for this. She is not at all sure she ever wants to come back here. She will see what Vinland has to offer – the land of vines, sweet-scented with honey. In her thoughts she is there already.

But she is melancholy just the same. Her father has turned out to bid them farewell. Freydis runs ashore and hugs him one last time. She rubs her nose in his great beard and inhales the rough, familiar salty scent of him.

Perhaps it is her imagination but she thinks she sees a tear in the corner of his eye, even though he has forced a smile and is wishing them all bon voyage.

Brosi is not himself, either. Normally, the lively dog runs about yapping and wagging his tail at everyone when he is not on guard duty over his sheep. But now he just lies there quietly at the chieftain's feet, staring at her sadly with his big brown eyes.

There is something about this leave-taking that makes Freydis uneasy. A foreboding, a cold weight that lies upon her heart. Why did her father insist on telling her all this stuff, almost compelling her to listen to it all?

Did he really need to teach her all about sailing? Her brother Torvald is a great mariner, almost as good as Leif. Besides, they are sailing with Karlsevne and Torhall. Both are very experienced mariners, especially Torhall, who has participated in most of Eirik's Viking voyages.

No, Eirik is surely not afraid that they lack people capable of commanding a ship. There must be something else, though she is not sure what. But she quickly forgets. The thrill takes over.

Torfinn Karlsevne's ship *Karlshode* is the first to sail out of the fjord. He has clearly made up his mind that he is the leader of the expedition, to the great annoyance of Freydis. She had imagined herself standing in the bows, watching the fjord open as they sailed out. Now she has to gaze at the stern of the *Karlshode* instead.

Their ship should be leading. After all, aboard the

Serpent are the son and daughter of the chieftain of Greenland, brother and sister to the man who discovered Vinland. And the third vessel is under the command of Torhall, one of Eirik the Red's best friends from Iceland. Yet this Karlsevne fellow demands the right to lead the way. Has he no respect for the bonds of blood and friendship? If this arrogant Icelander carries on pushing himself forward like this ... She does not finish that thought, but instead decide to enjoy the journey. The weather is fair, and people wave to them from various spots along the fjord. She waves back with both arms.

On the promontory where she had stood awaiting Leif's return two years ago, she catches sight of a familiar figure. A bent woman leaning on a stick.

Freydis shouts halloo and waves to the strange wise woman, but the other woman does not return her wave. As always, Freydis feels uneasy when she sees Torbjorg. How much does she know?

Freydis represses the thought. Instead, she saunters about the ship, chatting to people. Several people aboard the *Serpent* are thinking of settling in the new land. Others are more concerned about the treasure they hope to take home with them. It is no doubt the same on both the other two ships.

Karlshode is still in the lead when they reach the mouth of Eiriksfjord and set a northerly course.

'Is that Icelander going to be in charge of everything?' demands Freydis peevishly, glaring at her husband and her brother.

'So long as he is steering the right course, there's nothing to worry about, little sister,' says Torvald, smiling at her in that teasing way she knows so well from childhood.

Freydis snorts, kicks an empty water bucket and goes off to scold a few slaves she thinks are taking too long preparing a meal for the crew.

But they soon have something else to think about. A storm overwhelms them; the ship groans. First, everything is pushed downwards, then thrown up in the air. They do all they can to prevent people, animals, food and equipment from being swept overboard.

Torvald and some of his slaves are hard pressed to keep the ship afloat. Freydis hangs over the gunwale throwing up. She can't remember ever having felt so dreadful – not even when she was expecting Einar. The waves of nausea sweeping through her body feel much stronger than the waves of the sea.

So embarrassing, too, that she, daughter and sister of the great explorers, should be brought low by sea sickness. Luckily, not many people notice. They have their own troubles.

It goes on all night. Throwing up, again and again. Freydis is drained and dizzy. She can do nothing but surrender to the forces of nature, let them batter her as they will.

In a brief moment of clarity, she thinks of the tale her father told her about the eight kings of the wind. Has disagreement already broken out among them, although winter is still a long way off? She has emptied her stomach of all its contents. Now there is just a sour liquid that comes up now and then, but that too is decreasing.

But when at last it is morning, the sun peers forth again. Luckily the wind has abated, and people fall to the deck, exhausted. Even the animals have had a hard time of it, but there are no injuries.

None of the ships has lost anyone, but quite a lot of tools and equipment has been lost in the sea. Nor have they been blown substantially off course. They soon find their way again, thanks to Leif's thorough directions.

The ships sail northward for a stretch along the coast of Greenland. There is a lot of loose floating ice there, so they do not risk trying to land. Then they set their course due west, towards the open sea, in the direction of the other coast. This is where it starts.

Freydis watches Greenland disappear astern. Slowly she turns, and leaves the land of her birth, setting her thoughts on the new land she is looking forward to seeing rise before her eyes. And, as Leif promised them, after a couple of days of brisk sailing, they glimpse a land covered in glaciers and flat rocks. A shout of joy bursts out from all over the ship when they realise that they have reached Helluland. They are on the right course. They celebrate with ale and fresh fish, but they do not go ashore. The place does not look very welcoming.

But they row close enough for Freydis to catch sight of several beautiful arctic foxes. The fox is her favourite animal. She has met a blue fox so often in her rambles around Greenland that she wondered if it was the same animal. She fancied it was guarding her. If she ever gets a ship of her own someday, the figurehead on the bow will be the head of a fox. She decided that a long time ago.

Now they sail on down the coast in a southerly direction, and after a couple of days they see the land Leif called Markland. It is flat, wooded, and has long white beaches, but no areas suitable for pasture. Nonetheless, they decide to investigate.

Freydis has never seen such lofty trees. In truth, she has never really seen any trees except the stunted mountain birches. There are no real trees in Greenland. She has only heard her father's and Leif's descriptions of them. But she has seen tree trunks, for down the years many ships have come to Greenland bringing timber.

She feels a need to go and touch the living trees and inhale their scent, closing her eyes and rubbing her nose against the tree trunk. The odour is fresh and rather acrid, and yet at the same time something strikes her as menacing. It is as though the dark branches are reaching out to grasp her. She withdraws and refuses to go any further into the woods.

But her companions do not hesitate but take the timber they want. Both Icelanders and Greenlanders fell a few trees. They won't need to go looking for timber when they reach Leifsbudir and Vinland.

Now they are only two or three days away. Freydis sits quietly by the ship's side and gazes towards the land, the cool breeze blowing her hair about in a wild dance. Sometimes she closes her eyes and stretches out towards the sun, relishing its warm caress on her face.

There is a fever in her blood, and she is there already among the sweet-smelling flowers, where the streams gurgle. Every bit of her is alive, every finger and toe.

Now and then she glances towards the great expanse of the open sea. Far in the distance there is a line, a line dividing the dark-blue sea from the slightly paler blue sky. What lies beyond that line? Would you fall off the edge of the earth? And where would you land then? In the realm of the gods? In the yawning abyss, in Ginnungagap – the great abyss between fire and ice where all life was created between the giant Yme and the primeval cow Audhumbla? Or would the World Serpent, Midgardsormen, be there, the serpent which encircles the earth by biting its own tail?

Did her father not speak of this once, a long time ago? What was it he said? Did he say the world was round and had no edge that you could fall off? No, that couldn't be right. That line she sees there must be an edge. How far away is it in reality? She must think on it later, she cannot ask her father now.

LANDING AT LEIFSBUDIR

VINLAND, THE YEAR 1003

KARLSEVNE'S VESSEL has been in the lead the whole way. But early one morning when the sun is just beginning to make its presence felt, Torvald executes a cunning manoeuvre. He has learned a thing or two from Leif about the inlet to Vinland that the Icelanders are unaware of.

The *Serpent* is lying astern of the other ships. Torvald has allowed them to sail ahead. For this reason, they do not notice when Torvald suddenly changes course, so the *Serpent* is now sailing straight for her destination.

Soon it appears, the land of green pastures, more fertile than Greenland. Houses can be glimpsed in the far distance. That must be Leifsbudir; There can be no other buildings here.

The houses are bathed in the red glow of the

morning sun and look just as Leif described them. In the centre there is a large longhouse with several smaller buildings around. Soon they hear the crunch as the ship's keel touches the beach. They have arrived.

The Greenlanders raise their arms in the air, yelling in crazed enthusiasm, throwing themselves about each other's necks in a wild embrace. People roll about on the deck. The sheep bleat, the cattle bellow. Other people are struggling to keep the ship steady. There is laughter and singing.

Ravn the smallholder has composed a song, and soon they are all joining in, while they try to check everything they have on board.

Their pleasure is in no way diminished by the fact that Karlsevne and Torhall lag so far behind. Freydis flashes a broad grin at her brother. She has never felt such affection for him as she does at this minute.

And so it comes to pass also this time that it is the children of Eirik the Red who are the first to set foot on the new soil. Freydis generously allows Torvald to be the first to step ashore. He deserves it. Then Freydis climbs over the gunwales before the other Greenlanders rush after her.

They swiftly take possession of Leifsbudir. Freydis leads the way into Leif's longhouse.

The longhouse is light and in good shape. And large, indeed it seems even more spacious than Eirik the Red's house at Brattalid. This proves that it is easier to obtain timber here than in Greenland. Sturdy tree trunks support the house and no wood has been spared in the cladding of walls and benches. The work has been skilfully done.

The house shows signs of not having been inhabited for some time. The air is stuffy and stale. Freydis gives orders for it to be aired and washed.

Binna is sent down to the ship to fetch fresh water. They had filled up the containers from a stream in Markland. Freydis herself lights a fire in the hearth.

Freydis and Torvard set up house in the innermost part of the dwelling, while Torvald and his two concubines Aase and Ida occupy the outer portion. He has not taken a wife either; odd creatures, her brothers. The rest of the crew have to find places on the benches and floor in the centre.

When Karlsevne finally lands, he is blazing. They have had to sail a long detour. Now he marches irritably about the yard, snarling and yelling at everyone. He wants to evict the Greenlanders from the longhouse.

'I am the leader of this expedition. It was my place to go ashore first and decide how we were to arrange things here. There has never been any doubt about that,' he fumes, striding right up to Torvald. He glares at Eirik's son. They are the same height. Karlsevne's right hand grips the knife he carries in his belt.

But Torvald only gives a little mocking laugh.

'We got here first, and don't forget it was my brother who discovered this land and built this place. He is chieftain here, this is his farm, and he lent these dwellings to us, his own siblings. But we are kindhearted folk, and therefore we shall give you leave to use the other houses for the time being,' he says, staring Karlsevne straight in the eyes.

'And we will be happy to help you build yourselves new dwellings.'

Karlsevne mutters crossly, turns on his heel and goes away. Gudrid looks upset. She exchanges a brief glance with Freydis and thanks her for the offer.

She already has much to thank Eirik the Red's family for, and she knows how to show her gratitude. Was it not Leif who rescued them when their ship was wrecked on the reef off Eiriksfjord? Was she not married to one of Eirik the Red's sons? Was she not given her own house at Brattalid when she was widowed, and have both Freydis and Torvald not always treated her kindly? Her husband, too, should be grateful for the hospitality Eirik the Red has shown him and his people all winter. Moreover, he ought to understand that this land already has a chieftain, and that chieftain is Leif Eiriksson.

The livestock quickly find their feet at Leifsbudir where the grass grows fresh. Eagerly they fall upon the delicious pasture. It is early, and in the shade the dew is still on the grass. Freydis takes a break from arranging the places for people and animals. She sits down on the ground and runs her hands through the dew. Then she closes her eyes and tastes it. Never before as she tasted water so sweet as this. Leif was right; It is almost like honey.

The new settlers are animated and cheerful. Already the very next day after landing, they start building more dwellings. Karlsevne has spied a fine plot a couple of hundred metres to the south. Here he intends to build his longhouse. The other families and Torhall's people spread out around the area.

The men set off towards the great forest. They fell trees and haul them back to the building sites. They have great help from the horse Karlsevne bought from Eirik the Red before they left.

Freydis enjoys the spectacle of all these half-naked men hacking away at the thick tree trunks with axes and cutting with sharp knives. There is joy in the air, and the smell of fresh wood. They work hard, cutting sturdy support pillars and thinner planks. A couple of the men are also skilled wood carvers capable of more delicate work, making table chairs, troughs and other furnishings needed for the interior of the houses.

They also make a loom.

Before they feel the first breath of autumn in the air, sleeping benches have been made for all one hundred and twenty travellers. Soon they are engaged in building winter accommodation for the livestock and also several fodder storerooms.

The men go hunting and fishing. The fishermen come back with their boats laden to the gunwales with the gleaming treasures of the sea. The hunters are successful too, bringing home game of all sorts, both large and small.

'It's easier to get close to the game here than it is in Greenland,' says Torvard, grinning, holding up a large bird he has caught that morning.

'They are probably not used to being hunted,' smiles Freydis, rolling up the sleeves of her blouse before deftly gutting the bird and preparing it for roasting. She is happy that her husband seems to have settled well.

The women milk the cows, make cheese and churn

butter. They forage for berries, nuts and other edibles. The land offers an abundance of these, too. They gather grass, heather, moss and other vegetation which they dry; This will provide winter feed for the animals.

The storerooms are chock-full of dried meat, fish and berries. Several barrels of ale and mead are brewed.

Next summer they will investigate the possibility of sowing wheat here. The conditions look promising, and Leif had spotted wild wheat growing a little to the south.

They are unsure what to expect of the winter. Leif had said that when he was there it had been mild. But it could well be like Greenland and Iceland, where each year was different. They prepare for the worst-case scenario.

Towards the end of the summer, Karlsevne summons everyone to a meeting. He climbs up on a big boulder, sticks out his chest and surveys the gathering below him. The wind takes hold of the flowing blue cloak he wears.

'Silence!' he shouts.

Torvald looks at Freydis and rolls his eyes. She is just as tired as he is of this Icelander who loves to play the chieftain, when the natural leader should be Torvald, as Leif's brother. But both of them are curious to hear what the man has to say, so they keep their peace.

'Well, now we have all settled in this fertile land. We have sufficient provisions to keep us through the winter. I have decided that I wish to explore the country further to the south. This is the area where the grapes and the wheat were found,' says Karlsevne.

There is a buzz of eager voices in the crowd.

'Those who wish to join me can see me afterwards.'

'When are you leaving?' One man asks.

'In two days' time if the weather holds,' declares the self-important Icelander.

Both Freydis and her brother are keen to see more of this country; They share an adventurous spirit. But they want to do it in their own way. They do not want to form part of Karlsevne's party. Instead, they convince one of the smallholders from Greenland to go along with him, so he can tell them all about it afterwards.

Karlsevne gathers several men and two women. They sail along the coast, first eastward and then due south. After a while, they have to set a northerly course, and later a westerly one. To the south-west there is a fjord or more like a wide bay. They make several landings and investigate the terrain closely.

Far to the south, they discover an area that seems more fertile and welcoming than any other they have yet seen. The air is cool and pleasant. Here they find wheat, vines, fruit trees and many other types of vegetation growing wild.

Is it possible the area is inhabited? There are signs of human habitation: a pile of furs, a fireplace. But they see nobody, even though they make camp and tramp about in all directions. They find animal tracks, and there is plenty of fish.

Karlsevne calls the place Hop.

'Next summer I shall return and build myself a farm and settle here. This is my land, I shall be in charge here. Then I shall not have to endure the arrogance of Eirik the Red's offspring,' he says to Snorre Torbrandsson, the Icelander whose rank is closest to Karlsevne's own; but he also says it so loudly that the smallholder from Greenland hears it too.

At first they think Karlsevne is making it up, back at Leifsbudir, when he tells them about Hop. But then he shows them great clusters of grapes and ears of wheat. Then everyone decides they want to go there when spring comes.

While they were building their houses there had been a great community spirit among the little group of settlers, but there is much disagreement about how things are to be governed. Karlsevne has declared himself chieftain.

Freydis quivers with rage when she hears this man promoting himself. Imagine Gudrid being able to put up with such a fellow! Freydis would never. She is more fortunate in her own husband, after all, even though he still does not kindle her desire.

It does not seem that Gudrid is happy about the way her husband is carrying on, either. She is constantly going around smoothing people's ruffled feathers when he has upset someone. And on one occasion Freydis hears her taking him to task.

'You can't go barging about like that and acting the chieftain'

'I am the most powerful man here. I command the best ship and I have brought the most with me. Besides, I have the most beautiful wife, he says, trying to wink charmingly at Gudrid. But she is not impressed.

'Wealth is not everything. You must remember that this is Leif Eiriksson's land. It was he who discovered it. His brother and sister have more right to it that you do.'

'Huh, whoever said this was Leif Eiriksson's land? He isn't here looking after it, is he?'

'And you're not back home on your farm in Iceland either. Does that mean anybody at all can just take it over?'

'Womenfolk!' groans Karlsevne, throwing his arms wide and stomping off.

They soon divide into two camps, the settlers from Iceland who support Karlsevne, and all the rest, who certainly do not.

Nor can they agree on whether the White Christ or the Norse gods will rule in Vinland. This dispute crosses the borders of the two communities. Brynjulf the priest came in Karlsevne's ship. He thought it would be unacceptable to sail to a new land without bringing the true faith with them. Now he is going about trying to persuade people to build a church. There are arguments about where this church should be erected.

'This White Christ just causes disagreements. I don't understand what he is about,' Freydis complains one day when she overhears yet another heated exchange between adherents and opponents.

After that she avoids the topic and keeps her

distance from the man in the robe and all he represents. But to her great annoyance, Torvard gets involved with the building of the church.

Her brother Torvald, on the other hand, refuses to have anything to do with the building of the church. His opposition is only increased when he discovers that Brynjulf the priest is disporting himself with Ida, one of Torvald's concubines. He has had the gall to do this in the longhouse at Leifsbudir.

The church is erected a good way off from the dwellings. It was Torhall who saw to that. Eirik's best friend takes great exception to Christendom.

Now he is demanding that a house of sacrifice should be built. The Christians raise strenuous objections, but Torhall has sufficient support and the house of sacrifice is both built and taken into use.

Freydis spends much time at her new loom. It is not as good or as smooth through frequent use as the one she had at Gardar, but it works. She weaves clothing and rugs. When she runs out of wool, she sews clothing from animal skins, which are becoming increasingly abundant. At present she is sewing a winter jacket for Einar. Now that he is not under her feet, she finds she misses him. She imagines how wonderful it will be to see him again – if that ever happens.

Fetching water, tending the fire and washing and cooking she leaves to the slave girls. The men pass the dark hours telling stories, playing games – sometimes board games – singing and carving various wooden objects.

Gudrid runs the household for the Icelanders. One

chilly winter's evening she knocks on the door of Leif's longhouse and asks to speak with Freydis. They sit down in a corner away from the others.

'What brings you here tonight, Gudrid?'

'I think it is so sad that there should be quarrelling here in this good land. I hope we may find some way of stopping it,' she says, looking at Freydis with gentle eyes.

'I agree with you. But it is your husband who is mainly to blame for the way things are. He does not respect the rest of us.'

'Well, yes, there is something in what you say. I have been thinking about how we could resolve the situation. Could we suggest establishing a Ting? It could consist of a few from each ship's company. Then we could discuss the most important issues at the meetings,' she says.

The chieftain's daughter ponders this while she fetches some gruel and freshly cooked fish for them. The more she considers it, the more it appeals to her. This would give her a chance to become involved in the running of things.

'That's not a bad idea. But how would we ever get Karlsevne to go along with it?'

'We must both go around and canvass support for the idea,' Gudrid smiles, sipping the sweet gruel. Freydis smiles back.

The idea takes root, despite fierce opposition from Karlsevne. Freydis manages to get a place in the Ting meetings for herself and her brother as representatives of their ship. Many of the meetings are turbulent, but the quarrels grow fewer in number. The settlers are headed for a more peaceful time.

The winter is windy, but quite mild, and lasts less time than it does back home in Greenland. The spring sun is warmer than they are used to. Everyone is lively and cheerful, and they celebrate with a great feast. The last of the mead is served, and they have fresh meat from a whale some of the men caught the previous day.

Torvard and some of the men sail north to hunt the white bear, seal and walrus. It is the right time of year for that. They reckon they will be able to navigate the moderate amount of floating ice.

Two weeks later, the *Serpent* sails back to Leifsbudir fully laden with meat and furs. They share generously with the Icelanders, for there is enough for everyone and more.

The pelts are of the finest quality, and now they begin to talk about all the goods they will be able to trade them for when they return to Greenland. Most of them are seal and walrus skins; They only managed to kill one of the white bears. But it was a huge monster. That skin will fetch a high price. Torvard has also got his hands on a number of walrus teeth.

'Perhaps you'd like some new gold jewellery?' he says, smiling shrewdly at his wife.

Freydis shrugs.

'You still don't know what I want? It's not more jewellery,' she snaps, gathering up the newly washed clothes ready to take them out to dry in the wind.

No, it is not jewellery or other pretty things that set her pulse racing. She is happy enough in Vinland and enjoys the cheerful atmosphere between the new settlers. She is also glad to have a say in the running of things. Yet there is something lacking; She is not sure what.

Karlsevne fills his ship with able men and women who can cook. He intends to set up his home at Hop, the location he discovered the previous summer. He sails off, bidding farewell to Gudrid, whom he intends to send for later.

The ambitious Icelander quickly sets his people to work at Hop. He himself sets off with two companions to explore the area around. He wants to be seen as a great explorer, and everybody knows it. He does not intend to be outdone by Eirik the Red and Leif Eiriksson.

They find a fjord teeming with fish, with an islet outside it where the currents flow strongly, and they call it Straumsfjord, and the islet they call Straumso. There are many birds there. Further to the south they find a lake with a rivulet that flows out into the sea, and several streams full of fish. They dig out pits on the shore and catch halibut.

Then they return to Hop and sow wheat. The grain soon begins to sprout, and the building of the first house is coming along nicely. The timber is sound, and the men are enthusiastic.

Can it really be that they are the first people here? Karlsevne plays with the idea. If so, then it is only natural that he should name it after himself. He would not mind doing that. For now, he contents himself with naming the first house Torfinnsbu.

One day, their peaceful existence is disturbed. Nine skin canoes appear, heading for land. On board are people plunging wooden poles into the waters of the glittering lake.

Karlsevne and Snorre exchange glances and whisper something to each other. Snorre fetches a white shield. Karlsevne takes it and approaches the people in the boats. Behind him stand Snorre and some of the other men, hands on the hilts of their swords.

'We only want peace, not enmity and war,' says Karlsevne as the people leap ashore.

All of them are men. They are small and wear little clothing: only a loincloth. They have lots of dishevelled hair, large eyes and broad cheekbones. The two very different groups of people stare at each other for a little while without speaking. The strangers mutter in a language the Icelanders don't understand. Karlsevne approaches the man who appears to be their leader.

'In true Christian spirit we offer you food and friendship,' he says, bowing. With a nod he signals to one of the women, who fetches some dried meat.

The leader sniffs at the meat but does not eat. The Icelanders try to look friendly, but some of them are quaking with fear. The strangers whisper to one another and then trot back to the beach. They jump into their boats and row southward. That is the last they see of them.

The encounter makes Karlsevne and the others uneasy. Although it did not come to blows, and the people did not seem hostile, they find it all unsettling. A few days later they return to Leifsbudir to reflect on it all.

Freydis makes her own discoveries that summer, even though she does not stray beyond the area around Leifsbudir. Here in Vinland she rises at dawn as she always does. Silently she wanders around the flat fields. Usually she wears only a thin blouse and a skirt. A blue cape is slung about her shoulders, but it is mainly there for effect. Her hair hangs down over her shoulders. It is so very different from the steep areas around Brattalid and Gardar, but she likes it. The air is mild, fresh, luxuriant. She revels in the sea breeze and the rhythm of the waves on the shore. She enjoys sitting on the shore with some handicraft project, occasionally gazing out at the horizon and the hillocks and knolls on the islets and promontories out at sea.

In clear weather she catches sight of the line where the sea meets the sky. She still thinks about that a great deal. Sometimes it is dark blue against pale blue, sometimes dark grey against light grey, and other times the colours change continuously. She never stops wondering what lies beyond the line, and where you would end up if you sailed over it.

She is more and more convinced it must be the entrance to the yawning abyss, to Ginnungagap. If you don't end up in Ginnungagap, where else could you end up? In one of the other worlds, perhaps – in Asgard, the realm of the gods, or in the domain of Hel, goddess of death?

Suddenly she recalls a stranger who was on board one of the trading vessels that came to Brattalid. Did he not also claim the earth was round? But if that were the case, surely it would roll about and all the waters of the earth would run off?

No, the earth must have an edge somewhere or other, but she does not know where, and no-one else seems to know, either. The people she asks merely shrug their shoulders. They have enough to keep them occupied with their daily lives. But Freydis wants to solve the puzzle; If only there were someone who would sail with her there. Then there would be yet another explorer in her distinguished clan.

One sweltering hot morning she sets off on a new route. She passes the Icelanders' camp on her way, but it is completely silent. Nobody is awake yet. The only signs of life are two big lean birds flying about above the roofs of the dwellings. They make little sound as they fly around each other with their wide wingspan.

The little meeting house with the grass growing on the roof is bathed in the red glow of the morning sun, which throws long shadows across the fields.

After some time, she reaches a small bay. The sun is reflected in the still water; only a few small birds break the silence, and there is a wonderful sweet scent. She tests the water and finds it quite warm. Freydis is damp after her walk and decides to bathe.

She starts to undress. First, she rolls up her apron and lets her thin skirt slide down. Then she slowly pulls her blouse over her head. She stretches her arms out towards the sun and lets it warm her naked body. She shakes out her mane and lets the sea breeze winnow her locks. She feels a sense of freedom.

As she bends down to remove her shoes, she hears a faint sound from behind her. She stiffens. Is it an animal? She picks up a stone from the beach and spins round.

But it is not an animal. She sees a man, sitting in the grass behind some bushes. It is Bjarne Grimolvsson, the Icelander who is the helmsman on Torhall's boat. She has hardly ever exchanged a word with him, but he seems like the sort of man who can take a stand. He is not one of Karlsevne's puppets. He avoids conflict and is one of the most enthusiastic storytellers. He has made many voyages, experienced many things.

He is sitting in front of her, as naked she is. He looks alarmed. He shields his sex with his hands and tries to speak, but no words come out.

Freydis smiles and almost bursts out laughing. She reveals herself to him in all her glory, hands on hips. She knows herself to be irresistible when she parades like this. She lets him admire her shapely curves, her broad shoulders, large round breasts and tiny waist. Her hips are wide, her bottom just the right size, her legs long and strong.

The hair of her head and her pubic hair are the same red. Now she puts on her most seductive smile and looks at him with her deep green eyes.

The only parts of Freydis that cannot be described as beautiful are her sharp, slightly aquiline nose, her masculine fists and her broad flat feet. But most men do not notice these things.

She cocks her head to one side.

'Good to see you, Bjarne. Would you remove your hands so I can see you properly?' she teases.

He is so embarrassed that he does as she commands. His manhood stands erect. It is large, larger than either Sverre or Torvard could present. Freydis lingers, enjoying the spectacle. A familiar heaviness spreads through her lower body, and she breathes deeply.

She kicks off her shoes and goes over to him. Only a few steps. Boldly she throws her arms about Bjarne's neck and plants a kiss on his mouth. He responds quickly, thrusting his tongue into her mouth.

And soon he is kissing her all over, her face, her neck, her throat, her breasts and down over her belly. He lingers over her navel. Then he lifts his head, gazes at her with a dazed, distant expression, before he begins to stroke her from the knees upwards along the inside of her thighs. He bends down and toys with her sex with nose and tongue. Rigid with pleasure, she groans aloud.

'You liked that,' he says with a thick voice, grinning at her.

Freydis cannot reply, her throat feels constricted. Now she explores his body. He is tall and strong, hard as granite. She sniffs his rough skin which smells of sun and sea water, strokes his almost bald crown, plays with the soft hair on his breast and his beard, kisses the thick scar that runs down his back.

She rubs herself gently against his member before slipping him in between her legs for a second, then teasing him by wriggling away and standing up. He seizes her in his strong hairy arms and will not let her go. Laughing, she pretends to struggle free, wanting him to pursue her and catch her again. Then they both overbalance and tumble to the ground, giggling.

Soon they are rolling about on the soft, scented carpet of grass and then he holds her arms above her head and throws himself upon her.

Freydis is more than ready when he penetrates her, sending warm rays shooting through her body. He does not thrust long before he roars and lets his body sink down over hers.

Panting, she relishes the weight of this big man on her body.

But then it grows too much and she wriggles free. Lazily she allows the soft wind and the blazing sun to warm her. She dreams of butterflies and the laughter of children. But all at once she awakes and has a sudden urge to bathe. She shoves Bjarne off and nods towards the alluring lake,

'Are you coming?' she asks, with a crooked smile.

'Oh, I have bathed already,' he says rather hazily and rises.

But Freydis does not hear him; She has already thrown herself into the cool water. Soon he follows at a jog. They play like little children, splashing each other, diving under the surface, until they feel the desire to make love again.

The day is drawing on when they finally trudge back. They do not speak much, contenting themselves with smiling at each other. He has a lovely smile. It seems surprisingly mild and friendly for a man with such a tough, at times menacing appearance. Half-way they part, tacitly agreeing that nobody should ever know about this.

Torvard is in a bad mood when at last she turns up back at Leifsbudir.

'Where have you been? The slave girls had to deal with all the morning jobs without you,' he says crossly.

'I'm sure they managed just fine. I found some new

paths and got lost,' replies Freydis, starting on the laundry to avoid any more questions.

Torvard has been talking for a long time about going back to Gardar. He misses the farm, his son, his parents and the landscape of Greenland. But Freydis will not hear of it. Nor are any of their companions in any great hurry to leave. To Torvard's horror, it seems several of them intend to settle here for good.

'We promised we'd come back after one year,' he said to Freydis through clenched teeth.

'Well, I made no such promise. Why should we go home? We have a great life here,' she says dreamily.

'Don't you miss Einar and your family?'

But Freydis will not listen, so he walks dejectedly out of the longhouse.

Nobody asks where Bjarne has been. The Icelanders are used to him going his own way. When he reappears, he is carrying a brace of hares over his shoulders. He has been hunting.

Freydis is not as infatuated with Bjarne as she was with Sverre. Sverre was probably right when he said she was obsessed with him. Her passion frightened him. But Bjarne kindles a passion in her too, one she wants to feel again.

She seems to remember her father talking about Bjarne once. What was it he said?

Bjarne was the same age as her eldest brother. He says he grew up at the home of his father, Grimold, who was one of Eirik the Red's friends in Iceland. For various reasons Grimold chose not to accompany Eirik to Greenland but remained at home on his small farm at Breidafjord.

'You grew up with no mother. I did, too,' she says one day when they are huddling close under a blanket on the beach. Bjarne looks uncomfortable and makes no reply. Clearly this is not a subject he wishes to discuss. So Freydis leaves it. He tells her that when his father died, Bjarne sold the farm and built himself a ship.

'I am more of a trader and mariner than a farmer. I like the sea, I like going to new places, going on raids and having new experiences,' he says. 'And meeting pretty women, too,' he adds, grinning roguishly at Freydis.

'Have you met many such before you met me?' asks Freydis, gazing at him, wide-eyed and innocent.

'None like you,' he says, giving her a quick kiss on the cheek. But Freydis is persistent.

'Why have you never married?'

'I guess I never found anyone I wanted to marry. Before now. And you're already married.'

As time passes, their relationship becomes close. After they have made love they often lie closely entwined. Bjarne tells tales of his voyages, sometimes so hilarious that she bursts out laughing. He tells a new story every time, or an old one he has shamelessly embellished.

Sometimes they just lie still, enjoying each other's skin, the secret spaces, the sweet and tart smells. Tenderly she lets her fingers wander over his body, memorising it. He lets her. But when she runs her hand curiously over the ugly scar on his back, he grows silent, and removes her hand.

One time they snuck into the barns, which empty now in the summer, and are surprised by Gudrid, who is there to fetch something for the animals out at pasture. They are caught in the act: Freydis is riding her lover. Both are dripping with perspiration.

Gudrid has grown large and heavy over the spring; She is due very soon. Now she stands there like a queen, staring at them with her arms crossed across her belly. Bjarne is shamefaced. He creeps away, dresses quickly and disappears without making eye contact with the woman in charge of running things for the Icelanders. It is she who makes sure food is put before him every day.

Freydis takes her time. She is not ashamed. Why is Gudrid still standing there, silent and expressionless? Has she grown as arrogant and self-important as that husband of hers? Freydis is seething.

'What do you want? What right have you to judge me? Do you think yourself a saint now you've become a Christian? You, who have been married three times, and also shared a bed with Torstein the Black, they say. And ...' Freydis rages, and has to draw a deep breath.

'And what do you know about having to marry a man you don't love, maybe don't even like. But at least my husband is better than yours,' she spits the words out.

'I agree with you there,' replies Gudrid with a little grin. Freydis's eyes go wide. She is dumbstruck. Gudrid goes on.

'I'll tell you about Torstein the Black. If you promise to tell me about Sverre afterwards.'

Freydis just nods.

'He had just lost his wife. I had lost my husband – your brother. We comforted one another. Yes, we were together. To be honest, I had long had an eye for Torstein the Black. From the day we met, in truth. I had never felt so strongly about any man. But I am fated to follow the husband I have cared for the least, Torfinn Karlsevne. And now I have carried his child for so long that I have hopes of bringing it to term. That is all I live for.'

Understanding begins to dawn on Freydis. Gudrid has challenges of her own to deal with.

'I hope it goes well with your child. I've got a child already. Einar is Sverre's son. Unfortunately, he has his father's eyes, and his father betrayed me,' says Freydis, feeling again the old anger surge through her veins.

'Sverre had to take over the farm in Iceland. Otherwise it would have been ruined. Don't judge him too harshly,' Gudrid says, and continues: 'And now there's Bjarne.'

'Indeed. As you saw with your own eyes,' Freydis says, boldly meeting her gaze.

'I could not help it. He is well-endowed ... Bjarne, I mean.'

'That's for sure,' says Freydis, winking.

They giggle cheekily. Then they double up with laughter. Gudrid howls with mirth so loud and forcibly that she has to bend over her great belly, while Freydis curls up in the remains of the hay that will be the winter feed for the livestock. Finally, they get their breath back.

'You know I'm not judging you, Freydis. I've no right to do that, nor do you have the right to judge me. Only our gods can judge us, whether it be the White Christ or the Norse gods.'

Freydis nods. Someday it would doubtlessly become clear which gods were worth believing in.

In the early autumn Gudrid gives birth to a well-shaped boy child. Freydis assisted at the birth along with Maja. Gudrid christens her son Snorre in the little church, but she also allows a sacrifice to be made for the child. The baby is born just before the autumn equinox, so it is very fitting.

The winter that follows is even milder than the first. No snow falls. The livestock graze and feed themselves.

Freydis is pregnant again. She knows the child is Bjarne's, and she tells him so. At times he can be taciturn and pensive; He is not a man who shows his emotions. But when he hears about the child, she sees his eyes light up.

Torvard rarely sleeps with Freydis, but with sufficient frequency for him to accept that it is his child she is carrying. She feels no desire for him, especially now that her needs are being met elsewhere.

'Can't you ask Torvald to lend you one of his concubines?' she hisses, one time when he tries.

She sees he is crushed, and she feels bad for saying

it. He has always been kind to her and he doesn't deserve the treatment she gives him. But she never wanted to marry him. It was decided without her consent, by Torvard himself, and their fathers. She does not love him, however a good catch he may have been. And now she is tied to him forever.

HEROICS AND SACRIFICE

VINLAND, THE YEAR 1005

THE DAYS GROW LONGER and longer, and the air grows ever warmer. Springtime has taken root in the settlement. Early one morning, they hear splashing sounds from the bay. They soon see where the sound comes from. Five skin boats and ten small people rushing towards them. All men.

The small people, whom the settlers call 'skraelings,' jump ashore at Leifsbudir. Can these be the same people as those who visited Karlsevne at Hop the previous summer? It is hard to say, they all look the same, murmurs Karlsevne to the others who have gathered at the beach.

The settlers stand in a circle around them, unsure what to make of them. Some take care to have their weapons in hand. But the skraelings appear friendly. They want to trade. With gestures and body language, they explain what merchandise they want to buy. Red cloth, swords and spears. Karlsevne and the other men refuse to part with weapons, but cloth, cheese and other dairy products are exchanged.

They seem particularly delighted with butter. Samples are passed round, and lips are smacked in appreciation. In exchange the settlers receive the furs and skins of various animals. They have enough of these themselves, in reality, but they are keen to be on the indigenous people's good side. They try to smile pleasantly.

Suddenly the bull rushes at the skraelings with a roar. Karlsevne had purchased one of Eirik the Red's bull studs for the expedition; He was to serve the cows if they found they needed to breed more cattle. But the bull has behaved oddly since they arrived and has not covered a single cow. Perhaps the grass here is not to his liking.

Whatever the reason, the skraelings are terrified of this huge angry creature, the like of which they have never seen before. They leap into their canoes and disappear.

A fence is erected around the houses so they can protect themselves against the skraelings, in case they thought the settlers were using the bull to provoke a fight. Backed by Karlsevne's two guard dogs, a watch is set around the clock.

Their concerns were justified. Later in the summer, they return. Now they are many, and they do not come in friendship. They have painted their bodies with many colours. They paddle into the bay, howling and shrieking.

The settlers seize their weapons and run to meet them. There is a battle with arrows and spears, and several of the skraelings are injured. But they have a powerful weapon, a catapult which hurls blue stones as big as boulders. This throws the settlers into confusion and they flee, howling, to a small hill.

It seems the skraelings have surrounded them. More of them come running to join the attack from the land side, spears in hand. Karlsevne and the other men fight, but their odd are not looking good. They are outnumbered by the horde of indigenous warriors.

Freydis is changing her clothes in the longhouse when the skraelings attack. Dressing is a lengthy process with her growing belly in the way, and she has had to let out her red wadmal skirt. She has not had time to fasten her blouse when she hears the yells of the men. She does not bother with it but lets it stand open as she runs out to see what all the commotion is about.

Now she discovers that the settlers are fleeing before the arrows and spears and the dreadful slinging machine of the skraelings. She sees a great ball fly through the air; It falls to the earth with a crash without hitting anyone.

For a moment she meets the gaze of the man who thinks of himself the chieftain of the settlement. Karlsevne is displaying little leadership or heroism in the hour of need; He is making only a feeble attempt to gather the troops and organise a counterattack. In fact, it looks as if he is trying to run away with his tail between his legs.

Torvard and Torvald are not much use on the battlefield. But they have never been warriors. It is not in her husband's nature, and Tjodhild forbade Eirik the Red to teach his sons the art of battle. Serves her right, thinks Freydis bitterly. Now you will see your son Torvald slaughtered, because he was never taught the skills of a warrior. You have only yourself to blame, Tjodhild.

Torhall, Bjarne and a handful of their men are the only people offering any decent resistance to the skraelings. They fight bravely, like true warriors – true Vikings. Her father's best friend and her own sweetheart. They prove to be the only people who can be trusted when push comes to shove.

But there are many more skraelings, and Freydis sees that the settlers are losing the battle.

Eirik the Red's daughter and Leif Eiriksson's sister will show them what she is made of. The blood surges through her veins: She feels strong, stronger than she has ever felt in her life. She clenches her fists. And then she shrieks.

'Why are you fleeing from these wretches, fine men like you? Instead you should cut them down like cattle. If I had a weapon, I'd fight better than any of you!'

But nobody hears her in the heat of battle. Freydis strides purposefully towards the battlefield – slower than she had hoped, because of her advanced pregnancy. She follows the skraelings, who are driving her people into a trap.

But suddenly some of them turn towards her, their eyes burning with hatred. At the same time, she stumbles over a dead man. It is Torbrand, Snorre's son. He is stretched out on the ground in front of her with a stone axe embedded in his head. She sees at once that there is nothing she can do for him. She notices his sword lying beside him. Freydis picks it up. She rips off her blouse, which is only getting in the way. Now she stands there half-naked, the sword raised high above her head.

A handful of skraelings come at her, brandishing spears. The catapult hurls another ball; It lands just a few metres away. Freydis ignores it, but the skraelings are startled and for a moment they lower their spears.

Without a thought she lowers her sword and rubs it across her naked breasts. Then she screams as loudly as she can, a wild howl that makes the other embattled skraelings turn to look at her.

Seeing the half-naked, pregnant woman with her wild eyes and flying red mane, they freeze where they stand. Then she screams again and begins to move towards them, almost dancing, the sword still pressed against her breasts. The man who seems to be the leader of the skraelings yells something to the others, and they run screaming back towards their skin canoes.

Flushed with triumph, Freydis raises her arms in the air and sends a last long yell in the direction of the running savages, who cannot get away quickly enough. With lightning speed, they spring into their boats and paddle off southward. The furious paddles splash loudly in the water. Soon, they are out of sight.

Freydis still stands there, supporting herself on the

sword, her hands on the hilt and the sword point thrust into the earth. A strong gust of wind lifts her red mane and spreads it wide. She laughs. A moment of sheer happiness, breathing hard, her heart pounding. She is alive.

For the first time ever she is praised by Karlsevne for her courage and her quick thinking.

'That was a smart move, Freydis. You saved us today.'

Torhall gazes at her, eyes full of admiration.

'You are a true Valkyrie. Your father will be so proud of you,' he gasps out.

Torvard is not pleased to see his wife standing there grinning, bare-breasted and heavily pregnant, making no attempt to cover herself, even though the skraelings have long disappeared and the danger is over for the moment. On the contrary, she seems to be enjoying the fact that several of the men are gazing at her lustfully.

Torvard hastily pulls off his own jacket and throws it about Freydis's shoulders, then he seizes her by the upper arm and drags her home. She goes along reluctantly.

On their way they pass Bjarne. Freydis covertly exposes one swollen breast and much of her swollen belly to her lover's gaze. She casts him an alluring glance. He devours her with his eyes.

Back on the battlefield six men lie dead; two of their own and four skraelings. Three others have lacerations from the combat. They send for Maja. She quickly decides that their wounds are not life-threatening and begins to bind them up. One skraeling they have taken prisoner is locked up in one of the sheds.

The survivors return to their homes to reflect and to grieve. It is especially hard for Snorre, who has lost his only child, Torbrand, and also his best slave, Sigvard. Both had been christened, and they were buried by the church. The dead skrealings are rowed far out to sea and dumped in the ocean. They do not want their corpses lying about near their dwellings.

The field is cleared. The Greenlanders and the Icelanders resume the pattern of life they established when they came here. But the joyful spirit has evaporated. They are constantly looking over their shoulder, and they start up in alarm at the slightest unusual sound. They double the watch and remain in a constant state of readiness. Will they come back, the skraelings?

What are they going to do? More and more of them start talking about going home. They have come to a rich land, a good land, but they want to live in peace. They don't want to go about their work in perpetual fear of attack.

A meeting of the Ting is called. They discuss for a long time the possibility of making friends with the skraelings and trading with them, but nobody knows how to achieve such peace. Nobody speaks their language; Nobody even knows where they live. The skraeling they have captured, and who has such a prominent chin that he has simply been dubbed Chin, has not said a single word.

At the meeting it is agreed that they will sail for home as soon as possible, before the summer is over.

Freydis is the only dissenting voice; She calls the rest of them cowards. They are Vikings, they are bigger and stronger than the skraelings and they have better weapons. And now they have captured the catapult, she points out. The skraelings' most powerful weapon. They didn't manage to take it with them when they fled.

'And I can always flash my bosom at them and yell. It worked fine last time,' she puffs. She does not want to go back to Greenland. Not now.

But the others turn deaf ears to her arguments. The Norse settlers now spend the next few days hunting, drying meat and fish, gathering hides, timber and other riches offered by this generous land. They keep constant watch. The ships are made ready to sail back to Eirik the Red's dominion.

The pains begin on the very morning they have agreed for their departure. Freydis stands doubled up on the beach as the pain shoots through her back. She suddenly remembers the previous difficult birth in all its horrid detail.

'We can't leave, we must wait till the child is born. I can't give birth on the high seas!' Freydis shrieks.

She has to support herself on a stone as she curls up, hoping to ease the agony that overwhelms her. Nobody hears, except Bjarne and Gudrid, who keep sending her worried looks. But they are powerless. Karlsevne has spoken, and both her husband and her brother agree with him. She curses them at the top of her voice, and it makes not the slightest difference.

Suddenly Snorre rushes up.

'The skraelings are on the war path, war against us. They are coming,' he pants.

Terror seizes everyone. No-one is going to listen to the pleas of a woman in labour now.

They drag all they have on board, urging one another to speed up their efforts. Freydis protests, but is hauled on board, howling, by Torvald and Torvard.

Gudrid and Maja remain aboard the *Serpent* to assist with the birth. Gudrid has to leave her own little son in the care of a slave girl and the child's father, Karlsevne, on board the *Karlshode.*

Soon all the boats are afloat, and not a minute too soon. For here they come at full speed, brandishing their weapons: a whole army of skraelings.

There are many more than last time, and now they have painted their faces and upper bodies in blood-red warpaint. Furiously they run into the sea. Behind them the fleeing settlers see a skraeling with a stature equal to their own, a broad-legged, powerfully built man with long hair who shouts orders to the warriors. Is he their chief? They seem to have an Eirik the Red of their own.

All at once, the warriors stop, and they all begin firing arrows at the three ships which are now on their way out to the open sea. Most of the arrows thud into the ships' sides like a sudden shower raining on lead; They do little damage and drop feebly into the water.

But one of the arrows hits Torvald in the belly. The searing pain causes him to drop to the deck, doubled up in agony. As her own birth pangs grow ever stronger, Freydis has to witness her brother fight for his life. Torvald is a brave man.

With great courage, he pulls the arrow out himself. Maja runs briskly back and forth between Freydis and Torvald. With great determination, she attempts to staunch Torvald's bleeding with bandages, herbs and salves, and asks Gudrid to assist both with the birth and the wounded man.

They do not succeed in stopping Torvald's bleeding. Both he and Freydis shriek when their suffering reaches its peak. The rest of the crew keep silent. The Christians mumble quiet prayers that all may go well. They have shaken off the skraelings and set a northerly course. It is good sailing weather and they have a fair wind.

Torvald writhes in pain for hours while Maja and Gudrid fight to save his life. When it is all over, Eirik's son lies with his eyes peacefully closed on the bed they have made for him. With heavy hearts the crew look upon their helmsman, but there is relief in their expressions, too. They are glad his sufferings are at an end.

'We must offer him to the sea gods, to Ran and Aege, Freydis exclaims in a moment of relief between two pains.

The Christians on board protest. They want him to be buried in sanctified ground in Greenland. But Freydis gets her way. She is the closest relative of the deceased, and she and her husband are in charge of the ship.

Torvald never became a Christian and he was never baptised. Having a dead man on board the ship brings misfortune, says one of those who still believes in the Norse gods. Another says the stink will become unbearable in this heat. The voyage is estimated to take around two weeks.

The chieftain's son is wrapped in a white sheet and dropped over the side into the sea, to the accompaniment of prayers and heroic poems. Torvald is swallowed up by a tall foaming wave and quickly disappears from view.

Freydis hopes he will be embraced by Ran and Aege in the depths of the sea. She grieves for the brother she has become so much closer to since Vinland. But she has little time to mourn. The imminent birth demands all her strength.

The crew have been so preoccupied with Torvald that they have not noticed that the good weather has turned. A gale starts to blow, and soon they are in a storm. All at once, the waves tower like mountain tops and the wind brings rain squalls in its train.

Torvard and a few of his slaves have their work cut out keeping the ship afloat. The others do their best to secure people, animals and equipment on board so that they are not swept into the sea.

They do their best to steer the ship without Torvald, but are not very successful. Torvard the farmer from Gardar has never been much of a seaman. He is clumsy and unsure of what to do. The slaves are not used to being in charge of anything, and they wait for orders which never come.

Freydis sees it. She despairs at her husband's ineffectiveness and screams furiously that Hallvard Olavsson must take over the helm. Hallvard, a steady fellow from a farm further to the south of Greenland, was Torvald's right hand man on the voyage to Vinland. And, as far as Freydis can see, he appears to be a skilled sailor; the only one

capable of getting them through the storm.

Torvard moves over for Hallvard, who quickly brings the lurching *Serpent* under control.

They even out in the nick of time. A fog has rolled in, and they can only just make out the shapes of the other two vessels. It seems the gods of sea and winds are throwing everything they have at them. Did the offering not satisfy them, do they want more?

Meanwhile, Freydis is battling with even fiercer pains that seem to grow as the waves swell more violently. The sea throws her about from side to side. This birth seems as slow as her first.

Maja gives her an herbal drink intended to speed up the birth and rubs her abdomen with a salve she has concocted. Gudrid holds her tight and tries to rub her back when the pains come. At the same time Freydis gets seasick and spews in between the hard blows to the small of her back.

The cattle bellow in terror, the sheep bleat till their voices crack. The crew lie spread out in the bilges, desperately trying to grip on to something while also trying to prevent all their possessions from being swept overboard. A bucket comes hurtling through the air and strikes Gudrid on the head, knocking her out.

Now there is nobody to hold onto Freydis, and she rolls from side to side in time with the waves, which pull her down and then throw her in the air, while the pouring rain stings her face. Her hair and clothing stick to her body.

She yells and shrieks for her special goddess, for all the gods. Freya, Ran – goddess of the sea, Eir – goddess of healing, and above all the god her father honours most, Tor – god of wind and weather. But none of them come to her. Or at least they do not manifest themselves.

Instead, a huge troll appears before her, resembling a woman from the waist up. She has huge breasts, long arms, long hair, a head like a human being, big hands with webbed fingers. Her face is large and hideous, her skull pointed, her eyes wide; she has a big mouth and furrowed cheeks. Below the waist the gruesome troll resembles a fish with scales, a tail and fins. Might she be a sea troll?

She catches the troll's eye and a cold shudder runs down her spine. The troll begins to throw fish at the ship. What does it mean? What did her father say about this?

He himself had seen many a ghastly sea monster. Was this a sign that the crew were to fear for their lives, that one of them would be the victim of the sea? Or was it the other way around? She cannot collect her thoughts.

It does not appear as if anyone but she has seen the troll. Maybe she dreamt it. Instead she hears many of the ship's company crying out in prayer to the Christian god, begging for the forgiveness of their sins. One asks forgiveness for visiting his brother's wife when his brother was away, another for stealing a piece of jewellery, a third for having set out a child to die. More and more people join in. In the end Freydis can take no more.

'Shut up!' she howls, as a wave of pain surges through her racked body, and the ship creaks and groans ominously as the sea batters it brutally.

But the exhortations of the faithful grow louder and more insistent. One mumbles a Biblical verse. Another sings hymns. It is unbearable, and it is no help at all. For the Christian god does not appear, either. The tempest continues to rage, unabated. The Greenlanders are now so exhausted that they can hardly manage to cling on any longer. They lie dazed in the bottom of the ship allowing the forces of sea and wind to slam them about as they will.

Freydis too is about to give up all thoughts of coming out of this ordeal alive, but the imminent birth forces her back to reality.

At last Maja announces that the opening is large enough, and she can push. She summons up strengths she did not know she possessed. The experienced midwife has taken hold of the baby's head. Freydis does not need to push more than a couple of times before she feels it letting go, and the baby slips out.

First, she hears a little sob, and then a hearteningly loud shriek which for a brief second drowns out the ocean's persistent roar and the enervating howling of the gale. With a tired smile on her round face Maja declares that it is a boy. She sets to washing him in sea water. The water bucket has toppled over and there is no more fresh water. Freydis is thirstier than she has ever been in her life, but there is nothing to drink. Maja promises to see if she can find some mead for her. She does not think the mead barrel has been blown into the sea.

Few of the ship's company have seen that the birth has taken place; nobody manages to crawl over to inspect the newborn.

Maja rises slowly and holds the baby boy out to his mother. Freydis looks into a small face with big round pale blue eyes and thick brown hair. He is wrapped in a soft dark-blue blanket Maja has found for him. Freydis smiles. He is beautiful. She is enchanted by him at once. The wonderful baby smell wafts over to her, mingled with the salty tang of the turbulent sea. She cannot wait to hold him close and rub her nose and cheeks against his soft skin. Tears of joy well up.

But just as she stretches out her arms, smiling, to receive him, a massive wall of water strikes the ship's side. The ship is pushed down so powerfully that it feels as though it goes the bottom of the sea, and is then violently tossed in the air. Maja loses her balance and both she and the newborn baby boy roll over the gunwale and are hurled out into the roaring waves.

Maja sinks to the bottom. While the child, to whom in her heart Freydis has already given the name Storm, flies in the air with the blanket flapping round him. It seems to go on for ever – the child, flying through the heavy rain clouds. But in the blink of an eye, he lands on the top of a raging demon of a wave which immediately thunders away from them at lightning speed.

It seems that sea and wind are calmer for an instant afterwards. Are the gods pleased, have they received the desired sacrificial offering at last?

The image of the boychild on the blanket riding the wave, burns itself into the mother's retina for ever. It will never be obliterated. Again and again it will reappear in nightmares or in her ponderings. Could she have acted differently, could she have rescued Storm? Many a time would she bitterly reproach herself for not throwing herself into the sea after him. Perhaps she could have saved her son, or at least have travelled with him to the realm of the sea-gods.

Freydis is never told that they are close to land, and that the monster wave sweeps the baby boy right onto the beach, where he is found.

Bjarne and Torhall's boat is very close to theirs when the terrible accident occurs, but they are unable to rescue either Storm or Maja.

Briefly her eyes meet Bjarne's. His expression is as fathomless and dark as she imagines her own must be. She does not know that this will be the last time she sees him. Bjarne. Lover. Warrior. Hunter. Mariner. Father of her child. The man she has come to feel affection for. The man who has rekindled her dreams.

Now she screams out her sorrow and anger.

'Was my brother not enough? Did you have to take my son too?' she howls at the sea gods.

She attempts to stand up, but just then the afterbirth drops on to the deck, accompanied by a lot of blood and water. Her chest aches, her heart feels like a heavy stone. She tumbles backward, faints, and just lies there at Gudrid's side.

When she awakes, the ocean is calm, and the weather so fine that she has to shield her face from the sun with her hand over her forehead. She is lying under a blanket on a bench amidships. She is wearing dry, warm clothes.

Now she finds herself staring straight into the faces of Torvard and Gudrid, who have noticed that she is awake.

Serious, silent faces. And what is there to say?

'Please tell me I have been dreaming,' she implores them.

But they just look at her sadly and shake their heads.

Now she realises that she no longer has her swollen belly, and she feels the tenderness in her lower body. And there is no infant anywhere on the ship. Nor is there any sight of Maja. Sombre and battered, the Greenlanders are making the vessel ship-shape after the storm, salvaging what equipment can be saved. Not very much. Nothing much really except the timber, stacked in the bottom of the ship, and the skins lying between the planks.

There is a rip along one side of the ship. Luckily, it is so high that the vessel is not taking in much water. Two slaves are leaning over the side, attempting to repair the damage. The sail is also in tatters as a result of the gale. They did not manage to lower it before the storm struck. They are ready to sew a new sail, but it will not be as good as the sail Freydis wove.

They will likely have to row much of the way home. Several men have already taken to their oars.

Resolute faces, strong arm muscles flexing and relaxing. They will get them home, home to Greenland.

One cow looks about to collapse and has stopped giving milk. Two of the sheep have broken limbs and they slaughter them. They need meat, because all the food has been lost, swept overboard. There is hardly any mead left, either. But they have been ashore and fetched fresh water, which Freydis drinks greedily. She is not hungry, even though now it is a long time since she gave birth.

They tell her two days have passed since it all happened, that Bjarne and Torhall's ship and crew have vanished, and that Karlsevne lost four slaves in the storm.

She catches a glimpse of the Icelanders' boat a little way ahead. Freydis no longer cares that Karlsevne has once again arrogantly assumed the right to lead.

There is no room for anger, just an infinite dark misery.

She attempts to rise but she feels as though someone has placed a weight on her head. She totters. An overwhelming dizziness forces her to her knees. So she crawls. All the way to the bow, her favourite position on board. She settles herself, refuses to speak to anyone, begs to be left in peace.

She sits there quietly the rest of their journey, interrupted only by a slave girl who brings her blood food and milk. She forces herself to consume it, although all she really wants to do is to lie down and just fade away.

But the survival instinct is stronger.

As her strength is gradually restored, the familiar

fury returns. She rages against Ran and Aege, especially Ran – she is a woman, after all. How could Ran capture a newborn in her wicked net? A baby has no place at the gods' feast in the depths of the ocean. Were Torvald and Maja not enough, could Ran not have taken her instead?

She is also furious with Thor, who rules the thunder and lightning, the weather and the winds. Could he not have waited to unleash that storm until they had reached home? Has he so little control of the eight chieftains, his subjects? But she neither sees nor hears anything of the gods, no matter how often she calls upon them. As little now as in the hour of need.

Then her fury burns itself out. She collapses, exhausted, and falls into the dazed, hazy condition between sleeping and waking.

And then she appears to Freydis. The woman with the long black hair. The woman who only appears when something extraordinary happens. The woman Freydis does not know, yet who looks familiar. Her goddess. The woman's alluring green eyes entreat her silently to cease cursing the gods. This is part of her destiny, her life, she says. 'You must endure it, you must come through it. You are a hard woman; You will have a hard life.' But Freydis cannot accept the answer.

'Is it to punish me for Sverre? Did I have to sacrifice my son for that?' she flings the words at the woman. But she receives no response. The mysterious figure has already disappeared.

HOMECOMING

EIRIKSFJORD, THE YEAR 1005

THE *SERPENT* ROUNDS the familiar reefs at the mouth of Eiriksfjord, and then they sail into calmer waters. The oarsmen ply their oars more vigorously, but there is no rejoicing as the ship slides into the beautiful fjord, surrounded by the steep granite-grey cliffs, the fresh green meadows, the dark, dancing columns of smoke rising from the homesteads, the small blue-green icebergs floating in the water, each of them a natural work of art.

Heavy blue-grey clouds hang over them. There is little joy to be found at Brattalid, either. Karlsevne has already landed and is unloading his ship.

Freydis realises at once that something is wrong when only Leif and Tjodhild come to the beach to meet them.

Leif is leading a small dark-haired boy by the hand,

while Tjodhild, now grey-haired and bent, clutches at her staff for support. When she is told about her son Torvald's sorry fate, it is as though her back bends a notch or two lower. She too has bad news.

'Just after you left, Greenland was stricken by a terrible plague. Most of us were taken ill; we lay for days with fever and pain. Several people died. One of those who died was your father,' Tjodhild says quietly.

For once, her stepmother regards Freydis with sympathy. Yet that is the most dreadful look Freydis has ever received from that quarter. She sinks to her knees and collapses. She lies there, convulsed with weeping.

Does she not have a heavy enough burden to bear? Was it not enough to lose her newborn son, her lover, her brother? She had been so looking forward to her father's embrace and comfort, to pressing her nose into his beard and weeping on his shoulder. He alone could have got her through this, she had thought. And now she has lost him too.

And yet she is not surprised. She had an uneasy feeling when they left. Her father seemed so determined to convey every single scrap of information to her all at once. As though he sensed that he would never have the opportunity to do so again.

Suddenly she feels a cold nose tickling her cheek. She opens her eyes. Brosi, her father's faithful dog, has come to comfort her. He presses close to her. They lie there thus for some time.

Leif is now the master of Brattalid. The boy whose hand he is holding turns out to be his son, Torgils. A somewhat strange, peaceable boy with huge observant brown eyes. A child who seldom smiles and hardly ever plays with other children. The boy spends most of his time hanging around his father.

Freydis has to drag the story out of her brother. When Leif was away on his great voyage to Norway and later to Vinland, they were caught in a storm and spent most of the first summer in the Hebrides. There Leif had met dark-haired, well-born Torgunna and become attached to her. When the crew were making the ship ready to sail to Norway, Torgunna announced that she was with child, and that she wanted to go with Leif.

Leif refused. There was no place for a woman on the journey he was planning, he told her. But he presented her with valuable gifts – a ring, a Greenlandic wadmal cape, and a toothed belt.

Then Torgunna grew angry and told him that she would send him his son when he was old enough to go to sea with men, and that she herself would follow.

Earlier that summer, Torgils had arrived with a trading vessel, bringing back with him the gifts his mother had received from Leif. Leif took him in and acknowledged him as his son and the heir to Brattalid.

For a moment something approaching laughter springs up in Freydis, before it is quelled by the sorrow that weighs on her heart. But she manages to say what she thinks.

'So, you have a child by a woman you are not married to. You are not as saintly as you pretend to be, my revered brother.'

'That was before I became a Christian,' retorted Leif.

'Oh, and now you've become a monk?' she asks.

Leif does not reply. And Freydis is too exhausted to continue bickering.

Later, she asks Leif where their father is buried.

'You never held a Christian funeral for him, surely?' she exclaims.

'Mother wanted us to, but to the very end he cursed and swore and said he would come and haunt us day and night if we didn't bury him the old Norse way, so we didn't dare do anything else,' said Leif.

That gives her some kind of satisfaction when she is shown the burial site. Eirik lies beside Ragni, mother of Freydis, on a hillside just a few stones' throws below to the left of Brattalid. They lie on the hillside facing the sea.

Freydis wonders whether Leif and Tjodhild know that this is where Ragni is buried. Is she the only one who knows? Either way, she has no intention of revealing the fact.

'Father took with him many of his treasures and plenty of food for his life on the other side. He will lack for nothing, wherever he ends up,' Leif says, as the pair of them stand contemplating the grave.

'That's good. We have no idea what he might need on the other side. You can believe, but nobody really knows,' says Freydis.

'That's true.'

'Not even your priests,' Freydis adds, unable to resist.

Unlike many other great Viking chieftains, Eirik the Red was not buried with his ship, the *Dragon*, the ship in which he had sailed out to discover Greenland

and settle there. It would have been too large for the burial plot. Moreover, it was the only ship at Brattalid, Leif's ship having been borrowed to those travelling to Vinland. The people at Brattalid needed the *Dragon* for their hunting and fishing expeditions to the north. The ship was still useful, even though age and the constant battering she had endured on the high seas were beginning to take their toll.

But they had laid huge sharp stones in the shape of a ship round the burial mound. These symbolised what a great mariner Eirik the Red had been. Freydis sat down on one of the stones.

'I should like to sit here alone for a while.'

'I understand. Just let me know if you need anything,' Leif says, with a gentle look. Although the relationship between the siblings is not cordial, Leif feels sympathy for his sister, who has suffered so many losses.

He leaves her. She closes her eyes and allows her thoughts to stream in. Unbidden, a verse springs to her mind, a verse Eirik often repeated. Freydis thinks perhaps the words held a special significance for him.

Cattle die, friends die, a man dies the same way. One thing I know that never dies, the judgement of every dead man.

What judgement did her father receive? She knows that he hurt many people in the course of his life. He treated many harshly. People were either friends or enemies. Eirik wounded and slew the men he quarrelled with. He raided and plundered. He took the women he wanted, whether they were willing or not.

On the other hand, he was generous to his friends and associates. And he was bold and adventurous, a born military commander, a fabled mariner, a skilled and just chieftain – a man without equal. And not least: he was a good father, strict but loving. Had it not been for Eirik the Red, her childhood and youth would have been joyless. Her father was the only one who understood her. He, and sometimes Leif.

Weighing up the good and the bad, how would the chieftain of Greenland be judged? Did he himself ponder this question much? She will probably never know.

The memories continue to crowd in. She was still a little girl, maybe five or six, last time she sat in this very spot, perched on her father's lap. Eirik told her about her mother; told her this was where her mother was buried. That was why he liked to sit there.

'Ragni was a beautiful girl, slight, with long brown hair. Her loveliest feature was her smile, and she smiled often.'

Then Eirik said that Ragni had caught his eye the very first time he saw her. She was a slave, belonging to a neighbour, and she healed him one time when he was wounded. He liked her so much that he persuaded his father to buy her so she could become Eirik's concubine.

Freydis had asked him what a concubine was, and why everyone called her the concubine's daughter, as if that was not a fine thing to be.

'Don't you worry your head about that. It just

means that she was my woman, in the same way Tjodhild is. I was just as fond of her. More, in fact ...'

He told her he had taken two women with him when he set out from Iceland to find land in the west. He had come to realise they needed women to do the cooking and take care of their clothing. Ragni was skilled in the art of healing, which could be useful on a journey such as theirs. Then they found this land, Greenland.

'Ragni became pregnant, but not long after she bore you, she was taken ill. She had a fever for many days before she died. She knew a great deal about plants and how they could be used to heal the sick. She helped many other people, but she could not help herself.'

Her father seemed so sad that she refrained from asking him anymore, just hugged him tight. Then a thought struck her. It was her fault her mother had died. That, she thought, must be the reason so many people disliked her.

When she was a child, Eirik had often spoken enthusiastically about his childhood in Norway and their flight to Iceland. She heard of his friendship with the Earl Haakon of Lade, about his Viking expeditions and all the riches they found, the things they saw and experienced.

These stories were the seeds of Freydis's dreams. This was the life she wanted – to travel and experience new things, see new countries, new people.

Only later had she learned that Eirik's expeditions had not been jolly, friendly jaunts. Robbery, murder and rape. But she did not want to think about that, neither then nor now; no-one should sully Eirik the Red's name.

A tear rolls down her cheek as Freydis conjures up the image of her father. Then the dam bursts and the salty waters of all her sorrows overflow. She weeps not only for her father, but for Sverre, who deceived her, and for Bjarne, for her brother and her son, lost in the ocean deep.

And suddenly she remembers the story her father told about Bjarne and Grimolv. She is amazed she never thought of it before, while she was with Bjarne. There must have been something else going on in her head at the time. It seemed so strangely remote, although it was only a few days ago.

Bjarne's mother had also been a slave. Grimolv bought her because he needed a concubine. Soelvi, as she was called, was as fair as a flowery meadow in summer. But what Grimolv didn't know was that she was mentally damaged.

She had seen her whole family, her parents and her brothers, slaughtered by the Vikings. Her homestead had been set on fire and razed to the ground. She had been captured and violently raped by several of the Vikings. At the time, she was eleven years old.

She had experienced many dark things before she was sold to Grimolv at the age of fifteen. He treated her well, although he too demanded that she satisfy his lust. For two years she wandered round the farm in silence, quietly carrying out her duties both in the house and in his bed.

But when Bjarne was born, something inside her broke. She lost her mind. She refused to have anything to do with the child, or with Grimolv or the other people on the farm. She went about screaming without end. Nobody knew what to do with her.

One day, she seized a glowing iron and dragged it down over her son's back. For weeks the little boy shrieked in agony. Finally, herbs, healing plasters and time healed the wound. Now Grimolv did not dare allow Soelvi to go about freely anymore, so he locked her up in a shed. Here she sat day and night, wailing. After a few months of this she began to refuse both food and drink, and one day they found her lying dead in the hay.

Bjarne was hardly two years old when they carried his mother out and buried her at the edges of their farm. Poor Bjarne, Freydis thinks to herself. They had much in common, both losing their mothers so young. She feels closer to him than ever now. The loss of him strikes her savagely.

Now it is not only her eyes that are flowing. Her breasts are swollen, heavy and painful. Full of milk, with no-one to empty them. The milk flows out, soaking her dress. She has not stopped bleeding since the birth, either, although a couple of weeks have passed. Suddenly a great clot of blood falls into the cloth she has bound about her waist. Perhaps that is what was needed to cleanse her.

Eventually, when her stream of tears abates, she decides to bathe. She tugs off her sodden dress and her underclothes. Naked, she steps into the ice-cold water, welcoming its embrace, then swims briskly over to a small iceberg that looks rather like a bird that has been shot. It is floating on the edge of the shore.

She dives down deep and suddenly she is faced with a green, slender, shapely woman whose long floating hair almost envelops her. Slowly and gracefully she dances in the deep.

Can this be Ran?

But the woman does not state her name, just says she has seen neither Bjarne nor the baby boy. But Maja and Torvard, the brother of Freydis, have been guests at her banquet. They have come to a good place, she says, without elaborating further.

When Freydis later hurries ashore, she shakes her head over this encounter. She must have imagined it. Is she losing her wits? She saw Storm disappear with her own eyes, and Bjarne is gone, too. Maybe there are other sea gods who have taken them. She hopes they have gone to the same place, father and son.

The icy dip has done her good; She feels revived. Shivering, she wraps herself in the only dry piece of clothing she has, her warm woollen skirt. She smiles at a pair of foxes that are resting on Eirik and Ragni's grave mound. Their fur has a bluish tinge.

The chieftain's daughter has reached some decisions. She will live her life to the fullest, and she will endure her fate, whatever it may be. It can hardly be worse than it is, she thinks. Why must she lose all the people she loves? Surely, she must have made enough sacrifices by now.

Overcome with drowsiness, she dozes off. When she wakes, everything around her is in pitch darkness. Only the full moon and the starry sky cast their light over the mountains and create treasures of playful silver that shimmer on the gurgling water.

Now she sees a warm light oscillating towards her. An oil lamp. She recognises the smell from a distance. It is Torvard, coming to fetch her. They are to spend the night in Leif's longhouse until the next day. Then they must return to their duties at Gardar. Freydis sighs and trudges after her husband. Back to everyday life. She fears it may be even more excruciatingly dull than it was before.

EVERYDAY LIFE

Greenland, Gardar, the year 1005

Freydis wants to enjoy the son she has left, to forget that he has Sverre's eyes, and remember that in all other respects he resembles her own family, especially his late grandfather.

She had cherished high hopes of her reunion with Einar, but the moment he looks at her she realises it will be harder than she imagined.

Although not as strongly as before, she still feels betrayed. Over and over again. She tries to repress the feeling. She approaches Einar, wanting to hug him and lift him up. But he ducks and runs over to Bjadok, the Irish slave girl who has been taking care of him while they were away in Vinland. He hides in her green skirts. He does not care about the fine clothes his mother has sewn for him, which strangely enough resisted being washed overboard by the waves.

Torvard, on the other hand, soon establishes a bond with this son who is not his. Before long, the pair of them are running around the yard laughing. Einar is actually quite a handsome boy, with his freckled nose and long wavy red hair, which needs cutting.

Although he is more than three years old and tall and strong, there is still something babyish about him. Is this how Eirik the Red was as a boy? Einar is certainly very unlike Torvard, naturally enough. Her husband has become even more scrawny and pale after their sail to Vinland. It certainly has not done him any good. Not at all. And the journey home has had its ill effects.

Freydis ignores her son's indifference to her. Instead, she quickly takes charge of running Gardar. Her father-in-law, Einar, died of the plague like Eirik the Red. Since then the farm has been managed by the remaining servants and slaves, with the help of Leif and other neighbours.

Leif is the natural chieftain in Greenland since the death of Eirik the Red. A strong leader is needed in a land which has been shattered by the plague. Just before Freydis returned to Gardar, Leif invited her to walk with him in the familiar mountains behind Brattalid. It did them both good.

'I've been thinking. Father is dead, and of his children only you and I are left,' Leif says.

'Yes, there has been much trouble over the last two years.'

'And you lost your newborn son at sea.'

Freydis stops. Her throat is constricted so she

cannot utter a word. She leans against her brother. He hugs her close. It is just like the old days.

'There have been many changes in Greenland too. Many have been broken by the plague, these have been bad years. Many people are starving, especially on the smaller farms. These are bad times for us here at Brattalid, too, but we'll get through it.'

'Yes, you have been given a heavy burden to bear. But you will manage to make Greenland great again. I know you were born to do it.'

'I'll do my best. We shall all have to do our best. Hard times ahead.'

Freydis had been studying Leif as he stared ahead. He was still a handsome man.

'I don't suppose I'll ever get to Vinland again. Both Torvald and Torstein are dead. I'm the only one left to run Brattalid. And you are at Gardar. It is my destiny to stay here in Greenland,' he sighs.

'Yes, none of us can command our own destinies,' she replied.

They were silent for a while, and then she plucked up the courage to ask the question that was burning on her lips.

'You haven't thought of taking a wife? Brattalid needs a mistress.'

'No, there's no hurry. We have plenty of capable women on the farm.'

'How about that Torgunna? Won't you go to the Hebrides and fetch her?'

'No, she'll have to come of her own accord.'

'Don't you think she'll be hoping you'll come for her?'

'No.'

Leif snapped so sharply that she asked him no more questions. She was happy to be back in his good books, just the same.

Torvald's mother Bjarghild, once so stubborn and sharp-spoken, is unrecognisable. She wanders about, confused, hardly recognising her son and daughter-in-law. But they allow her to go on living in the old long-house. She has help with the daily chores from her faithful slave woman, Unni, who is almost as old as herself.

Freydis sees that, despite his grief for the loss of his father, Torvald livens up now he is back at his home-stead. His health improves. And now he has taken Bjadok for his concubine. Nobody has mentioned it, but not much goes on at the farm that Freydis does not know about.

But she does not care; She is happy enough to escape her marital duties. Even so, she cannot resist treating Bjadok more harshly than the other slaves.

'Haven't you milked those cows yet? They are standing lowing like mad,' she shouts at her.

'I'll go now,' Bjadok replies meekly.

'There's no water, and you haven't washed Einar yet either. Useless girl, what am I going to do with you?'

Bjadok sneaks away, and Freydis immediately regrets her tone. Bjadok is competent. In a moment of self-awareness she realises she is turning into Tjodhild. Why is she being so hateful?

Sometimes Freydis amuses herself with the crew of visiting trading vessels. These men are easy to seduce.

She knows that the tale of her feats in Vinland is passed around among Icelanders. Freydis is made out to be like a goddess who saved them all from certain death. They bombard her with questions, they want to know all the details, they want her to show them exactly what she did to terrorise the skraelings. It excites them.

And Freydis enjoys it, lays it on thicker than she needs to. The events were sufficiently dramatic already, but she likes to be reminded of them. She remembers how alive she felt, although her life had never been in greater danger than at that moment. She still does not know what came over her and made her act the way she did. And yet, her pleasure is not unmitigated. Too many terrible things happened in the wake of it.

In the area surrounding Gardar there are many spots where she can hide, alone with her temporary lovers. Freydis builds an invisible shield around her heart. She will never allow herself to become obsessed by anyone as she was by Sverre, nor get close to her, as Bjarne did. Never again.

She has decided that she will not conceive any more children. No more ghastly births, no more sons who will reject her or who will be sacrificed to the gods. She has procured an herbal brew from a wise woman at Herjolvsnes, and she drinks a mouthful every day. This potion will cause her womb to reject any child that tries to take shelter there.

Sometimes on her morning rambles Freydis meets Torbjorg. The soothsayer often pops up out of the mist like a troll woman from the other world. But she has never spoken, except for that one time when she prophesied Leif's return, and Torbjorg still never looks her in the eye.

Freydis does not consort with other women, apart from her slaves. She is not like other women, certainly unlike the women living here in Greenland, stolid farmers' wives each one of them. They have accepted the distribution of tasks; The men go hunting and fishing, while the women take care of everything to do with the home. They seem to have no dreams, or none they dare to share. And now many of them have become Christian, too. They sing hymns, say grace before meals, and worship a half-naked man hanging on a cross.

Most of the other women think Freydis is bold and behaves like a man. Besides, there are rumours about her loose behaviour with the men from the trading boats. The righteous believe a sinner like her will burn in hell.

The only woman Freydis considers a friend is Gudrid. She is more free-thinking than the rest. They grew close while they were in Vinland. Often, the pair of them had to team up against the men over important matters. Also, Gudrid was the only woman who praised Freydis for her courage and quick thinking when she saved them in Vinland. In retrospect, Gudrid actually thought the whole thing was hilarious.

'To think they were scared off by flaunting a bare bosom and a few shouts! Men really are simple creatures, whether they be skraelings or Norsemen,' Gudrid had told Freydis when she visited her in the longhouse in Vinland just after it happened.

'How right you are! The simplest creatures in the world!'

Then the two women had laughed long and hard.

But now Freydis has lost Gudrid too. She has left for Iceland with Torfinn Karlsevne and their son, Snorre.

'I must go and start spawning this great dynasty I've been promised that I shall leave behind me,' she had said with a slight air of mockery and a roll of her eyes, when she took her leave of Freydis on the beach at Brattalid. Freydis had laughed.

'Yes, many of us have to live lives we never wanted. Our fates are not dissimilar. We have both sustained heavy blows, and we must take what comes.'

Then they had hugged each other, shedding tears, and wished each other good luck and a happy life, knowing all too well that they would never meet again.

The years pass, and the wall she has built around herself grows more robust. The men from the ships are now no longer so easy to seduce. All the Icelanders avoid her as soon as she approaches them. At first, she is mystified as to the reason for this – she is still as fair, as desirable as before, and the story from Vinland is still fresh in people's minds.

One day it becomes all too clear. The rumours about Sverre have begun to spread like the autumn storms at sea. She is the cause of it all, this madwoman Freydis Eiriksdatter of Gardar. The shameless heathen, the bastard child, the witch. They dare not risk being cursed by her, as he was.

For Sverre, it appears, has become a bitter man, alone on a big farm in Iceland, with only a few slaves to help him. It is said that he goes to church every day to pray. But to no avail. He is praying to the wrong gods, thinks Freydis. Why does he not pray to the Norse goddess of love, Freya?

But she does not waste any pity on him. There is hardly anything in her life that sets joy rushing through her veins, opens up the floodgates of her laughter, sets her soul on fire. There is only cold. The sort of cold that bites the palm when she places it on an iceberg. Cold like the eternal winter on Greenland's mountains. A still, lifeless cold.

As the years pass, she grows no closer to her son, despite her repeated efforts. She is fond of him in her own way, but he rejects her. She brings him along on walks to show him animals and plants, she takes him on a boat on the fjord, she tells him stories about the family and the Norse gods.

He goes along, he listens, but there is a cloud of resentment surrounding him. He would prefer to be with Bjadok and the men on the farm. Only then is he animated.

Oh, Freydis hates living here; She longs to return to Vinland, to the rich country where all was going so well, until the return journey which she has decided she is going to put right out of her mind and not think about anymore.

They did not achieve their goals there; They did not explore the country, nor did they manage to bring home the wealth they had accumulated. It was all washed overboard in the sea. Deep in her heart there is a flash of hope. Was it Ran who spoke to her that time, in the depths of the ocean? Was she speaking the truth when she said that she had not taken Storm and Bjarne? Could they had survived and made it ashore in some other land?

ANOTHER VOYAGE TO VINLAND

Gardar and Vinland, the year 1009

The days drag on by. Each is a grain that settles in the jar of life. She feels doomed to spend the rest of her life here at Gardar, staring into this jar. When the jar is full, she hopes she will be able to travel to wherever her parents and Bjarne and Storm are.

Then something happens. A ship from Norway sails into Eiriksfjord and steers straight for Brattalid. On board are two brothers of Norwegian and Icelandic blood, Helge and Finboge. They are lively lads thirsting for new adventures.

'We'd like to stay here for the winter and get to know this land we have heard so many good things about. If we may?' Finboge asks, shaking hands with Leif, who is bidding them welcome.

'We're a hospitable folk. Everyone is welcome here. How many of you are there?' Leif replies, uneasily trying to estimate how many people there are on board the ship.

'There are thirty of us, all told, freemen and slaves. The ship is also laden with timber, grain, malt, honey, iron pots and many more things which we'll give you in return for your hospitality,' says Finboge.

It is late summer already, and Brattalid, impoverished by the plague and a series of cold winters, is not ready to support so many souls for a whole winter.

Gardar is asked for help. Torvard and Freydis have food, and plenty of room. The longhouse stands empty now since the recent death of Bjarghild. So, since the winter has tightened its iron grip and the fjord can now be crossed both on foot and on horseback, Finboge and his household move into the old longhouse.

Finboge has brought his wife, Reidun; two half-grown sons, Soelver and Sverre; Geirmund the hunter; Sveinung the wood carver and five slaves, two men and three women. Freydis suspects the fairest of the slave girls, Silfa, is Finboge's concubine, but for some reason he makes every effort to conceal this from the others.

Reidun is an unusually hard-working woman; She is not afraid of doing the heavy lifting on the farm. But even though she has muscles like a man, her body is neat and slender.

In fact, she is rather good-looking. Good features, healthy brown hair often bound up in a scarf. But her expression is grim, and she never smiles. She expresses her thanks most courteously for food and shelter, but there is something about her that seems off.

Freydis shrugs off these tiresome misgivings and tries to feel pleased that the family is doing their share and more of the work on the farm. They erect a new barn. Laundry and cooking are much easier with so many hands, and there are more hunters, so they kill more animals than ever before. And it is a good thing, too, for the winter is both hard and cold.

For the most part, the people living at Gardar stay indoors and get to know one another. Freydis is thrilled when she learns that both Helge and Finboge want to sail to Vinland. Leif has told them of this rich land in the west.

'And you have actually been there! What was it like, was it as Leif describes it?' Finboge asks, staring at the Gardar couple with wide blue eyes.

'Yes, it's a wonderful land. Milder than here, greener too. There are massive forests with all sorts of game, and the waters are rich with fish – both fresh water and salt water. There are berries and fruit, and wheat grows easily.'

Freydis is extolling the land's virtues while she serves ale and newly cooked fish. But Torvard interrupts her.

'It is possible to have a good life there. But there is trouble, too. Twice we were attacked by skraelings. They fired arrows at us, they hewed at us with axes, and they had a strange slinging machine which allowed them to hurl a great stone a long way. In their first attack they slew two of our men, and in the second attack they fired a deadly arrow that struck Torvald, the brother of Freydis, and killed him. And on the return journey we were caught in a storm which cost us dearly ...'

Freydis scowls at her husband. He is ruining everything as usual. She sees that the enthusiasm of Finboge and the others has been dampened by Torvard's words.

She quickly takes command of the conversation.

'These skraelings are tiny creatures, much smaller than we are. And their weapons are not terrifying so long as we are prepared. We were caught on the hop last time.'

'Yes, we heard you behaved like a Valkyrie and scared off the skraelings,' Finboge interjects, with a wry glance at Freydis.

'Yes, as I said, these skraelings are easy to deal with.'

She sees that Torvard is about to butt in again and raises her voice.

'Besides, Karlsevne captured one of the skraelings, Chin. He's a slave at Brattalid. He often goes along on the hunts. A little dark fellow with squinty eyes. You may have seen him about. He speaks the language of the skraelings, and I'm sure he could be used to negotiate a peace agreement or a truce.'

The Icelanders have plenty to think about. During the winter, they speak together. They occasionally include Leif, Freydis and the others who have been to Vinland. They speak with Chin to learn more about the skraelings. He says his people are peace-loving, but that they will not hesitate to take up arms if they feel threatened.

With dreamy eyes he speaks of their chief, the great Ullakhan, admired by everyone. If they can make an agreement with the chief, they will be able to live in peace, Chin thinks. (He has another name, of course, but nobody bothers to ask him what it is.)

When at last the spring sun starts to melt the snow which surrounds the Greenland farms and the thick ice in the fjord, they have come to an agreement. They want to go, but they want experienced people with them on the expedition.

They ask Leif first, but he points out that he has responsibilities both for the farm and for the land as a whole. He is also expecting the arrival of Torgunna. He cannot be away from home when she sails into Eiriksfjord.

Then they ask the master of Gardar and his wife. Freydis is excited. Secretly she makes a deal with the brothers that they will each sail with his own ship, taking thirty men and five women each, and that all the riches they discover shall be shared equally between them.

She also makes an agreement with Leif that she may borrow the *Serpent* again. The ship has long since been repaired after the storm that battered her on her return voyage from Vinland.

Freydis says nothing to Torvard until the deal has been made. He is far from delighted.

'We've been to Vinland and it was not that great. Haven't you had enough of it? You can't have forgotten that nightmare journey home, when we lost the baby and nearly our lives, too.'

'You know very well that I am not happy, locked up in this valley, every day the same. I'm going. If you aren't coming along, I can still go. I'll borrow the ship and the crew from Leif,' Freydis says briskly.

Torvard sighs. What a terrible hand fate has dealt

him, doomed to love this woman all his life, whatever she gets up to.

'And we were attacked by those skraelings!'

Torvard begs and protests, in a desperate attempt to dissuade her.

'We cannot let ourselves be cowed by those little creatures. We'll take weapons. And if worst comes to worst I can always flaunt my bosom again,' says Freydis with a coarse laugh and looks pointedly at Torvard.

'It had been better for your mother if you had been born a woman. Because that's what you are, a silly old woman, if you daren't come with us to Vinland,' she snaps.

Her broad stance makes it look like she is nailed to the ground. She crosses her arms over her chest.

Torvard stands quietly beside her with his eyes closed and lets her stream of curses rain down over him. At last he gives in. Again.

'Right, I'll make ready for the voyage, then,' he says wearily, turning and trudging slowly off towards the longhouse.

Freydis flies about like an autumn gale. She sees to it that they have enough dried meat and fish for the voyage. They will bring with them two cows and a few sheep. Clothes and shoes, kitchen equipment and weapons. So many details to think of. Flints to light the fire, for instance. They carefully choose which slaves get to go along. Adventurous folk from the poorer neighbouring farms flock in to join them, lured by the thought of grapevines, the mild climate, and especially by the promised abundance of food. These have been lean years in Greenland.

At last they have thirty-five men and five women. That is five more men than Freydis had agreed on with Helge and Finboge. Freydis points this out to Torvard, but he cannot say no to anyone. She decides it probably makes no difference.

Freydis is pleased with her ship's company. She has got hold of a skilled helmsman from Herjolvsnes. There are farmers, hunters and fishermen. There are strong men who can row. There are women who can take their turns at laundry and cooking. She brought a slave to be her assistant so that she can spend all her time leading the Greenlanders.

Freydis is excited. She recalls her first encounter with Bjarne by the bay. Could she ever experience anything like that again? She sighs without thinking. Torvard hears it.

'What are you dreaming about while the rest of us slave away?'

He has been like a thundercloud of late, bursting with rage every now and then. Freydis shrugs and gets on with her work.

She has almost forgotten about her son Einar. He is old enough to understand what is happening, and he clings like a leech to Torvard, snivelling. He ignores his mother completely. Oh, how she wishes she and Einar could love each other! But she loses all the people she loves. She would probably lose Einar too, if she did love him. It is best to harden your heart.

On the day they set sail, Greenland shows itself at its most beautiful. Sunshine floods the landscape and spirits are high both at Gardar and at Brattalid. Many people have turned up to wave them off. Some are sitting on the grass, enjoying food they brought with them, others are helping them carry aboard the supplies. There is laughter and cheering, barking and bleating. They take two dogs with them aboard the *Serpent*. They will be on guard in case the skraelings turn up.

While rolling up woollen blankets in the longhouse, Freydis catches sight of a familiar figure. Torbjorg Lillevolven. The soothsayer is more crooked than ever and walking down towards the ship. She turns to Torvard. He is giving orders to a slave who is tethering the sheep onto the ship. The crone says something to Torvard. He replies.

Freydis hurries over to hear what Torbjorg has to say, but before she gets there, the soothsayer has disappeared.

'What did she say to you?' she asks her husband.

'She warned us not to go. She said there will be a kind of Armageddon, a Ragnarok, in Vinland while we are there. And you will do a cruel deed, she said. Yet another reason to stop this madness now. She is usually right, that soothsayer, isn't she?' Torvard says sternly.

Freydis is seething. Why did Torbjorg go through Torvard instead of speaking with her?

'It doesn't change anything,' she snaps and walks hastily away from her husband.

Outwardly she gives no sign that the soothsayer's words affected her, but they were haunting her just the same. What had Torbjorg foreseen? What was going to happen to them in Vinland?

Finally, everything is ready. Freydis is dressed in her best clothes: a dark-blue dress which shows off her figure. Her red mane is loose about her shoulders, sparkling in the sun. As though she were the queen of Greenland – which is nearly true – she stands tall in the bows of the ship, waving to the smallfolk on the shores of the fjord.

At last she is alive again, every heartbeat pulses through her with a fierce joy. She feels like shouting aloud. She is alive! Torvard does not understand that the urge to travel is in her blood, the blood she has from her father, her father's father and ancestors beyond.

Eirik the Red's great-grandfather was the legendary Oksna-Tore. Oksna-Tore's brother was Nadodd, who discovered Iceland. They are a whole dynasty of explorers.

Freydis would gladly sail to Iceland and Norway too, just to experience new things. She has often dreamt of leaving Greenland for good and sailing away on one of the trading vessels, but the idea never bore fruit. She even asked Leif whether they might sail together to the Hebrides to fetch Torgunna, but her brother never assented.

'She'll have to come to me,' he had said when she asked again.

'Maybe she's waiting for you to come and fetch her. I'd really appreciate that, in her place.'

But Leif just snorted.

They agree that the *Serpent* will sail out of Einarsfjord from Gardar, while the brothers' ship, the *Wolf*, sails out of Eiriksfjord from Brattalid. They will rendezvous in the archipelago at the mouth of the two neighbouring fjords when the sun is at its zenith in the heavens.

As they approach the rendezvous, Freydis binds up her hair in a knot and dons everyday attire. She asks five of the men to conceal themselves beneath some blankets. She has neglected to inform the Icelanders that they are carrying more men than was agreed.

This is not discovered until they reach Markland, where they go ashore to fill their freshwater reserves.

The Icelandic brothers are angry when they count the *Serpent*'s ship's company. They are not surprised, because they have heard many bad things about this chieftain's daughter. Of course, she is renowned for repelling the attack of the skraelings in Vinland, but she has also done many evil deeds. Finboge clenches his fists and goes up to Freydis; his eyes flash angrily when he meets hers.

'You have deceived us. You've brought five men more than you should have.'

'So what? You've brought along more women than we have. That evens it out,' she says, looking at him scornfully.

'What do a few women matter? You know full well it's not the same,' Finboge snarls, aiming a large gobbet of spit which lands just beside her left foot.

She sends him an icy glare and then spins round silently as a cat and strides away to the crew who are loading the water containers.

In bitter rage Helge and Finboge get the ship ready for the last stretch southward. The brothers decide to break their agreement that they will all stay together. A few days later, as they are approaching the site of Leifsbudir, Helge and Finboge make a break for it.

They reach land first and quickly take possession of Leif's longhouse. When Freydis sees this, she flies into a rage. As soon as they touch land, she swings herself over the side. She rushes up to the house and hurls herself through the door. Panting for breath, she shouts:

'My brother built these houses. He has lent them to me, not to you,' she thunders, hands on her hips.

All the Icelanders, who a moment before were rushing around busily doing various things, freeze in their tracks. The atmosphere in the room is as cold as a midwinter Greenland night. Helge and Finboge whisper to each other. Helge turns to Freydis and glares at her.

'We certainly can't beat you when it comes to wickedness.' he says.

Then they carry all their possessions back out and take over some of the houses built by their compatriots. They assume this is in order. From what they have heard, neither Torfinn Karlsevne nor Gudrid Torbjornsdatter intend to return.

Freydis does not wait long before visiting the brothers to ask for fair weather. She apologizes for bringing more men than agreed and offers to lend them to the Icelanders.

The brothers accept, and there is a cessation of hostilities. They realise that they need to stand united against the skraelings. They all immediately set about hunting, felling trees and gathering what food and other resources they can find.

They had had high hopes for Chin, the skraeling, and were confident he would help them broker an agreement so they could live in peace. But no sooner had they landed, than he escaped their camp. The Icelanders tried to pursue the barefoot native, but he shook them off in the deep forest. Neither Chin nor any other skraelings have been spotted since, though the settlers have kept watch since the very first day.

The brothers suggest they should occupy themselves with various sports. Running, wrestling, throwing. All is fine for a while, but then ill-feeling breaks out again. One of the Greenlandic wrestlers is too violent, and his Icelandic opponent ends up with a broken arm. The feast they had planned after the games is cancelled. After that, the households keep more to themselves.

This winter is colder and windier than the two they experienced the last time they were here. Freydis usually stands at her loom, which is luckily still in good shape. The half-finished coverlet she had been working on last time she was in Vinland, the one with the blazing sunrise at the line where the sea meets the sky, was still in place on the loom. In fact, the skraelings have not done much damage. All that is gone are the axes they did not manage to take with them when they fled, and a few buckets and bowls. That is all.

One of the smallholders who joined the voyage is a gifted bard. Almost every day he composes a new verse about their experiences. Games and stories comprise the evening's entertainment around the long fireplace. At times like these Freydis finds herself missing Bjarne, the best storyteller of them all.

When they are all gathered together it can be crowded and noisy. But while Freydis works her many coloured yarns, she dreams away the time. Then the racket the others are making fades, and she has peace to explore her own inner universe.

In the latter part of the winter, the Greenland contingent decide they will try to mend fences with their neighbours. They collect cheeses, butter and spun yarn as a peace offering. The Icelanders did not bring any livestock along, so they do not have these commodities themselves.

Freydis, Torvard and a handful of the others carry them. Helge meets them at the door.

'We would like there to be peace between us, and we hope you will accept these gifts,' says Freydis.

'Thanks. That's fine,' says Helge curtly.

There is a silence. The Greenlanders are not invited in. Freydis tries again.

'We would also like to invite you all to a feast tomorrow. We have newly brewed mead.'

'We'll see,' he says.

Finboge is busy mending a broken axe and clearly does not think it worthwhile to rise and greet them. His wife Reidun stares hard at Freydis. Reidun dislikes her, there is little doubt about that. She was just the same back at Gardar. But why? What has Freydis ever done to her?

But something is afoot, and it has nothing to do with the Greenlanders. Freydis can sense it.

Although the households have little to do with each other, the Greenland and Iceland slaves talk to each other. Many of them are related. Among them are a pair of siblings who were separated as children and are now reunited. The slaves say an icy front has been established between Helge and Finboge.

As far as Freydis knows, there are two reasons for this. One has to do with the ship. Freydis always thought the brothers owned it jointly between them. But it turns out that the *Wolf* belongs solely to the older brother, Finboge. Helge has long wished to build a ship of his own, and he saw the possibility of doing so when he learned of the masses of timber available in Vinland. He wanted to build himself a ship there and sail her back to Iceland and Norway. According to Helge, Finboge promised him the services of Ulf, a highly skilled Norwegian shipbuilder, to assist him in this project. Ulf is a soft-spoken free man who has lived and sailed with Finboge for many years.

Finboge denies ever having made such an arrangement with his brother. He has plenty of other work for Ulf to do.

The other source of disagreement concerns the slave girl Silfa. She belonged to Helge. He had bought her off a neighbour in Iceland. She grew into a beauty and soon became Helge's favourite concubine. When they came to Greenland and Finboge and his household moved into Gardar, Helge lent Silfa to his brother's family to assist Reidun.

But now Helge has discovered that Finboge has been enjoying Silfa's company not only in Greenland but also here in Vinland. That is the reason Finboge was so keen to hide the truth from everyone.

Freydis understands very well how men could be bewitched by Silfa. She has long flaxen hair, big blue eyes, full red lips and a sweet little nose. She is slender but shapely. She has good teeth and a modest demeanour. Many of the Greenland men, including Torvard, have cast longing glances in her direction.

Silfa reminds Freydis of a younger Gudrid, but she lacks Gudrid's natural strength and her frank, open nature. Nor can she, as a slave, behave with the same freedom.

Now Silfa is with child, and it is uncertain which of the brothers is the father. Although they live in the same house, they no longer speak to one another.

When she hears this, Freydis has to laugh. After a little reflection she decides there is nothing she can do about it. And it is no concern of the Greenland people.

But she is soon proved to be drastically wrong.

The reason Reidun hates her is also revealed. Freydis catches Reidun red-handed, milking one of her cows. Freydis is angry and rebukes her sharply. Reidun tries to defend herself by saying one of her sons is sick and she thinks fresh milk might help him.

'Why didn't you say that? Why didn't you ask? You know we'd have given you the milk,' Freydis sighs.

'How could I know that? You are not a person to be trusted,' Reidun retorts bitterly.

'What is it you have against me? What harm have I ever done to you? Weren't you taken in at Gardar, given food and everything else you needed by us?' demands Freydis.

Now Reidun lets the cow's teat go, swings round on the stool and locks eyes with Freydis. She draws a deep breath.

'I am the sister of Sverre Sigurdsson. You know

very well what you did to him. You ruined him. A witch, that's what you are!' she rages.

Freydis stands motionless, like a tree trunk whose great root system stretches far and deep. Sverre's sister. This is why Reidun hates her. Now that Freydis studies her features carefully, she can see the resemblance. The same nose, the same colour hair. But the sister lacks her brother's beaming smile and his charisma.

For a second, the sense of loss overwhelms Freydis, and a surge of rage at the way he deceived her. For once she is lost for words, but she tears herself free. She dismisses Reidun, saying:

'I have no idea what you are talking about. Get out of my cowshed.'

The days grow longer and the sun warmer. The spirits of Freydis and the other Greenland people improve. But there is no sign of a truce between the warring brothers. It is as though a wall of ice separates them. One morning when Freydis is out rambling, she overhears a violent quarrel between them. Helge wants to sail to the south in the *Wolf* to find good timber for the sip he intends to build. It is said that the trees that grow in the south are more suitable than the trees around Leifsbudir. But Finboge has other plans; He wants to sail north to hunt seal and walrus.

She shakes her head hearing their angry words. The Greenland group are also preparing to sail north to go hunting. They estimate that the sea and fjord ice has melted sufficiently for them to avoid getting stuck with their ship.

Freydis is going along. She participates in the preparations, brimming with anticipation. She takes charge of all the provisions and the sleeping arrangements, while Torvard is in charge of everything required for the hunt. He smiles, laughs cheerfully; at last he is doing something he enjoys.

Freydis hands over the running of the household at Leifsbudir to Gerd, a sturdy farmer's wife she knows she can rely on. She is ready. She has sewn herself a pair of thick wadmal trousers. She has no intention of running about after seals stumbling in a skirt. She likes this practical outfit. Had she only been a man, she could have worn trousers every single day. Let the others whisper and giggle. She does not care.

After sailing for a couple of days, they reach their destination. The icebergs are closer together than they expected, but they just about manage to scrape the *Serpent* safely through between them.

The great walruses lie dozing on the ice floes. Such a delightful sight. Such a shame they have to be slaughtered, thinks Freydis. But they have to.

On Torvard's command, they charge forward. Soon a dozen lifeless carcasses lie on the ice, which is now more red than white.

A white bear passes slowly in the water, only its head and part of its back visible. It is clearly on the look-out for an easy meal, and it circles the dead seals and walruses. The skin of the white bear is highly sought after, so Torvard and one or two others spring from ice floe to ice floe with their pickaxes at the ready.

But the bear senses the danger, quickly dives and vanishes.

Torvard slips into the ice-cold water too, shrieking. Luckily, the other hunters realise what is happening and manage to drag him out before he freezes to death.

Freydis is livid.

'Whatever possessed you to go hopping about on the ice floes? It's lethal!' she shouts, tugging off his wet clothes.

'I had to, to get close enough to the bear.'

'Instead you nearly ended up as bear fodder yourself! We'll just have to hope you don't get sick.'

'Oh, I won't,' he says, smiling.

Freydis feels her anger fade. This is in fact the way she wants him to be. She orders half of the crew to butcher the animals and the others to set up camp on land.

At twilight they are all sitting around the fire roasting fresh meat. There is nothing better than this. The skins are lying round drying. Their spirits are high. They have had a good day. Some of them sleep on the ship, others lie down round the fire, and so does Freydis.

She rolls out some of the furs and wraps a blanket around herself. As soon as she lays down her head, she is asleep.

As usual, she wakes before anyone else. A light morning mist envelops them. She rubs her eyes and sees the *Serpent*, emerging like a ghost ship from the haze. Then she turns her eyes landward, wondering whether to go for a quick walk. Then she stars in surprise. For right there, only a few metres from the camp, stands a group of people. Skraelings. She counts eight of them, five children and three adults. A family?

She reaches for the axe that lies beside her and is about to yell to wake the others. But something stops her. The skraelings are standing perfectly still; They are unarmed and show no signs of wanting to attack. All they do is to stare at her and at her sleeping companions.

Now she studies them more closely. There is something about one of the boys. He looks different from the others. His hair is fairer, he is taller and slimmer, his eyes more round. Are they blue?

Suddenly recognition surges through her like a flood of joy. It must be Storm, her son. Is it possible he was washed ashore and taken in by the skraelings? The boy standing before her looks to be the right age. Her blood runs hot, then cold. Her breathing is fast and heavy.

Quickly she gets to her feet and goes towards them. But the group have retreated almost imperceptibly; She sees them pulling into the forest. She runs after them shouting, but they do not wait. And then they are gone, as if the forest floor had swallowed them up.

In desperation she runs to and fro in the woods until at last she collapses on the ground. Now they come towards her, the long twisted branches. The branches that seek to catch hold of her and choke her. In her haste she had forgotten her loathing of woods. And now she has no idea how she is going to get out of it. She screams as loudly as she can. Soon two men from the *Serpent* appear and take her out of the forest.

'What are you doing here, Freydis Eiriksdatter?' one of them asks.

'How come you couldn't get yourself out?' the other asks, helping her to her feet.

'Storm, skraelings, mist, branches!'

At first Freydis answers in single words. They know not what to make of her reply. She is not herself. The men simply shake their heads and exchange glances.

They spend a few more days hunting and then load up the ship. But they see no further sign of the skraelings and the strange boy. In the end, Freydis decides she must have been dreaming; The vision came to her because she so longed to see Storm again.

By midsummer they had already collected so many animal pelts and so much timber that they had no more room on board. And they had dried large amounts of meat and fish down by the beach. They want to go home.

The Icelanders are in no hurry. They seem more preoccupied with their internal squabbles than with acquiring valuable goods.

THE BATTLE

VINLAND, THE YEAR 1011

ONE MORNING FREYDIS is awoken by a long drawn-out scream. One of the slaves comes running into the longhouse. Waving his arms wildly, he declares that the *Serpent* is gone.

The whole household pull on their clothes and rush out to see. The slave was right. Freydis paces to and fro on the beach, teeth and fists clenched.

Initially, they suspected the skraelings. But the dogs would have warned them, or the Icelander, who had been on watch that night. Then they realise that Helge is gone, too. As are Ulf the boat-builder, Silfa and a handful of others, including the man who was on watch. Helge must have stolen Leif's ship and sailed away to the south in search of timber so he can build his own ship.

Freydis is fuming. She marches right up to the equally wretched Finboge.

'You have stolen our ship. You see to it that we get it back right away.'

'I wasn't the one who took your ship. You'll just have to wait until Helge chooses to return home.'

'And when will that be?'

'That cowardly brother of mine will soon be back with his tail between his legs,' says Finboge, shrugging dismissively.

'It wouldn't have happened at all if you'd lent Helge your ship to go and get timber.'

Freydis leaves him, still furious. Her wrath lasts all day, and keeps her awake the next night, too. She sits on the sleeping bench beside a snoring Torvard, arms clasped around her legs, resting her head on her knees. She rocks from side to side, thinking hard.

They are in real trouble. Their ship is gone, and they have no idea if or when it will return. What if Finboge and his crew sail off in the *Wolf*? They will be stranded here alone with no ship. It is true that they have masses of timber, but there is no boat-builder among them. Helge has taken with him the only man who was skilled in that craft.

If that happens, they are doomed to remain here at Leifsbudir forever. She is the one who thrives most here, but she hates the thought of not being able to leave if they want to. Of having no choice in the matter.

Is nobody else pondering this the way she is? Her husband must not be, else he would not be sleeping like a baby, she thinks, looking at him in resignation. A plan begins to form in her head.

As soon as the sky begins to grow light, she rises. She dresses but does not take the time to put her shoes on. It is summer, after all. She throws Torvard's big warm cloak about her shoulders. The dew on the grass is cold, and she jogs quickly down to the brothers' house. The door is ajar. She pushes it open and stands on the threshold.

Finboge is lying in the centre of the room. He is wide awake.

'What are you doing here, Freydis Eiriksdatter? Didn't we say everything there was to say last night?'

'I want you to get up and come outside with me. I want to talk to you.'

Finboge complies. They sit down on a bench.

'How do you like it here in this land?' she asks.

'This land seems a good, rich place to be. We'd like to stay here longer, but there is unfriendliness between us, and that's not good.'

'You are quite right. But we have gathered enough treasure and we've decided to sail back to Greenland. We want to go now, but the *Serpent* has gone, as you know. I am asking you to lend us your ship, so when Helge returns you can take Leif's ship. We can change back again once we are in Greenland. You can keep the livestock if you want.'

Finboge is silent for a moment. Then he says, without looking at her:

'I'll go along with that, if it pleases you.'

Freydis glances at him in surprise. That was easier

than she expected. Perhaps too easy, she thinks. But she can read nothing in Finboge's square countenance.

'Good. Then we'll start packing up right away, and sail off in a day or two,' she says, standing up and setting off towards Leifsbudir.

But as she passes the door to the brothers' house, she discovers Reidun standing there, arms at her sides and a fierce grin on her face. She has clearly overheard the entire conversation. She looks down at Freydis's bare feet and rolls her eyes.

'You whore. You'll never get hold of our ship.'

There's just the hint of a twitch at the corner of her mouth. She whispers so quietly that only Freydis hears.

That does it. Freydis does not believe for a minute that the Icelanders will keep their promise to her. She will have to put her reserve plan into action.

Hastily she walks back to the longhouse and jumps into bed to warm up her feet, now ice-cold and soaking. Torvard wakes up and demands to know what is going on.

Freydis tells him about seeing Finboge, her request to him and his response.

'But they are plotting something, and it isn't anything good. They are planning to get away with their ship and abandon us here alone. We'll never get home to Greenland.'

'How do you know that? What have they said? What have they done? Didn't Finboge promise we could borrow the *Wolf* to sail home?' Torvard asks, staring at her round-eyed.

He looks so naive that Freydis flares up in anger, at him and at the Icelanders who are the bane of her life.

'I just know. And when they've gone, it'll be too late to do anything. We'll have to stay here for ever. Besides, they show no respect for me; They treat me rudely. As for you, you wretch, you won't do anything about it. You won't avenge me. If you don't do something, I'm going to divorce you,' she says bitterly.

Her wrath is boiling over; She cannot contain it. She asks Torvard to gather everyone together so they can outplay the Icelanders. Torvard sighs heavily but does as his wife says. The men take up their weapons, but they agree that if at all possible, violence must be avoided. The best thing would be to lock the Icelanders up inside their house and make sure they do not escape before the Greenland party have sailed away in their ship.

Shortly after, they gather in the farmyard and run to attack the Icelanders, brandishing spears, swords and axes.

Finboge and his people are taken by surprise. Many of them are half-naked, washing in the water close to the longhouse. Some are sharpening tools and hunting equipment, others repairing damage to their ship. The women are preparing to serve breakfast.

They run about like headless chickens in terror when the Greenland party storms in. Torvard and the other people from Greenland stop in the yard and yell that those who value their lives should go into the longhouse now, and they will be spared. Only a handful comply.

The rest refuse to surrender without a fight. Finboge is among the first to fall. A well-aimed sword thrust removes his head from his body; It rolls across the grass. Others are felled by an axe in the back or a rock to the head. Some try to flee into the forest, but are caught. They are given one more chance to go into the longhouse, and they surrender.

Soon the Greenland party think they have the upper hand. There are eight corpses stretched out on the grass. One of them is one of their own – one of the men sharpening his weapon slew the son of a farmer from Greenland.

Now they wander back to Freydis. In her white blouse and bright red skirt, she stands proudly on a flagstone in front of Leif's longhouse. She turns her fierce gaze to Torvard and wants to know the outcome of the attack. Torvard informs her that the plan was successful. All the Icelanders are either dead or in the longhouse, under guard.

'Good. You are sure nobody got away?' she demands sharply.

'Finboge's wife and some other women are in one of the barns. They are refusing to move,' one of the men says.

'We can't use force against the women, or behave violently towards them,' another says.

There is complete silence in the yard at Leifsbudir. A long silence.

Without a word, Freydis goes into the toolshed and fetches a heavy stone axe. Then she asks the man who spoke up to show her where the women are hiding.

She drags open the door and quickly sees five women huddled together against the far wall of the barn. Reidun is sitting furthest to the left. Her eyes flash with hatred.

'So, it is Freydis Eiriksdatter herself who deigns to honour us with a visit. The great witch among witches,' she spits.

These are the last words she will utter in this life. The stone axe strikes her head so hard that blood spurts all over the barn. The axe also hits Reidun's faithful slave girl Hild, who was sitting next to her. Both die instantly.

Freydis feels the blood surging through her veins, and her heart pumps so hard and fast that it seems about to leap out of her breast. She is beside herself. The feeling is enthralling. This must be the way her father felt on his pillaging raids. She raises the axe again, wanting to sustain thc intoxicating blood rush.

But just as she is about to wield it anew, she meets the terrified eyes of one of the women, more a child than a woman in truth, maybe thirteen or fourteen summers at the most, and heavily pregnant. No doubt another one that duplicitous pair of brothers have been disporting themselves with. Poor girl.

Slowly Freydis lowers her axe. She stands there, leaning on the shaft while she recovers her breath. Then she gives permission to the three surviving women to proceed in safety to the longhouse. All three accept her offer.

'So, we have two corpses and three living ones in the longhouse,' Freydis says, walking into the yard in front of Leif's house.

Her blouse, her hair and face are splashed with

fresh scarlet flecks, the axe she carries in her right hand is dripping with blood. The men stare at her in horror. Torvard hustles her into the house so she can change her soiled clothing and wash herself.

The Greenlanders work swiftly. A mass grave is dug for all the dead. The *Wolf* is laden to the gunwales with timber, skins and furs of various types, dried meat and fish. Tools and equipment are also loaded. There is plenty of room aboard the Icelanders' ship, which is both larger and newer than the *Serpent*.

They leave a cow and the sheeps and take the rest on board. They also leave food in the larders. The Icelanders in the longhouse must have some means of survival until Helge returns and takes them home. If he ever does...

Only two days after the battle, they are ready to set sail. The weather is good, the wind fair. They take one of the Icelanders along with them. The door to the longhouse is locked on the outside.

Just as they are about to sail out of the bay, Freydis discovers that the pin she uses to fasten her cloak has disappeared. She jumps over the side at once and runs back to find it. She runs around Leif's house, looking everywhere. In the end she has to give up.

It has probably fallen into one of the bundles of clothes and blankets she was packing, she thinks. But it is not there. The pin is lost.

The pin would not be found until almost 950 years later, by Norwegian archaeologists.

Just before they sail, they free the Icelandic farmer they had taken on board, so he can release his friends who have been locked in. He runs towards the longhouse.

The wind is fair and the sun is warm. This journey home promises to be much pleasanter than the last one they made from Vinland.

Freydis has plenty of time to enjoy the sight of the northerly coast. When they sail past the place where they went hunting seal and walrus, she pays extra attention, scanning the landscape. She has not forgotten the skraeling boy she saw, the boy she fancied might be her own son, Storm. But she sees no sign of other human beings.

A little further north she catches sight of a small group of men clad in loin cloths, carrying arrows and spears. Skraelings out hunting? Their leader is a tall, robust-looking man, nearly bald. Can he be their chief? Ullakhan? He does not look much like a skraeling. Her heart skips a beat.

No, Freydis, she reprimands herself. Now you really are losing your mind. That is not Bjarne. That is the chief of the skraelings. She draws a deep breath, closes her eyes and leans back, allowing the sun to warm her face.

Nobody on board the *Wolf* sees a tall man with very little hair standing on the bluff astern of them. He waves his arms and bellows at them. Bellows words in Norse. But nobody hears.

The days pass, each one with sunshine or light cloud cover, and they have a following wind. They have crossed the open sea now and are making their way down along the coast of Greenland. Soon they are home.

But the mood is subdued. Many speak in low voices of the violence and the killing. Was it really necessary to take such a hard line? When it came down to it, the Icelanders had been their friends.

Will they still be talking like this when they come home and are among their own people in Greenland? She needs to stop this. This concerns their reputation – what is said of her in Greenland, in Iceland, in Norway. Freydis decides that she must step forward as the person commanding the ship and explain why the use of so much force was necessary.

She finds a solid wooden box, which she places in the bows alongside the figurehead – the grotesque wolf's head. She dons a dress of sky-blue wadmal, climbs onto the wooden box and calls for silence, and asks everyone to pay attention to what she is about to say.

She tells them frankly about her despair after Helge stole their ship. She leaves them in no doubt that it was extremely unlikely they would ever have got home at all unless they had taken action.

'Nobody knew where Helge was bound, or whether he would ever return. We tried to make an agreement with Finboge whereby we could sail home with his ship, but we could not trust his word.'

She does her best to make them understand that they might well have ended up stranded in Vinland for the rest of their lives.

'Everybody was offered the opportunity to save their lives by going into the longhouse. Many did so. And before we left, they were released. We even left them food and livestock,' she points out.

She pauses, letting her words sink in. Then she promises them all, even the slaves, a fair share of the skins, timber and all the other things they have brought home with them. But she asks them to keep their mouths shut about what took place. She fears the peace-loving people of Greenland will find it difficult to accept why they acted as they did.

She instructs the ship's company to say that the Icelanders wished to remain longer, and that they will come home later in Leif's ship, the *Serpent*.

'That may well be true. Helge may come, but we don't know that.'

After this the mood is slightly easier, but not everyone is happy.

Freydis decides the wisest thing would be for them to sail into Eiriksfjord first, so she can tell Leif what has happened right away. He is the one who must have the *Wolf*, because it was his ship that Helge stole.

They are made welcome at Brattalid. Leif is surprised that they have come alone, and aboard the Icelanders' ship. But he accepts the explanation they have agreed on.

He feels quite hopeful that Helge will bring his ship back. He had him as his guest at Brattalid for a whole winter, and his impression of him was that he was a man who could be trusted.

Everyone is invited to a feast Brattalid. A successful voyage to Vinland must be celebrated, and heartily so.

The mead barrels are rolled out, the very best victuals are fetched from the larders, and the Vinland voyagers make their own contribution to the feast with good, tender meat from the land to the west. Things are almost as they were in Eirik the Red's day.

Before long, rumours begin to spread. What really happened? The tale that Freydis urged them to fight is circulating, and the story of the slaying of the women is passed round. Some say little, others say more.

The main gossipmongers are two men. One is the Greenland farmer who lost his son in the fight with the Icelanders, and the other is Hald, a slave from Brattalid. Hald was the twin brother of Hild, the slave girl of the Icelanders, who unfortunately got herself killed when Freydis wielded her axe against Reidun.

The twins had not seen each other since they were small. They had been sold separately as slaves and were thrilled by their reunion. But now they were parted for ever, and Hald had developed a bitter hatred for Freydis.

Every time the story is retold, it grows more brutal. Soon, every soul on Helge and Finboge's boat was slain and Freydis personally beheaded all the women and children. The story continues to spread, not only in Greenland but also in Iceland and Norway, passed on and embellished by the crews of visiting trading vessels.

The stories reach Leif's ears. He can hardly believe his sister capable of such cruelty, but he knows that unfortunately she has inherited a good deal of their father's intemperate nature.

She has behaved like a man, acted in a manner

unbefitting a woman, she has refused to be baptised. Leif had decided to accept this; She was, after all, the only surviving sibling he had. But killing women was a step too far.

'Freydis is my sister, I will not sentence her to the punishment she deserves. But I hope that she and those who come after her will never find peace,' he says grimly.

Once again, the atmosphere between the siblings is as chilly as a polar night in Hel, the Norse gods' realm of the dead.

To Freydis, it feels like a blow from a clenched fist in the belly. She implores and begs, tells him frankly and openly about everything that occurred.

'It really isn't as bad as what you've heard. Helge ran off with your ship, and we couldn't see any other way out.'

But it is like talking to a steep Greenland cliff.

'You lied. You should have told me everything right away. How can I ever trust you again after this?' he says harshly.

Leif has grown bitter. He is a shadow of his former self. Freydis cannot remember the last time she saw him smile. He has never married. He is still waiting for that Torgunna.

The years go by. Torgunna never comes, and a few years later Leif dies. He and Freydis were never reconciled.

Now Freydis is generally disliked. People avoid

her. They always approach her husband Torvard, her son Einar, or someone else on the farm if they have any business at Gardar. She is used to being ostracised, used to being different, so she just keeps quiet and takes it.

But sometimes she is overwhelmed by a lonely darkness and a heavy sense of being abandoned. On cold winter evenings she lies on the bunk feeling vulnerable as the sense of loss surges through her, forcing her tears.

At such times she wonders why this always happens to her. Why she was born with this nature, why she is always deserted, always disliked. What does it all mean? Is this life, is this all there is? She asks the animals, especially the pair of foxes she often encounters. It seems she is the only one who sees them, other people do not see blue foxes. They do not think they live around here at all, or else they are hiding.

'It's a good thing there's someone who likes me,' she says loudly to herself, feasting her eyes on the sight of the beautiful creatures with their bushy tails.

It is a long time since she has seen the dark-haired goddess. Has she, too, deserted her? But Torvard continues to be infatuated with Freydis, even though he too was horrified when she came back bloody and crazed after slaying Reidun and Hild.

She has reflected much upon that incident. She never felt such fury, either before or since. Did she have to be so merciless, could she not simply have tied them up and shoved them into the longhouse?

It might have been all right, but for Reidun's conduct and her poisonous tongue. She does not regret killing Reidun. But she should have been more careful. She ought not to have killed Hild too. She has begged Hald, the brother, for pardon, and tried to present him with timber and animal skins. She has offered to buy his freedom from Brattalid. But he rejects it all. He hates her. She just has to live with it.

She accepts Torvard's advances more often now when they lie together on the bunk. In time, she even comes to enjoy their rather tame lovemaking.

She is gratified by the thankful looks he sends her. He does not kindle her passion as Sverre and Bjarne did, but she likes him for what he is, and always will be. Torvard's love is all she has.

She has stopped taking the herbal contraceptive. She wants a child to love, a child who will love her in return.

But the years pass relentlessly, and no child appears. She is approaching forty. Is she too old? Or is it Torvard who cannot give her a child? He has not successfully impregnated his concubine Bjadok either. Although she is his concubine, she does not think he visits Bjadok these days.

Suddenly, her son has grown up. He is soon to be married to a girl he met on a farm when he was away in the north on a hunting trip.

Perhaps she should be hoping for a grandchild rather than a child. That looks to be a more promising prospect, she realises, when the girl Einar is to marry comes to Gardar.

Bjornhild is broad and wide in every respect. Her face, her smile, her shoulders, her hips, her feet. Her breasts are already swollen when she ambles around the farmyard a week or two before the magnificent wedding celebrations at Gardar. Freydis cannot resist; She grins teasingly at her son.

'It was so cold up there in the north that you had to warm each other up, eh? A good Christian like you? For shame.'

But as usual, Einar totally ignores anything his mother says to him.

Just before the wedding, something happens that changes everything.

FREYA'S LEGACY

Gardar, the year 1022

It will be a bedcover, a cover for the marriage bed. A cover of many colours, woven with all the affection she has never been able to give to her son. A cover showing the landscape of Greenland. Green grass, yellow and purple flower meadows, blue icebergs in marvellous shapes carved by the hand of nature herself, the dark-green sea, a blanket of sparkling white snow.

She tries to include the sun, the waves, the reindeer herds, the white bears and the grey mountains sharp as swords. Her realm. Einar's realm. They were both born here. Both live here now. Both of Norwegian and Icelandic blood.

One evening as she stands at her loom in the glow of the malodorous oil lamps, working on her wedding present, there comes a loud knock on the door. She glances at Torvard, who is whittling a ladle. But he merely shakes his head. They wait.

It is Agnar, a crafty, scrawny farmer from a small holding near the ice-fjord. He has walked and ridden far, he is exhausted and needs to be refreshed with a jug of ale and some cooked fish before he can deliver his message.

He says Torbjorg Lillevolven has been staying with them for a few days.

'But now she is ill and bedridden. She says she does not have much time left. She knows about such things,' says Agnar, gulping his ale heartily. Then he looks straight at Freydis and draws a deep breath.

'She wishes to speak with you before she dies. It's really important that you go to her.'

'Me? Why on earth does she want to speak to me? She only ever spoke to me once, and that was over twenty years ago.'

'She didn't mention that.'

Freydis does not understand a word of it, but she dares not evade Torbjorg. She is also curious as to what the mysterious soothsayer wants of her. It must be something important. Hopefully she is not being called in for a mere scolding. Well, she shall have to smile and bear it either way. The wall she has built around herself lately is a sturdy one.

Next day at dawn they set off, she and Agnar, each riding their own horse. Agnar is not a talkative man. But he says Torbjorg has been staying with them now and again.

'She stays in various places, sometimes at farms, sometimes in caves when the weather is warm. She does not take much with her, just a very heavy satchel. There is something strange about it.'

'What do you mean?'

'I don't know. But when you are close to it, you feel uneasy. No doubt it's to do with witchcraft.'

They arrive in the afternoon. Torbjorg has been given a fine sleeping bench in the heart of the long-house. Agnar and his wife take good care of her; They dare not do anything else. They want to keep in with the woman who possesses such impressive powers.

Torbjorg is lying on her back, her head resting on a pillow. Her eyes are closed, her toothless mouth is open. Her scrawny chest rises and falls with a whistling sound. Her dishevelled hair is spread out, as white as her blouse. Her pale twisted hands lie on a blue blanket. On the middle finger of her left hand she wears a ring with a large green stone. A smell of decay permeates the room.

Freydis takes a seat on a chair close to the strange soothsayer. She waits until Torbjorg wakes of her own accord, even though she is itching to hear what she wants of her on her death bed. Previously it has always seemed like Torbjorg was trying to avoid her. Did she not address her warning to Torvard rather than Freydis before the last voyage to Vinland? And why has she sought refuge on a poor farmstead like Agnar's rather than Brattalid or Gardar? Who is she really, anyway?

Time passes, her eyelids grow heavier and heavier. But suddenly she starts up. Torbjorg coughs. She wakes up and begins to talk. She turns towards her but stares straight ahead as though she were blind.

'Have you come now, Freydis Eiriksdatter?' she demands hoarsely.

'Yes, I'm here. What do you want with me, Torbjorg Lillevolven?'

'I wish to speak to you of your mother, of Ragni.'

'My mother, did you know her?' Freydis asks, astonished.

'Yes, indeed I did. She was my sister.'

'Your sister!'

Freydis almost spits out the words. She rises so abruptly that her chair falls over, and she begins to pace the floor, her mind buzzing.

Then she spins round and points an indignant finger at Torbjorg.

'And you never mentioned this till this moment. You are the only relative I know of on my mother's side. And you, you've treated me like dirt. You've only spoken to me once in all these years, you never look me in the eye. You should have been a mother to me, for I had none other.'

Freydis draws a sharp breath deep in her belly before she continues:

'Even Tjodhild took more care of me than you did. At least she spoke to me and looked at me.'

Torbjorg says nothing. Freydis stands still, feet firmly planted on the floor, her hands at her sides. She waits. Then suddenly she can bear it no longer.

'Well, I've got to go now. I have to prepare for my son's wedding. We are expecting two hundred guests, so I have plenty to do.'

At once Torbjorg turns her head and stares straight at Freydis. It is like being sucked into a bottomless crater. Freydis feels like she is falling into it. She grows dizzy and has to grip onto a table to stop herself from crashing down to the hard floor.

'Now you see why I have always avoided looking people in the eye. It is probably to do with my ability to see through people, how their lives are going to turn out, foretell what is going to come to pass,' Torbjorg says, turning away again.

'You are right. I should have taken care of you. It was not very maternal of me. Ragni, by the way, was the only one of us nine sisters who became a mother. But then we had a peculiar mother ourselves,' she said in a monotone.

Then she tells her that all the nine sisters possessed different skills; One could talk with the dead, another could speak with animals, one could staunch blood, one could conjure up love, one could command the tempest to abate, one could make it rain, one could fly like a bird.

'And you know what I can do. Your mother, who was the youngest of us, could heal, both with her hands and with herbs. Unfortunately, she was unable to heal herself after she became ill after giving birth to you. I knew it was going to happen, but I could not stop her when she went off with your father to Greenland,' Torbjorg says sadly.

Freydis wants to hear more about Ragni. What was she like, what did she look like, how did she become Eirik the Red's concubine? She has a stream of questions but Torbjorg waves them away.

'Ragni will come to you when you are ready to receive her.'

'What about those two foxes I keep seeing? I have been wondering for a long time if they could be my mother and father. Could that be right?' Freydis asks.

'I don't know,' Torbjorg says, attempting to smile.

She begins to speak about her own mother, Freydis's grandmother. She was a great woman who was close to Freya, the goddess of love. According to Torbjorg, there were many people who believed that she was Freya herself. Torbjorg does not know who fathered herself and her sisters.

'There is much we don't know about our origins. Each of us received her skill as a birth gift, but we also received another legacy which is hard to bear. Now the others are dead, I bear it alone.'

Freydis learns about an incident among the Norse gods of which she had been ignorant. The story concerns the World Serpent, the evil Midgardsorm, son of Loke and brother of the Fenris Wolf and Hel, the goddess of death. It has been foretold that the serpent will play a crucial role in Ragnarok, the twilight of the gods.

When Freya was walking round her kingdom, she discovered the World Serpent. He had spawned four small serpents. She thought this was no good thing, for he would have more help during Ragnarok. She concealed herself and waited until the serpent left to find food for his offspring. Then she ran out, melted her gold jewellery and poured the molten gold over the small serpents. When the gold had cooled, she took the serpents up in her sack and vanished. The World Serpent was furious when he discovered this, but he could not find out who had stolen his offspring.

Freya found that in spite of the gold, evil still resided within the serpents. But she thought it would be possible to defeat evil and use the strength of the golden serpents to fight their father at some time in the future, when Ragnarok came.

Torbjorg pauses briefly in her tale. When she resumes, her voice is deeply serious.

'I have one of those serpents in my bag.'

Freydis needs time to digest Torbjorg's story. Eirik the Red has told her much about the serpents in the Norse belief system. The World Serpent, driven into the sea by Odin, which grew so huge that it encircles the earth and bites its own tail. She knows the great serpent will come to play an important role in Ragnarok. Her father also mentioned Nidhogg, the dragon which gnaws at the roots of Yggdrasil, the tree of knowledge.

Serpents and dragons have great powers for both good and evil. It all depends. Her father and many others who shared his beliefs always did their best to play along with these powerful beings. It was not for nothing he chose a dragon's head to be carved into the prow of his ship. It was to guard against the perils of the deep.

'I see. You've got a golden serpent in your bag, and it's allegedly the offspring of the World Serpent. Why are you telling me all this? What's it got to do with me?'

'Don't you understand? I said this was the inheritance of our clan. For a long time I have been the only living member of my generation. And you are the only member of the next generation. It will be your inheritance.'

Torbjorg tells her that taking care of the serpent will be the most important task in her life.

'That is why I came along when Eirik the Red decided he was going to settle in Greenland. I had to be near you, so I could hand over the legacy.'

'Then the only reason you were here was the serpent. Did you never care about me? Did you never have any affection for me?' Freydis asks, almost in tears.

'I'm fond enough of you in my own way. But I've always been a lone wolf, with many deep abysses in my mind. After your mother died, I understood that it was my fate to live the life I've lived. You've had a tough life, Freydis. You have a warrior mentality which has spoiled many things for you, but you have strength and goodness in you too. And I have no right to judge you.'

'No, you don't.' The silence rings through the room.

Torbjorg asks her niece to fetch the worn brown satchel that stands in the corner furthest from them. Immediately, Freydis understands what the farmer Agnar meant when he said he felt a great sense of unease when he was in the presence of that bag. A wave of nausea sweeps over her. When she pulls out a heavy iron box and cracks the lid open, the feeling intensifies. But she manages to catch sight of some golden thing moving within, before she quickly slams down the lid again.

'You must take good care of it. You must not let it use its powers. You must hide it somewhere where neither the Midgardsorm nor anyone else can find it,' Torbjorg commands.

Freydis is overwhelmed. She has so many questions, she does not know where to start.

'But, but ... how am I to do that?' she stammers.

'You have one who accompanies you, a family goddess – a woman in a white dress, with long black hair, right?'

Freydis just nods.

'She is your maternal grandmother, or maybe Freya herself. You weren't given the name Freydis for nothing. I reckon Ragni knew who was going to be your goddess and gave you that name. Listen to that woman.'

'That's easy for you to say. She hasn't visited me for many a year.'

'She'll let you know when she has something to say to you.'

Now Torbjorg closes her eyes and falls silent. Freydis infers that she has said what she wanted to say and quietly leaves the room. Before she is out of the door, she hears Torbjorg's voice ring out behind her. She turns.

'You will have another child, a daughter.'

'Well, I hope you're right,' Freydis says quietly.

'It's the serpent's doing. As well as the power of evil, it has the gift of fertility. Take good care of your daughter. You will have some good years together. But you yourself will also have thirty years of loneliness.'

That same night, Torbjorg Lillevolven dies. Freydis

sees to it that her body is transported by boat to Brattalid.

There she is buried alongside her sister Ragni and Eirik the Red. Freydis sits a long while at the graveside, mourning and reflecting. Here lie three of her closest relatives.

She has felt angry with Torbjorg and the choices she has made, which are still incomprehensible to her. But now she mainly feels pity for her. For the life she led, wandering the world restlessly, living in caves or on smallholdings. Eirik the Red would certainly have allowed her to stay at Brattalid had he known she was Ragni's sister, and she would also have been welcomed by Freydis to stay at Gardar.

They might have been close. But it is too late now, too late for all that might have been. Time marches ruthlessly on. When it has passed, it does not turn back.

BIRKA TORVARDSDATTER

GARDAR, THE YEAR 1024

BIRKA TORVARDSDATTER WAS BORN on the floor of the Gardar longhouse, while the sun was at its zenith and a mild spring breeze rustled the grass. Her feeble cries filled the room with gladness.

Freydis exhales with relief. This time it had been much quicker. She had felt the first spasms in her back that very morning while she was washing the milk buckets. And now here she is at last, the longed-for daughter. The daughter she was promised by Torbjorg.

Freydis clutches her to her so hard that the baby begins to whimper and wave her arms about. But Freydis calms her, laying her to the breast. The baby girl sucks greedily. Her blood sings, the sun shines, and an unusually early butterfly flutters in through the half-open door. She has a child she will love with all her heart.

Birka is little and fragile, with a mass of thick fair hair and a tiny nose. She has inherited Torvard's best feature, his deep blue eyes. Torvard notices this at once, too. She can see by his beaming expression that he understands that this child is his. He almost certainly realises that he is not Einar's father, but he has never mentioned it.

Otherwise it seems as though the baby has the same fine features as her uncle Leif. Freydis does not see much of herself in her daughter, but that is just as well.

'I will do everything in my power to make sure things are better for you than they were for me. At least you have a mother who loves you,' she says tenderly, dressing her daughter in the little dress she has made for her.

The baby girl responds with a little whimper and grips her forefinger hard with her own tiny fingers.

'And you are strong, too. That's good,' Freydis says, laughing at her.

'She is lucky to have you as her mother,' Torvard says, coming up behind her and putting his arms around her. Freydis turns and embraces him, tears welling up in her eyes.

Mother and daughter sleep beneath the same blanket. Freydis is reluctant to hand her over to the slave Astrid, a freckled girl Torvard got to help look after their daughter. Freydis likes bathing and nursing the baby herself, likes rubbing her nose against the soft skin. She feels the honeyed scent of hope.

Birka is hale and hearty and rarely cries. She soon

learns to focus her eyes, and it is easy to make her laugh. Freydis can spend hours gazing at her as she sleeps in her white nightgown. She is especially charming when she lies on her back on the soft reindeer skin, eyes closed and arms out to the sides, her tiny chest moving quietly. Those are the best parts of her day. Freydis feels a calm sinking over her. She no longer feels the urge to get out or run away.

Her daughter grows into a lively girl who loves running about the yard and down to the sea.

There are several children running around at Gardar. Einar's eldest Tor is two years older than Birka, while Inna is the same age. Then Eirik and Viljar appear, and after that Bjornhild decides she has had enough and shuts Einar out of her sleeping alcove in the heart of the house.

The whole household can hear him yelling and hammering his fist against the wall, but he is not admitted. Einar grows increasingly desperate and begins to look about for suitable concubines among the slave girls. He really wants Astrid – he likes big, solid women – but Freydis will not let him to have her, so he has to pursue his quest elsewhere.

'I know someone at Herjolvsnes who can brew a remedy so you don't conceive. I can get you some. I've used it myself,' she says to Bjornhild one day, encountering her by chance in the yard.

'What's the point of that?' Bjornhild demands, pursing her lips.

'You can be together with Einar without getting pregnant.'

'I have borne that man four children. I've done my duty. He can just go and find a concubine or two, I don't care,' she snorts, stomping off so determinedly that the water in the buckets she is carrying splashes over her skirt.

Her mother-in-law stands shaking her head and wondering whether Bjornhild's nether regions are as buttoned up as her mind. Does Bjornhild take no pleasure in being with a man? Freydis finds it incomprehensible. Or maybe she no longer loves Einar. Freydis feels sorry for her son.

But otherwise there is really nothing about Bjornhild anyone could criticise. She is industrious. She is up with the lark, wakes the slaves and sets them to work, lights the hearth, dresses the children, milks the cows, does the washing and cooking. Bjornhild is energetic and will make an excellent mistress of the house one day. Better than herself, Freydis has to admit. But Bjornhild has so much respect for Freydis that she makes no attempt to usurp the title of mistress of the house.

It is Freydis who holds the belt with the keys, except when she is away, which is almost constantly.

Once again, she has started to find the daily grind on the farm enervating. As often as she can, she goes off on errands that take her all over Greenland. Perhaps to order wrought iron, to buy new cauldrons or other household items, to purchase wool for her loom.

She may not be well liked, but she is courteously received. She is, after all, the daughter of Eirik the Red and mistress of the second largest farm in Greenland. And perhaps they are a little afraid of her, too; They have heard the tales from Vinland and know her reputation for ruthlessness.

Birka often accompanies her. Everyone loves Birka. It is not only in appearance that Birka is unlike her mother. She is calm and gentle, sweet and a little distant.

The only interest they share is the long rambles alone in the countryside, and the fact that they often shirk their domestic duties. Birka can sometimes sit on a rock gazing into space for ages.

'What are you doing while you're sitting on that rock?' Freydis asks one day.

'There are so many stories in my head. They just come to me, and I have to receive them. I need to sit quietly to do that,' Birka smiles, and runs off quickly, her increasingly thick golden plait thumping on the back of her dress.

Sometimes her head is so full of thoughts she needs to express them. She entertains both Einar's children and the others on the farm with wonderful tales of gnomes and trolls, animals, people both real and imaginary, and also of the Norse gods about whom Freydis has been at pains to instruct her.

Some of her stories are about the Christian god, Jesus, and other figures from the Bible. Torvard has insisted that the girl should be taught about them, too. Greenland is a Christian land.

'You look like Saga, you know,' Freydis says one day when they a riding out to visit a farmer's wife further up the fjord. Saga is the goddess who collects the stories and passes them on.

'Yes, I like Saga best of all the gods. Who do you like best?' Birka asks, turning to look at her mother.

'I like many of them, but perhaps I like Freya best of all. She is the greatest of the goddesses. She is the fertility goddess, and the goddess of affection and of love ... Well, you'll understand more about that when you are older,' she says, slightly embarrassed.

She does not tell her daughter that Freya may be her family goddess and perhaps even her great-grandmother. Freydis finds it almost unbelievable that she herself could be the granddaughter of Freya herself. She does not feel much like a goddess. But then Torbjorg was not sure it was correct, either.

'I like Thor,' she adds. 'But that's probably because my father had the greatest respect for him, and father and I are very alike.'

Freydis likes talking about her father; she wants her daughter to be proud of her grandfather.

She says that among the Norse gods there are both male and female gods, and in fact there are more goddesses than gods. In many of the most important areas of life there are gods of both sexes. For example, the gods of love, Frey and Freya, and Ran and Aege who rule the seas.

'In some areas the women rule, and in others, the men. The goddesses deal with healing, peace, confidentiality, death, eternal youth and praise. The male gods rule over forgiveness, trials, fishing, silence and light.'

Freydis tells her again and again about the norns and the Valkyries, who are all women.

'The three norns, Urd, Verdande and Skuld, are sisters. They are the goddesses of Fate. They spin the threads of life for people, then they measure them and cut them. This happens at Urd's well by Yggdrasil, the tree of knowledge. They are the past, the present and the future.'

Freydis has already had her future foretold by Torbjorg. So far, the prophecy has come true. Now she would like to talk to Skuld to hear whether there is any chance of changing her destiny; She can hardly bear to think of the thirty lonely years that lie in store for her. But Skuld does not reply, nor does she reveal herself.

'The Valkyries are the beautiful spirits of death whom Odin sends out to keep an eye on all warriors in battle and decide who is to die. Then they carry off the fallen warriors with them to Asgard. Half of them come to Odin in Valhalla, and half to Freya in Folkvang, her afterlife field,' says Freydis.

Birka imbibes everything that fuels and fires her imagination.

But when Torvard gets sick, neither the Norse nor the Christian gods can help. He has been looking poorly for a long time and has lost a lot of weight. With increasing frequency, he has had to lie down and rest. He has started to spit blood, and now all he wants to do is sleep. A slave girl nurses him and tries to get him to take a little soup. But he continues to weaken.

Freydis understands that he is nearing his end when he asks her to sit down beside him. He clasps his cold white hand around her warm one. Then he forces her to meet his eyes.

'I just want to thank you for the life we have had together,' he whispers.

'What have you got to thank me for? I haven't been very nice to you,' sniffs Freydis.

'I have loved you since the first time I saw you as a grown woman. I know you have not always loved me. But I think in these last few years you have grown to like me.'

Freydis nods, biting her lip as she tries to stop her tears flowing, without success.

'I know I'm not Einar's father, and that you have had other men. It hurt, but even so I have been grateful. It wasn't just because you are beautiful that I fell for you that time when you danced at the feast at Brattalid. You have an inner light, Freydis, a life force I have never seen or experienced in anyone else,' Torvard says.

He has to ask for a sip of water before he can continue, and again he fixes his eyes on her face.

'Whatever you may have done or not done, I forgave you long ago. Live well, and promise me you'll look after Birka. Use your strength for something good.'

Now Freydis lies down on the blanket he has wrapped himself in, and bursts into loud sobbing. Her dying husband strokes her hair.

Birka is inconsolable. She spends as much time as possible at her father's side, talking to him when he is well enough. She is the one at his side when he draws his last breath. Freydis is outside when it happens. She hears her daughter burst into loud weeping. Birka sits holding her father's hand in hers. Torvard stares stiffly and lifelessly at the ceiling. Gently, Freydis closes his eyes. Then she hugs her daughter. They stand for a long time embracing.

Freydis grieves, too. The loss takes the wind from her sails. She has to summon up all her fortitude to get through the funeral in the little church Torvard had built, and which had been such a great thorn in her side all these years. For this was where Christians from the neighbouring farmsteads came to hold weddings, christenings, funerals and other Christian rituals. Gardar was the only farm in Einarsfjord with its own church.

They are growing fewer and fewer, those who remain true to the Norse gods, and Torvard wanted a Christian burial. But just to make sure her husband reaches the right place, the recent widow sacrifices a sheep. The guests are quite ready to enjoy the feast. They are not picky as long as the meat tastes good.

Torvard's last words come back to her again and again, especially in the evenings when she tosses and turns on her bunk, and sleep evades her.

She had always believed that Torvard loved her for her good looks, but then he had spoken of an inner light and a strong life force. Nobody has ever said anything like that to her before. What can he have meant?

And he said he was grateful in spite of all the bad things she had done. Torvard had been a good man through and through. If he is not in the best place on the other side, then nobody is. The question is, where will she end up?

But Freydis has little time to feel how empty the house is, for one day her son stands in the doorway asking to speak with her. She and the grieving Birka are just finishing a silent meal.

Einar stands leaning against the wall. He waits till Birka goes out to help the other youngsters with their morning tasks. His eyes are hard, his mouth narrow. She senses this is going to be bad, and she is right.

'You know that I am the master here now.'

'Yes, you are,' says Freydis. She rises, turns her back on her son and begins to clear away after the meal.

'And Bjornhild is the mistress. So now you need to give her the keys to the main storeroom.'

Freydis spins around and is about to protest. But he has not finished.

'We are moving into the longhouse. We need the space.'

'And where is the master of the house going to put his mother?' she asks acidly, her cracked hands gripping the cauldron tightly.

'I don't want you here any longer. You'll have to leave. I've talked to Torgils at Brattalid. You can move there and take over Tjodhild's old house. It's stood empty for a long time.'

Freydis is so horrified she drops the cauldron of hot water on the floor. It falls heavily, the cauldron is tipped over and the warm water runs towards Einar like a river in spate.

'How dare you treat your mother like this!' she fumes.

'Mother, yes, a good kind mother you've been,' he says mockingly.

'You're a whore. I know full well Torvard wasn't my father. It was likely some Icelander called Sverre whom you bewitched with your spells. You've amused yourself with other men too, so I've heard. How do you suppose Torvard felt about that? And then there's all that business in Vinland.'

'You don't know the first thing about Sverre and me. And you've certainly no idea what went on in Vinland. You just listen to gossip. I can tell you the true facts about all of it, if you have the time to listen.'

'Spare me the details,' he snaps.

'What gives you the right to accuse me, you who are supposed to be such a good god-fearing Christian? I know you've had concubines. One of them is apparently with child. I am to be a grandmother again. Do you actually know how many children you've fathered?' rages Freydis.

Einar's eyes flash sparks.

'My life is none of your business. Oh, and Birka will stay here. I take it she's Torvard's? Nobody else wanted you by the time she was conceived. It's unbelievable he managed to put up with you. You think he was weak, but he was the strong one. The only one who could manage you.'

The harsh words swirl around, as though he were stirring salt in an open burning wound. And part of what he says is true.

'In reality Birka is the real heir to Gardar. She is Torvard's only child. She needs to stay here,' he says, preparing to leave.

It dawns on Freydis that he is serious about keeping Birka.

'You can't take Birka away from me. She's mine. I'm in charge of her!' she shouts.

'I have said all I wanted to say,' Einar declares, marching out of the house.

Freydis sinks down on the bench and cries into her apron, her body trembling with grief.

Birka is devastated when she is told she must part from her mother. 'I have to lose both my father and my mother? How cruel you are!' she shouts at her half-brother as streams of tears run down her cheeks.

Einar realises that he has been too harsh. Freydis has been a good mother to Birka. He is also fond of the girl, thinking of her more as a daughter than as a half-sister.

In the end it is agreed that Birka can stay with Freydis at Brattalid every summer and visit her fairly often. In the end, she accepts it, although she cannot understand why her mother cannot remain at Gardar. Birka does not want to be separated from her nieces and nephews, Inna and the boys. At Brattalid there are no children to play with.

Brattalid is a pathetic shadow of its former self. Long gone are the days of Eirik the Red, when the place teemed with people and animals, and the trading vessels that visited Greenland called in here first.

Freydis remembers how excited they were when the ships came sailing into the fjord. She and the other children would run along the beach, trying to catch a glimpse of the people on board and guess where they came from. Most of them were from Iceland or Norway, but sometimes ships came from strange lands further to the south. But now, trading vessels are rarely seen at Brattalid. Instead they go to Gardar or other large farmsteads.

Now only Torgils and a handful of slaves are left at Brattalid. When she comes sailing in, her brother's son is standing on the shore, waiting for her. She has come without Birka this first time. One of the Gardar slaves rows her ashore.

She has brought clothing, shoes, skins and a chest containing her most precious possessions – jewellery, pins, her father's knife. Freydis has packed the iron casket containing the wicked golden serpent with particular care. As always, having it close to her fills her with uneasiness. She needs to find some cave to keep it in. Her nephew stretches out a hand to help her ashore.

'You haven't brought much with you,' he says, lifting the bag containing the iron box. It does not appear to have any negative effect on him.

'I don't need much. So long as I have my loom, I'll manage. Thank you for allowing me to live here,' she says, trying to smile.

Torgils simply nods and begins to walk towards Tjodhild's old house. Leif's son has never married, nor does he have any concubines or children. Instead, a slave named Loke has moved in with him into Eirik the Red's longhouse.

Loke, even darker and gloomier than Torgils, greets

her with a cold sweaty handshake and a curt nod. Two tall thin men with hard brown eyes and dark bushy hair. They could almost be twins, she thinks.

The other four slaves, two women and two men, are more approachable. The women take care of all the household chores, while the men go hunting and fishing.

One of the women, Gudrun, has washed and prepared Tjodhild's rooms. She is a rotund, friendly woman about the same age as Freydis. She will be her daily assistant.

'I've lit the fire and warmed some water for you. You'll probably want a wash. I've tidied up and got hold of some blankets and furs so you can have a rest. Meanwhile, I'll make some food,' she says.

'That's great. Thank you,' Freydis smiles.

After they have finished eating, she revisits her old haunts. Nothing has changed, and yet it is a melancholy sight. For the whole place is falling into decay. The houses are dilapidated and there is grass growing untamed on the roofs. One of the barns has collapsed; Nobody seems to have made any attempt to repair it or tidy it up.

Inside the houses contain the same items as before. Even the pots in the longhouse where Torgils and Loke live are the same ones she remembers from her childhood. Rust has begun to eat away at them.

The big farmhouse her father was so proud of is a ruin and the corners are full of spider webs and dirt. The cheerful pictures she wove, which Eirik liked so much that he hung them on the walls, have been thrown into a box.

She picks a couple of them up and has to laugh at the way they radiate her own youthful confidence. Love has many faces, not all of them merry.

But in truth it is painful to be in here and to witness the decay. She has a sudden desire to re-establish the house of sacrifice as it was in its glory days.

On her way back she enters the longhouse and encounters Torgils, who is bringing in peat for the fire.

'Would it be all right if I tidied up father's house of sacrifice?'

'Yes, do as you please. I don't use it,' Torgils says, and gestures for her to follow him into the longhouse.

'When Eirik the Red was in charge here, there were always feasts going on in the house of sacrifice. Wouldn't it be grand if we could use it again?' she says, smiling at Loke, who is resting on a fur.

'What would be the point of that? Nobody ever comes here anyway,' Torgils shrugs.

The current master is obviously not interested in feasting and fun. Nor in sacrifice. Freydis cannot quite figure him out. She is not sure if he is a heathen, as many call the adherents of the Norse gods, or if he is a Christian.

'Perhaps you feel more at home in Tjodhild's church?'

'No, none of these gods means much to me. I don't really care which of them people believe in. What matters is how people are and how they behave.'

Freydis falls silent and takes a sip of the milk her nephew has set before her. She reflects on his words.

'Wise words. You are quite right. I want you to know I am grateful you took me in when my own son threw me out. Where else could I have gone? Most people here in Greenland dislike me. I know the dreadful stories have spread like wildfire not just here, but in Iceland and Norway too,' she sighs.

'Oh, I doubt that, and there's certainly nobody here at Brattalid who has anything against you,' Torgils says, his all-knowing eyes boring into her.

'I really appreciate that. But your father held a very different view.'

'Father changed his opinion of you. He came to the conclusion that what you did in Vinland that time was the right thing to do. Even though he disapproved of you for lying about it.'

Freydis opens her eyes wide but says nothing.

'He regretted many things towards the end, but he was too stubborn to do anything about it.'

Encouraged by her conversation with Torgils, she takes up her work at her loom as soon as she is back in her new home – the house her stepmother had built when she fell out with Eirik because he refused to be converted to Christianity.

Imagine her having to move into the house of the woman who bullied her throughout her childhood! Freydis laughs scornfully at the thought. She decides she will take life as it comes. That is what she has promised herself. And now she feels pleased about her nephew's kind words. Imagine, Leif thought she did the right thing in Vinland! And she is beginning to warm to Torgils, even though he is not a good farmer.

Tjodhild's house has been quite well maintained compared to the rest of the buildings at Brattalid. But it is chock-a-block with crosses and crucifixes, cloths and covers displaying religious images. There are also several skins hanging on the walls with what are presumably depictions of Bible stories.

The first thing Freydis does is to get rid of all this clutter. She intends to decorate the house in her own way. She already has a few thoughts about how she will go about it.

Tjodhild's church is still in use. But while there used to be a priest living permanently at Brattalid, now there is a peripatetic priest who holds services in the steadily increasing number of churches all over Greenland.

The autumn comes suddenly. One morning, Freydis is staring at her own reflection in the water tub. She is over fifty. Her eyes are still large and clear, but she sees she has a few lines in her face. And her thick red hair is flecked with silver. She gathers it in a ponytail and binds it at the back of her head.

Her body is still firm. She has kept her figure much better than most women her age, who are growing bent, fat and sickly. She cannot recall being ill for a single day, apart from sea sickness.

She changes into her brown everyday wadmal dress and puts on the stoutest pair of shoes she has, feeling a sudden urge to go for a ramble in the mountains around Brattalid. She has been thinking of places she liked going to as a child. Everywhere there are signs that nature is gearing up for the cold white season. The flowers are dying, the grass is wilting, the birches and heather are turning red, and there is sticky frost in the mornings.

She goes to the vantage point that was their secret place, hers and Sverre's. She feels a secret thrill down there as the memories come flooding back. There will not be much of that kind of thing in her future. She expects there will not be much chance of getting together with men at Brattalid. So few come that way. Perhaps she ought to throw herself on a male churchgoer now and then, or ingratiate herself with one of the slaves. She laughs bitterly.

Freydis sits there, lost in the view, until it grows dark and raindrops begin to fall from the grey skies. On her way back to Brattalid she almost stumbles over a pair of foxes on her path. Are these the same foxes she has seen before? she wonders, but she has no answer.

The foxes glance at her and go off in the opposite direction.

When Birka comes to visit, the oppressive, old-fashioned atmosphere at Brattalid is lifted. The daughter of Freydis, smiling and agreeable as she is, gets on with virtually everyone.

Even Torgils and Loke loosen up and run about the yard with the young girl.

Freydis shakes her head, unable to understand that this is her daughter. Even as a child, she herself was unpopular.

After the daily chores have been done, she strolls around the farm with her daughter, showing her her realm.

The chuckling stream, the rocks on the shore that she used to build houses with when she was a child, the caves she hid in, the most beautiful flower meadows, the most stunning views. Often mother and daughter do not come home until evening, their hands full of twigs and turf which will provide fuel for the winter. They must make themselves useful.

Sometimes they can also go fishing with Torgils and the male slaves. They are not allowed to go hunting, but Birka has no desire to do that, anyway. Animals are her friends and she does not like to see them killed. She ought to know how much her father used to enjoy hunting, Freydis reflects, with a touch of melancholy.

In the evenings they often gather in Torgils's longhouse, and Birka tells her stories with great feeling. These wonderful summers with Birka at Brattalid are memories Freydis will one day conjure up when her spirits are at their lowest.

For the days will be cut short. Suddenly and brutally.

The summer of her seventeenth birthday, Birka does not come to Brattalid alone. A fair-haired young man with eyes sparkling like stars comes with her in the boat which brings them to the farm. They are both wearing clothes of the same blue colour. They gaze at each other, laughing. The man holds Birka's arm tenderly as she climbs out of the boat. They suit one another, thinks Freydis as they come walking towards her.

'Mother, meet Sigurd. We're going to be married,' Birka blurts out without preamble.

Freydis can hardly take in the news immediately, but she quickly extends a hand. Sigurd has a warm, firm handshake and his smile is open and friendly. She likes him.

Birka tells her Sigurd is with a trading vessel from Iceland, which came to Gardar some weeks ago. Now the ship has sailed north to hunt whales.

'I couldn't leave Birka. I wanted to get to know her better,' he says, blushing furiously.

It has already been arranged that the ship will pass Gardar on the way back and pick Sigurd up.

'And now I'm going too!' says Birka.

They giggle, the pair of them, almost unable to keep their hands off each other as they speak. Birka's simple words weigh heavy as a mountain that crashes down over Freydis and crushes her. Birka is going to move to Iceland to be with this Sigurd.

'Can't you stay here in Greenland? You could take over Brattalid after Torgils and move into my house. I can go and live in the slave quarters.'

She hears the note of desperation in her own voice. But Birka just lays her arms round her and hugs her. Then she looks at her with her warm eyes and smiles.

'Mother dear, Sigurd already has a farm in Iceland that he's promised to take on. It's a fine farm, lying near the sea, in a sheltered bay. And there are great glaciers there, just like in Greenland. And volcanoes that spew fire. I am so excited to see them!' Birka beams and continues to talk about all the wonders that await her: Sigurd's family, the farm, all the livestock.

She takes hold of her mother's arm and forces her to meet her eyes.

'This is what I want, mother. I want to go to Iceland. I want Sigurd,' she declares excitedly.

A few days later the Icelandic ship sails out of Einarsfjord, bearing the newly-weds Birka and Sigurd. Freydis stands on the beach at Gardar with Einar and the rest of the people from the farm, waving good-bye.

Just before they sailed off, she had had a serious talk with Birka.

'Birka, I have done many bad things, and there are many stories circulating in Iceland about terrible things I have done. Much of it bears little relation to the truth. But my advice to you is not to tell people that you are my daughter. It would just make things difficult for you.'

'I expect I've already heard most of the stories, and I've also heard that you were a courageous heroine. You are bold and quick-tempered, mother, but I love you and I will never deny you. It is honourable blood that flows in my veins,' Birka said firmly.

'But ...'

'And besides, I have Sigurd at my side, and he will support me.'

'Yes, you are fortunate to be able to marry the person you want,' Freydis had replied, embracing her daughter.

She could have tried to stop the marriage and selected some suitable husband for her from Greenland. But Freydis knew with all her being that this was right for Birka, this was her destiny. And since Einar, too, saw no reason to prevent her marriage to the farmer from Iceland, the pair got what they wanted.

But the pain of losing Birka is almost unbearable. It surges over Freydis at night like a wild tide, and in her nightmares both Birka and Storm are consumed by the waves. Sometimes she dreams that they tumble off a mountain or into a chasm in the glacier, down to the deep black abyss. And she falls after them, but she cannot find them. They are gone. Gone for ever.

Her life becomes suffocating. She feels suffocated in her house, suffocated by her daily chores on the farm, the never-ending sequence of tasks that must be done over and over again, and to what purpose? Why does she have to milk the cows every day, cook, wash, weave? The pettiness of her existence becomes stifling. What more is she waiting for? Will there be no more adventures to fire up her blood with joy?

Nobody wants to go to Vinland anymore. And even if they did, they would not want to go with her, the blood-thirsty Freydis Eiriksdatter, the woman who wears trousers. She freezes to ice, grows as hard and cold as the icebergs the glacier gives birth to every summer.

She needs to get away from this closed, depressing life.

THE SKRAELING

Brattalid, the year 1041

She is well dressed, the woman who trudges along the side of the fjord, in over the glacier and the eternal white plateau. A thick brown homespun dress and warm, close-fitting leather shoes lined with wool.

Her sack is full of clothes and reindeer skins to sleep on. She also carries several days' supply of food and a knife and snares to catch game. She intends to be away for a while. How long, she does not know.

The day is fine. The air is chilly, to be sure, but the sky is cloudless and there is very little wind.

She has been walking for many hours before she decides that she wants to find a spot to camp. A hollow beneath an outcrop fits the bill. It is sheltered and soft, covered in earth and moss. She eats a little of the dried fish she has brought along, rolls out her skins and settles down. The sun is ready to set, too. It sinks lower and lower in the sky, turning the grass a reddish orange. The fjord turns deep blue, reflected in the icebergs.

The woman sleeps, her mind at peace, and she does not wake before a sunbeam shines on her nose next morning.

A bird has been caught in her snare. Freydis plucks it and lights a fire to cook it on. She munches half of the bird before she sets off again. She parcels the remainder up for supper.

Several days pass in this way. Nature provides what she needs to survive. Now she is approaching the great glacier. This is where she wants to be. She wants to see what there is there, and what lies beyond, if indeed anything does. She has heard tales of the glacier. People who have walked across it for days have seen nothing but the cold white expanse, with hardly any sign of life. But she remembers that Unar the hunter came home with two white bear skins once.

But there are many who were never seen again after they set out across the glacier. What became of them? Perhaps they lost in a battle with the white bear, perhaps they ran out of food, or froze to death, or perhaps they found a new land beyond the ice. The glacier could well be part of Nivlheim, the northerly reaches of the world where there is only ice and cold everywhere. And if she walks far enough, perhaps she will reach the land of fire, Muspellheim.

And then she will see the gap between the two worlds, the yawning abyss, Ginnungagap, where all life was created in the interplay between cold and warm. Maybe Ginnungagap is quite close, and not at the line between the sea and the sky, as she has always thought.

Is this where the sun goes when it rests during the night? There are so many unanswered questions, and nobody has the answers, not even her father, despite all his talk about the Norse gods.

But is it really Ginnungagap that attracts her, and is she ready for it now? It feels good to ponder these matters, to ask herself these questions as she trudges along. The crackling noise of her shoes on the surface of the glacier calms her restless spirit.

She realises that to trudge across the glacier with no idea where she is, without seeing naked mountains, green meadows or the sea, would be the same as death. There is little to live on here, unless she manages to catch some of the creatures that live here, but they are either elusive or dangerous. She has seen white bears before, but only from a boat. To meet a bear on the glacier would be very different.

There is nowhere to hide here, either, no caves or knolls. It is just cold and white, hard and pure. It sparkles enchantingly when the sunbeams touch the glacier, as they often do. She has been lucky with the weather so far. She decides to head north across the glacier, always making sure she keeps dry land in her line of sight, so she can monitor where she is and look out for places to camp.

Each day is like the one before it. But suddenly the ambient noise changes. The glacier is no longer silent and crackling. She hears an ominous rumbling sound. At first, she imagines the sound was coming from her own belly, for it is a long time since her last meal. But she quickly realises the noise does not come from her but from the snow and ice beneath her feet. Now it begins to groan and creak. She is not sure what is happening, but she knows she needs to get away quickly. She hurries off the glacier towards the mountain on her left side. Half-running, half-crawling, she clambers up the mountainside. The roar of the glacier grows louder and louder. Now there is a deafening crash, and many small sounds.

She has just about reached the top when it all breaks apart. A great cliff of snow and ice on the bridge of the glacier below her begins to move. It tips up high and then falls, the whole thing tumbling down over the fjord. Now several glacier cliffs that were unmoving before rise skywards and then fall down with a soft thud. The movement spreads and soon the whole arm of the glacier is in motion.

A floodwave of ice and snow pours down, rushing towards the fjord and the sea. Here the massive icebergs invite the water to join the dance, forming huge waves. Accompanied by a deafening roar, creaking and groaning, they float out into the water. Despite the tumult and the violence of the spectacle, there is something serene and beautiful about it too.

Mouth and eyes wide open, Freydis stands watching as the whole fjord is filled up with huge implacable mountains of hard ice. I hope nobody is out on a boat today. They will be trapped, caught and crushed, she thinks to herself.

Now she is beginning to understand why her father warned her about the ice. You should never imagine you know the ice. The ice lives a life of its own.

She remains sitting on the mountainside enjoying

the colossal forces playing out before her eyes. More and more icebergs roll down and splash into the water. As they float out into the fjord, many of them crack loudly and split up into several pieces, creating extraordinary shapes. This is something I must record on the loom, she thinks.

She seeks shelter for the night in a mountain cave and falls asleep to the sound of the glacier as it repairs itself after the avalanche.

The next day before she sets off again, she casts a glance at the fjord and the glacier below. All is quiet.

A couple of days later, she walks around another mountain and follows the glacier due south. After a few more days of walking she comes to a spot where she can glimpse the sea at the bottom of the glacier bridge, and she decides to camp there for the night. Maybe she will be able to do some fishing, too.

She is almost down by the water when she notices something. She stops, listening attentively. Something is moving by the glacier's edge. Is it an animal? A dangerous one or one she can kill? She grabs the knife that is attached to her belt and cautiously creeps forward. The fur-clad figure is only a few metres away when it suddenly rises to its full height.

She gapes in astonishment when she realises it is not an animal but a human being. A man. He is not one of her people, that is plain to see. Nor does he resemble the men who come from southern European lands aboard the trading ships. He looks like the skraelings in Vinland. But he is taller, about her stature, and he looks peaceable.

The man is looking at her calmly. Expressionless. He silently runs his eyes over her and then turns his head and moves slowly, indicating for her to follow him. She sees that he has dug out a dwelling for himself deep in the earth. Not exactly a house, it is more of a cave.

She peeps inside and is struck by how spacious it is. There is a bench made from stone and earth. Behind the dwelling he has lit a fire where he is cooking the meat of a freshly killed reindeer. The skin lies stretched out on the ice, surrounded by hot splashes of blood. The horns lie beside the fire. He probably intends to use if for fuel.

The man in the furs extends his hand towards a rock and nods to her. She sinks down on the rock, and he sits down on another one. She takes the time to scrutinise him more closely. The skraeling, as she calls him in her mind, is deeply tanned, with narrow slanting eyes and a round face, deeply lined around the eyes, mouth and forehead. She reckons he is about her age. Possibly slightly older.

But what she finds most exciting about him, which is why she is staring at them, are his hands. Large, brown, rough. Tough short nails edged with dark brown skin. Working hands, yet strangely sensitive. They almost seem to be dancing as he twists and turns the meat, massages it, chops it up with his knife. At last it is ready, and he hands her a morsel of the smoking pungent meat.

She is hungry and she accepts it, smiling. For a

second, one of his rough fingertips touches the back of her hand. A tiny scratch, a scraping movement that sends pleasant sensations rushing up her arms and down her breast.

It has been so long since she has felt anything like this. So very, very long. At the same time, she is shocked by her own reaction. Does she really feel desire for a skraeling, has she completely lost her mind? She takes a deep breath and avoids looking at him, but she senses that he is studying her.

Slowly they eat in silence. He does not seem ready to say anything. When she has eaten she thanks him politely for the food. But he does not appear to understand. She rubs one hand round and round over her belly, smiling at him and nodding. He nods back. It seems her body language is effective.

Then she points to herself, holding his eyes.

'Freydis.'

'Akku,' he replies, with a deep, lilting voice, and rises abruptly.

She follows suit and goes up to him. He takes hold of her hands and again she feels that glow, that strange, soaring sensation. Without thinking what she is doing she tugs off his fur cap, revealing a thick greying mane, which she strokes.

He makes no objection either when she starts to remove his heavy fur jacket. He is wearing nothing underneath, just his own skin. It is white. Unlike his hands and his face, the rest of his body has not been burned by the blazing rays of the sun.

Then she allows her own wadmal jacket to drop to the ground and begins to remove her blouse. She senses that he enjoys the sight of her breasts, still round and soft. Clearly, the skraelings are not so different from the menfolk of her own people.

When he runs his warm hands down over her body it is as though he kindles a fire which has long smouldered but been almost extinguished. Softly they let the rest of their clothing fall to the ground, sinking down on top of them. Almost silently they explore and enjoy each other's naked bodies, alone on the edge of the glacier, until the late summer sun bids the world farewell.

Afterwards they gather up all their clothing and furs and settle on the bunk in the shelter. There they sleep, closely entwined, throughout the chilly night.

Akku does not speak much, but every day they learn new words from each other's language. After a while, they are able to conduct brief, tentative conversations. She learns that he has four children, and that he is a shaman. This means, among other things, that by beating his magic drum he can become one with nature. He also has the ability to see into the future. Not so long ago he had a vision that he would leave his people and set out on his last journey. That is what he has now done.

He also saw that on this journey he would meet a woman, a woman with hair of flame, a woman from another people. He stares at her as he says this, and his lips twitch. A smile?

He must mean her, who else could it be – even though her hair is more greyish-white than flaming red these days.

At times he takes up his holy drum. When he beats

it, he creates an all-absorbing sound which seems as though it will never end, it infects everything around. It is as though it releases something within her, something hard and powerful. It surges, roars, eddies and flows.

Sometimes when he plays in the evening it seems to set the stars above them soaring and whirling. It also seems he can conjure up the green ribbons that flicker across the sky.

The late summer is unusually warm that year, and in the daytime they go about virtually naked. This gives her the opportunity to study his body. It has been used roughly; It bears the marks of a life lived to the fullest. He is broad, strong and firm. But his chest and upper arms are like children's stick figures, criss-crossed with deep scars.

'How did you get those scars?' she asks one day, caressing them.

'They come from a fight with a white bear. I had to use my magic to escape. But the bear got in his attack before the magic worked,' he explains using words and gestures.

Freydis tells him about her life, especially her two expeditions to Vinland, which brought her more harm than good. Akku nods; He is probably aware of this already. It seems he knows most things about her. It feels safe to confide in Akku, even though she is not proud of all the things she has done. She tells him about her warlike encounters with the skraelings.

'They are a little like you. Are they of your people?' she asks.

Akku does not exclude the possibility. He gazes distantly at the gleaming glacier.

'My people come from the east. We have always walked on the ice. Maybe it stretches all the way to Vinland.'

'But you are peace-loving. They weren't.'

'Most of the inhabitants of the earth are peace-loving, so long as they are not threatened or do not go hungry for too long. You did not speak the same language; You did not understand one another. They were probably scared. You had many strong men with you. It is quite a different thing when a beautiful lone woman comes strolling over the ice with the sun shining on her hair,' he growls teasingly, snuggling close to her.

His member is not the longest but thick and demanding. Freydis enjoys every second of their encounters and with the rest of the man. It has been so long, and now she has so much.

When winter has set in in earnest even in this dreamy corner of Greenland, they spend much of the day lying in the shelter, snuggled close under heaps of furs. Despite the cold, Freydis feels she is thawing. Slowly but surely the icebergs that have formed in her heart are melting.

Surviving the winter is not a problem. Akku throws ropes at passing reindeer. She sets up snares. They go out fishing, too, before the fjord freezes over.

Akku has a small skin canoe. There is water nearby, and they have firewood.

The summer that follows their first winter together is also very warm. There is no sign of any other human habitation. They are far away from both Akku's people and her own.

Freydis resumes her habit of early rambles in the surrounding area, wearing nothing but her leather shoes. It is such a relief not to have to trudge about in her heavy clothes. The baking sun, the silent glacier, the tracks of a hare, the scent of the flowers, sleeping to the regular murmur of the wavelets on the fjord with a fine man at her side – life holds nothing better than this. Even the midges do not bite her. She walks about, smiling. She has almost forgotten all the bad stuff. All that she has lost.

One morning, she indulges in a fresh dip in a mountain stream. Afterwards she lies beside the water on a large flat rock, hair and arms spread wide, legs to the side. She lets the tender sunbeams dry her and warm her.

Suddenly she feels like someone is staring at her. Not Akku. He almost never goes so far afield. Are there other people here, after all? She swings around quickly, trying to cover herself up.

Her fears subside when she sees who is watching. Two foxes. Are they the same ones? No, impossible. It is a long time since she saw them last, and that was at Brattalid. Yet they look the same, with that same bluish tinge to their coats. She waves to them. They pause for a while before they wander off, waving their tails in farewell.

The next winter is colder and windier than the one before. Akku is not in good shape, and mainly stays inside the cave except when he has to undertake necessary errands. He breathes deeply at night, tosses and turns, but never complains. He refuses to admit he is unwell.

Now it is Freydis who has to go out and get food, water and all the rest. But she does not mind, and she likes being inside with him when the west wind blows. It is good to creep into Akku's arms. They make love more seldomly now, but no matter. The closeness is enough. She feels Akku is weakening. It is increasingly difficult to get him to accept food and drink.

She begins to reflect on what he said about this being his last journey. What did he mean, she asks herself repeatedly. He does not answer, he just looks at her sadly.

But then one day, when the spring is turning into summer, Akku is sitting on the reindeer skin completely naked when Freydis returns from her morning walk. He is leaning his back against the wall. His shaft has risen and there is a magical glint in his eye.

When Freydis enters he takes up his drum and begins to beat it. The insistent rhythms make her dance around before him. With a sensuous smile she discards one article of clothing after the other, dropping them to the ground. In her younger days she would have thrown herself onto him and made fierce love to him. Now she takes her time. There is no hurry. She sidles up to him and begins to stroke the thick bushy hair on his head, lets her fingers glide tenderly over his face, his neck, his arms. She kisses his scars, down his belly, the inner thighs, his member. She listens to his heavy breathing, his groans. She draws in the scent of fresh sweat off his warm skin and the smoke that has settled in his pores from the open fire.

Then she allows him to again discover her secrets, her folds which have grown deeper with the years, the place that is the source of all her pleasure, the pleasure he kindles by softly rubbing her just right.

At last she lowers herself over the unexpected love, his roar of joy filling the whole space with something she cannot define, something not of this world. The swirling beat of the drum trembles in the enclosed air, although the drum itself is silent.

Afterwards she lies content on her side, Akku's left leg across her waist. He is well again! she rejoices, before giving in to her exhaustion and falling asleep.

When she awakes next day, the space beside her is empty.

On Akku's skin bed lies a piece of jewellery – a stout walrus tooth on a leather strap. This item is the only thing he never removed from his person, not even when they made love.

All his clothes and the animal skins lie where they did the previous night. But his canoe and his drum have vanished. There is no doubt. He has left her. He too.

Freydis picks up the walrus tooth and fastens it about her neck. An invigorating warmth permeates her body, and yet it is weighed down by sorrow. She lacks the energy to rise, she lacks the energy to meet the sunlight outside. She huddles beneath the skins.

Now they flow freely, all the tears she has collected inside her, and they are plentiful. The glacier in her heart has melted. There is a great deal of water to expel.

In the evening the rain pours down outside. It hammers on the rocks like drumsticks. She goes out, takes off all her clothes, lets the icy showers embrace her.

All at once the rain ceases, and she thinks she hears a familiar sound. A trembling tone that persists, that locks itself into the landscape like pack ice. Akku's drum?

RAGNI'S SAGA

GREENLAND, THE GREAT GLACIER, THE YEAR 1043

NO TEARS LEFT. It took some time. It had to take time. Freydis is chilled to the bone, even though it is summer, and she is wrapped in furs.

She collects all her fuel supplies and makes a great fire. Then she sits down on the boulder he assigned to her upon her arrival. It would later become her permanent seat when they ate their meals outside, here, in the special place she shared with Akku.

The two of them. Alone for two winters, almost three summers. They were like Ask and Embla, the first people on earth. She toys with that thought, seeing them before her. But Ask and Embla could hardly have been created here, because they were created from trees. There are no trees in Greenland.

Slowly the warmth returns to her body. It grows dark. She sits close to the rock. She stares into the beautiful yellow-orange pillars of fire that rise and turn into thin grey smoke high above. The crackling sound is comforting. The smell is sharp and dry, but also reassuring and familiar.

She starts suddenly. Two pairs of eyes are staring at her from the big flat rock where Akku used to sit. Sharp eyes surrounded by soft fur. The foxes. Confused, she calls out to them.

'What is it you want with me? Are you real, or are you spirits?'

She gets to her feet and wants to approach them, to touch their fur. To reassure herself that she not losing her mind. But before she can do so the foxes have disappeared. She sees their silhouettes in the moonlight, dark shadows fleeting over the glacier.

The stone they were sitting on, Akku's favourite seat, is warm. She drops down in her own rock again, clasping the only memento she has of Akku. The walrus tooth. It calms her.

When she lifts her head again, she meets the gaze of a female figure. She wears a simple brown dress with a white apron, in which her hands are resting. She has dark-brown hair and large, warm brown eyes with a hint of sadness in them. There is something kindly about her. She means her well.

But who is she? The woman says nothing; It is almost as though she is waiting for Freydis to begin. She looks like a younger, gentler version of Torbjorg Lillevolven. The same figure, the same aquiline nose as Freydis herself.

Suddenly she is ice-cold. Every muscle is tense. She knows.

'You're Ragni, aren't you?'

'Yes, I am, Freydis. I am your mother.'

There is complete silence. Gone are all the questions Freydis has thought of asking through the years. All she has wondered about, all she has resented. All gone now. Finally Ragni breaks the silence.

'I want you to know I am sorry I passed away and was unable to be with you while you were growing up. But that was my destiny. My wish was to live here in Greenland with you and your father.'

Now the questions come flooding back to Freydis. She wants to know all about Ragni.

The nine sisters grew up on a wealthy farm beside the fjord leading to Nidaros in Norway. Each one of them possessed magical powers. But their mother was the most powerful of them all. Many came to her – the sick seeking to be cured, the lonely looking for love, people who wanted to learn about their future.

Things did not go well for the sisters. Two had a weakness of the lungs and died young. Three of them drowned. The four surviving sisters were home alone when a ship put in to the shore. A gang of men stormed ashore and plundered the farm. They slaughtered the two eldest sisters after raping them.

Freydis sees that it is hard for her mother to speak of these things, and to relive the terrible experiences she has endured.

'I was the youngest. I was only ten years old. I was taken prisoner and dragged on board a ship. Torbjorg was twelve. She was in the barn when they came, and she hid.'

The ship's crew raided three other farms on their way out of the fjord. Running footsteps, ear-splitting screams, axes whistling through the air. Then they set a course for the open sea.

Ragni and the other prisoners were gathered amidships. They were given food and drink from time to time. Most of it was soaking and rotten.

After many long days and nights at sea they eventually reached a new land, Iceland. Here the prisoners were sold as slaves to Icelandic farmers. Ragni came to a farm in Hornstrendene, in the north-west of Iceland. A harsh, weather-beaten area.

'The rain was often more horizontal than vertical. It used to whip me in the face so hard I could hardly keep my eyes open,' she tells Freydis.

The household counted seventeen people of all ages. Ragni was the youngest of the five slaves on the farm, and all the work they were supposed to do they dumped on her. It was sheer misery. Silently she cried herself to sleep each night.

But then the mistress of the house, Signe Torsdatter, realised that the young Norwegian slave girl had unusual gifts. It all began with a cow with mastitis. Ragni had laid her hands on the painful udder, leaned her head against the cow's burning hot belly and begun to hum a strange tune. The next day the cow was cured.

Then she helped one of the daughters, who had got a wound that refused to heal. In the winter the oldest son, Knut, lay in bed with sickness of the lung. He grew weaker and weaker. His ribs were visible against the snow-white sheets, and his eyes grew increasingly black.

Ragni persuaded him to sip an invigorating herbal brew and laid her hands on him. When spring woke everything to life, Knut was out running about with his siblings.

After this, Ragni was given the responsibility for the youngsters and for the health of the household. Life grew simpler and more pleasant. And things were about to get even better.

One day when she and two of the children were picking berries and moss, she discovered a figure behind a knoll. A woman. One she recognised at once. She felt her heart stop and then joy overwhelmed her. Torbjorg.

The sun was setting when Ragni finally got away and was able to meet up with her sister again. It sent its last rays over Torbjorg, illuminating her as she sat looking out over the sea. Torbjorg had grown thinner, her face was more drawn, but otherwise she was just like before. Side by side they sat together. They saw how the sun gleamed, how the clouds, pink and blue, were reflected in the bright water. A bird flapped across the sunset. A fish leapt and then disappeared in the depths again.

'I am so glad you found me. I was so lonely,' said Ragni, leaning in close. Two sisters. Brown eyes, brown dresses, brown hair. They held hands as they talked of all that had passed, things that could never be recaptured. And about the future.

'A man will come and take you away from all this.

He is a man whose fame will last hundreds of years. A powerful man with many friends, and also many enemies. But you will see sides of him that nobody else will ever see,' Torbjorg says.

'And you will have a daughter,' she sighs.

The summer Ragni is fourteen, a new farmer settles at Hornstrendene. His name is Torvald Asvaldsson. He has a fourteen-year-old son, Eirik Torvaldsson, who will later become known as Eirik the Red.

Torvald was declared an outlaw at Jaeren in Norway and moved to Iceland. He had to sail around half of Iceland before he found a place to settle. All the best lands were already occupied, and many of those who had already settled were hostile. But at the windswept Hornstrendene, they were well received. They were given a plot of land where they established their farm, Drangar.

In the late summer the people of Drangar gathered at a feast. Torvald led the conversation with the hosts. He was a thickset man with a booming voice and a handsome appearance. But what Ragni noticed most was his red-haired son. Eirik could hardly be described as handsome, but he had a certain unique radiance. It was as though he had been chosen by the sun. Ragni could not take her eyes off him. Suddenly he spun around and looked her straight in the eyes. His green gaze held her own.

A few months later, Torvald came riding at full speed into the yard. Eirik had had an accident. During sword training he had received a long, deep cut in his thigh. And now he was bleeding to death. Torvald had heard of Ragni's skill in healing and was asking for her help.

Quickly she gathered what healing herbs she had and rode back to Drangar with Torvald. Eirik lay in an alcove in the centre of the house, almost unconscious. A blood-soaked cloth was wrapped around his left thigh.

Ragni sliced the cloth away quickly. The whole thigh was like a crater. She knew it had to be sewn. Eyes closed, she held her hands over the wound until the blood stopped flowing.

The wound was cleaned with an herbal mixture. Then Ragni took some horse air and her thinnest bone needle. Eirik awoke with a scream as she plunged the sharp needle into his flesh, but in the end she had ten stitches in place.

The wound was healing well, but Eirik had lost a great deal of blood and spent most of his time asleep.

'In my eyes he grew handsomer each day,' Ragni says dreamily to Freydis. 'I began to wonder whether Eirik the Red was my destiny, the man Torbjorg had spoken of.'

When at last Eirik came to himself, he and Ragni slept together in the alcove. Eirik was keen to continue the arrangement and persuaded his father to buy Ragni. And so, for the unheard-of price of two cows, Ragni became Eirik's concubine.

Eirik the Red was the most skilled at sword-fighting, and one of the best hunters. At sea, he had an understanding of the waves and wind that exceeded that of any other mariner. He was quick to anger, and if anyone crossed him, he was ruthless. Once, when a guest insulted Ragni, he hacked off his arm.

He had been sent out in charge of expeditions at the age of 18. Torvald had lent him a ship and crew. Not long afterwards, Torvald became mortally ill and died soon after.

In the late summer, Eirik the Red landed on the beach at Drangar. They had been to Norway, Ireland and the Hebrides. He leapt ashore with a triumphant roar. He allowed his hair and beard to grow, and he smelled different, too. Ingrained sweat, saltwater, fish guts and a smell Ragni could not quite place. The raw smell of a grown man.

Ragni knew he had committed savage deeds, that he had taken other women, that he had stolen the treasures he brought home with him – weapons, silver candlesticks and bowls, gold jewellery.

'He wanted to give me a beautiful piece. But I didn't want it. I kept thinking about the woman he stole it from,' she told Freydis.

Even so, Ragni could not resist him when he came to her that night. The fearless Viking grew tender in her arms.

He grieved bitterly for his father. But outwardly he showed only fortitude. Ragni was the one who had to kiss away his tears.

'He always came to me when he was down. I don't think he confided in Tjodhild in the same way, or the other concubines he acquired as years went by.'

It was soon after his father's death that Eirik married Tjodhild Joerundsdatter. She was chosen because she was high-born, descended from a Norwegian family from Breidafjord in south-west Iceland. There they established an impressive farmstead.

The following year, Tjodhild gave birth to their eldest son, Leif, in the longhouse. But his Viking blood gave Eirik no peace. He had barely cast eyes on his newborn son before he was off to sea. He brought incomparable riches back with him. But Tjodhild was furious. She had been left to run a huge farm on her own.

Torvald and Torstein were born, and Eirik did his best to play the dutiful farmer, but he had soon picked quarrels with several of his neighbours. When he was made an outlaw, he set sail for the west.

'I conceived during the voyage to Greenland, but sadly I never got to know you,' Ragni says.

The two women fall silent, reflecting on how things might have been different had Ragni lived.

'Where are you, mother, and where will I go when I die? Ginnungagap?'

'All I can say is that it is all connected.'

'What do you mean?'

'You are a good person, Freydis my dear, and I am proud of you. But you have lost so much, and you have done many things that were wrong. You must atone and do good deeds,' Ragni whispers, gradually dissolving and at last vanishing into the night sky.

'Mother, don't go. I have so many questions. How is father? What about the serpent I inherited from Torbjorg?'

But there is only silence. All that can be heard is the murmur of the wind and laughter of the brook. And later Freydis is not sure whether she was awake or whether she dreamt it all. But that she had encountered her mother, that she was sure of. The meeting had done her good.

A few days later, she packs up all the furs and cooked meat she can carry and sets off on her journey homeward.

Torgils and the slaves hardly raise an eyebrow when she strolls into the yard at Brattalid. It is as though she has only been away for a single morning. Her house stands untouched, just as she had left it, including the half-finished blanket on the loom. All she needs to do is brush off the dust and carry on.

She has many rugs to weave.

THIRTY YEARS OF LONELINESS

Brattalid, the years 1043–1073

Thirty-seven steps down. Forty steps up. She counts them every day, the distance from her house down to her favourite rock on the beach at Brattalid. Every afternoon she trudges down there, lays a skin mat on the rock and sits down with great care. Often she will sit there until darkness falls.

Although she is over sixty, she is busy all day long. First a short morning walk in the mountains, carrying two tubs which she fills with turf or berries, unless the snares have trapped animals, and she has to carry those instead.

When Freydis returns, her room is nice and warm. There is half a bucket of milk standing on the bench, and Gudrun is busy preparing a meal. Freydis has made a friend of Gudrun, even though she is a slave. The two women, both of an age, get on well.

'Good morning. I hope you'll enjoy some fresh fish and milk,' Gudrun says, placing the food on the table.

'That's great. Thank you. I could do with some food now. A hare was caught in the snare, and it was heavy to carry.'

'I understand. But it'll make a fine meal at dinner-time today,' says Gudrun, warming water for the washing up.

Freydis studies the slave woman. Her back has grown more bent lately, and she pants more and more when she lifts the heavy cauldron full of water. Freydis looks at her weather-beaten face. There is something familiar about her, something she recognises.

'Take the hare and the rest of the milk for yourself and your husband. From now on I'll do the washing myself, but it would be great if you'd help with the cooking,' says Freydis.

'But ...' stammers Gudrun.

'No buts. Go now,' Freydis commands.

Gudrun bows and curtseys in gratitude as she leaves the house. From then on, Freydis takes care of her clothes, the house, the pots and pans herself. She shears the sheep and cards and dyes the wool, so that she has enough yarn for the loom during the long cold winter evenings.

After all of that, it is good to rest on her rock. There is so much to see. In winter the fjord often freezes over. It stretches right in front of her – bright, peaceful and still as the skin of a white bear. Sometimes animals run across it, leaving their imprints. When the sun is out it glitters. On very rare occasions, people come walking across the fjord, but not many visit Brattalid anymore.

The most beautiful thing in winter is the green light that dances across the skies. Heimdall, the god of light, is out and about, and the green light is the bridge between earth and the realm of the gods. Is this the bridge you cross when you die? Freydis muses.

But it happens mostly in summer. Then the sea takes on a palette ranging from light blue-green and green to blue and grey-black, depending on the whims of the heavens and the weather gods. In the summer, too, icebergs come pouring down out of the ice fjord on the other side of the fjord. They drift out in various directions, and some remain floating just off the beach at Brattalid.

As she watches the icebergs melt away, breaking up or moving, she has plenty of time to think. That was what they had said, her goddess, and her mother too, that she should think – atone and think, purify herself, become free.

She has to have a reckoning with her past. Whom has she wronged on her path through life? Who must she find the strength to forgive, and can she manage to do any good in the years that are left to her?

Her first memories are from leaving Greenland when she was two. She remembers the sea voyage, her father's safe arms, the meeting with Tjodhild and the three brothers from Iceland. She remembers how she cringed under Tjodhild's icy glare. That woman never liked her, she sensed that, even though she was so little. Back at Brattalid Tjodhild treated her quite differently from the way she treated the boys. She was treated like a slave and was always called the concubine's daughter. She paid her back by dodging her duties and talking back at her. But why was Tjodhild like that with her?

For the first time, Freydis tries to put herself in Tjodhild's place. She begins to see that even if Eirik was the best father she could imagine, he was not the best husband.

He had handed his wife a child he had fathered by his concubine, expecting her to take care of it. It was hardly surprising it had made her mad. Freydis would have been angry herself. Tjodhild had still been wrong to take it out on Freydis. Her stepmother had spoiled her early years with her bitterness. The memories come flooding back. All the humiliations. And yet she feels sorry for Tjodhild. Two of her sons and her husband, lost in the course of a few short years. No wonder she went about like a crooked old crone, almost unrecognisable during the last years of her life.

'I forgive you, Tjodhild!' Freydis cries to the heavens. Her words come back to her like an echo. Just then, a black bird flies up from a rock further down the beach, circles around her a couple of times and flies off towards the fjord.

She has no unfinished business with her father or her two younger brothers. But she regrets bitterly that she was never able to be reconciled with her favourite brother, Leif. She understands that he was disappointed in her because she did not immediately tell him the truth about the last Vinland voyage. But why could he not forgive her?

Leif had turned into a bitter man while he waited and waited for Torgunna, who never came. Torgils had said his father had many regrets towards the end of his life. Freydis is keen to hear more of this.

One early summer's day she decides she will try to get in contact with Leif. She goes to his grave outside Tjodhild's church. He is buried close to his mother. She sits down heavily on his grave and stays there with her hands in her lap and her eyes closed, letting the sun beat upon her face.

Suddenly, something tickles her nose. She opens her eyes and stares right at two brightly coloured butterflies. Smiling, she closes her eyes again. She hears Leif whisper: 'I have found Torgunna. We are together at last. You were right. She was waiting for me to go and fetch her. I should have done it while I had time, but I was stubborn and wouldn't listen. It was you and Torgunna who had to suffer for it, and for that I'm sorry.'

Freydis asks her brother's forgiveness once again for lying about Vinland, and senses with all her being that she has been forgiven. She sees the last of the butterflies as they flit away, swarming around each other, heading for the mountains.

At that very moment Leif and Torgunna's son comes walking towards her. Torgils says nothing about her sitting on his father's grave, he just stands there looking at her with his dark inscrutable eyes.

'We've roasted a reindeer. Would you care to come and have a taste?'

'Thank you. That sounds great,' she says, bringing herself to her feet. As they trudge off in the direction of the longhouse, she tries to interrogate him.

'Did you miss your mother? She never came.'

'I think I did, the first few years. But I always knew she wouldn't come. One of the last things she said to me was that Leif would have to come and fetch her.'

'Did you ever tell him that?'

'I did try, but it didn't seem as though he was listening to me.'

So, it was not only Freydis who had tried. Freydis shook her head over her brother's obstinacy. Leif, who had been so handsome and sociable, the best of mariners – but he had had no understanding of women.

The time had come to reflect on the men she had known. She had suffered losses, but she had never been easy to live with.

Love is difficult. It comes in so many forms. She has experienced most of them. The demanding, all-consuming passion. The quiet, deep affection. The momentary, fleeting kind. The insidious kind that softly sneaks in over the course of time. The love that is there always, that never fades.

Sverre. Love at first sight. She still feels that thrill when she closes her eyes, relives and sees images of their urgent love. A whole year where every part of her, both body and mind, was obsessed with that man. She can still remember the agonising pain when he left, but it is only a faint echo of how it really felt. It must not have been easy for Sverre either. He had to take over the farm in Iceland. He was probably grieving, too, for his father and brother, lost at sea.

Now, finally, she accepts that the curse she put on him was worse than what he did to her. She cursed him with a life without love.

Now she appears to Freydis again, she who could well be her grandmother, or even Freya herself. The goddess looks at her questioningly.

'Grant him a few sprightly years at the end of his life. He deserves that.'

'Are you sure? You did say forever?'

'I'm sure,' Freydis says with great determination. The goddess smiles before she vanishes.

On Iceland's west coast a bitter man in his sixties wakes up with an erection. This is the first time in forty years. He can hardly believe his eyes – he has to touch it. He is not seeing things, it is as hard as an iron bar! He throws off his blanket, runs naked out to the courtyard and hops about like a colt, shouting with joy.

His slaves hear the commotion and run outside. They laugh cheerfully at their master, who is usually so strict and taciturn. Everyone can see why he is so happy.

A well-built grown-up slave woman, Brynhild, literally takes the matter in hand. She thinks it is most embarrassing that the master of the house should disgrace himself in this way before the servants. Without hesitation she marches up to him, grips him by the arm and manoeuvres him back to bed. Soon afterwards groans and loud yells can be heard from the longhouse.

Ten years later, Sverre Sigurdsson dies happy. He leaves a wife, four legitimate children and five children by his concubines. And Einar, his son by Freydis Eiriksdatter.

Bjarne disappeared at sea. He was taken by the storm. She has no unfinished business with him.

She was unkind to her husband, Torvard, who loved her all his life even though she deceived him. But she grew fond of him in the end, and he forgave her everything as she sat beside him on his death bed.

Akku was sick and did not want to be a burden to her. He set out on his final journey, as he said he would. He could have bidden her farewell, but she feels no resentment towards him. And she has his most treasured possession, the walrus tooth ornament. She carries it with her always. They met at a time when they most needed each other.

As she continues her soul-searching, she notices that Gudrun is getting to be in very poor health. Living in the cold, draughty little house she and her husband have tried to make comfortable cannot be good for her.

'You and Aslak are to move in with me. For good.'

'But can we do that? We are only slaves.'

'My mother was a slave too, and I've got plenty of room.'

A few months later, Gudrun is bedridden. The end is near, and one day she asks to speak with Freydis.

'You have been a good mistress to me, and I thank you for that. But I'd like to ask you to do me one last favour.'

Freydis nods.

'Could you please have me buried next to my sister?'

'Your sister? You had a sister here in Greenland?'

'Yes. Her name was Sigrid, and she was a slave in the house of Eirik the Red. I think you knew her.'

Freydis jumps to her feet and begins to pace up and down the floor. Sigrid, who ended her life so tragically after the baby son she had by Eirik the Red was set out to die. Gudrun is her sister. That explained why she had felt there was something familiar about her.

'Yes, I knew Sigrid. I liked her,' Freydis says, sighing deeply.

Then they speak of Sigrid and her sad fate. Before long, Gudrun is buried beside her sister and her son. Freydis sets up a stone on the grave and hires a man skilled in runes to carve their names.

She and Aslak sit looking sadly at each other.

'You must go on living here with me.'

'There'll be gossip.'

'Gossip is the thing that troubles me least in all the world.'

Now it is at its coldest, she summons him to sleep with her. It is wonderful to feel another person's skin against her own. Aslak, whose real name is something quite different, has Russian ancestors and he is a good hunter.

For two years they keep one another warm before he too dies. She is alone again. But that is her fate. She will outlive them all.

There are still many of the thirty lonely years to be lived through. She continues her soul-searching. Her mother was sick and died. She cannot be blamed for that. Now at last Freydis exculpates herself. She bears no blame for Ragni's death. She had never realised until this moment how much that had preyed on her mind.

It is more difficult with her mother's sister. Torbjorg concealed their relationship until just before her death. Freydis still does not understand why Torbjorg never stepped in when she saw how her sister's daughter was harassed and bullied.

She has difficulty accepting the explanation Torbjorg gave her, that she had no maternal instinct.

Now Freydis goes to her grave and rains down curses on her. But the grave is silent. At last she has said all she has to say. There is nothing for it but to accept it and forgive. One summer evening she does just that while the farm, the fjord and the mountains are bathed in the red of the setting sun.

Torbjorg had no easy life. She must have felt lonely as she wandered from place to place with no fixed abode. And she bore a heavy inheritance. The golden serpent. Freydis has hidden it in a cave in the mountains. She does not want it close to the farm because of its evil powers.

Yet still peace evades her.

'Is there more to come?' she shouts so loudly that the slave passing by, Stina, drops her water buckets.

Then she remembers the women she slew in Vinland. Sverre's sister, Reidun, and Hild the slave girl. She closes her eyes and face of the goddess glance.

'I never meant to kill Hild. I asked her brother's forgiveness, but he would not forgive me. Reidun despised me even though she didn't know about everything that went on between Sverre and me.'

'Did you ever try to tell her?' the dark woman demands pitilessly.

Freydis is forced to admit that she did not.

'I didn't do anything worse that the things I've heard that my father did. Am I to be punished because I am a woman? You took a newborn baby from me, and I myself had to grow up without a mother. I have lost so many.'

'Your punishment will not be worse. Eirik atoned for his crimes both while he lived and afterwards. He lost a son, and Ragni, the woman he loved most of all, and he lived to experience one of his own sons and his own wife turning against him.'

Now Freydis concludes that she will also beg forgiveness for what she did to Reidun.

She has often wondered what became of the people they left behind in the house they abandoned. Did Helge ever return, are they still living there, were they attacked by the skraelings, or did they move to some other place?

Then there are the slaves; They are people too. She does not think she has been downright harsh with her slaves, although she has bullied some of them from time to time. The only one she is conscious of treating badly is Bjadok, the Irish girl. That was because Einar preferred her to his own mother. And later she became Torvard's concubine.

Apparently, Bjadok came from a good family in Ireland. Now Freydis sends for her and serves her some fish.

'I have decided to buy your freedom from Einar,' Freydis says, studying the slave woman. She is looking good for her age, almost as good as herself. Bjadok nods, but her expression is impassive.

'I have not always treated you well, and for that I am sorry.'

'You were no worse than another,' says Bjadok, taking a piece of the fresh fish.

'I'm grateful for all you've done for us, especially looking after Einar.'

'Einar was a good lad,' Bjadok says, with a hint of a smile.

'You can have a house of your own here at Brattalid, and you won't have to work in your old age.'

There is a moment's silence.

'I thank you for that, but I want something different.'

Bjadok embarks on the next trading vessel that arrives. She does not wish to spend one more day in Greenland. This is the start of a voyage home to that much greener land further south.

Suddenly Baldur appears to Freydis, the god of forgiveness who was slain by a branch of mistletoe. He smiles, then vanishes in a kind of fog. She interprets this as a sign that he is pleased with her.

Her father's old house of sacrifice has been tidied up and all the debris has been removed. The great table and benches have been polished and cleaned. They are now fine and gleaming. Feasts for guests can now be held here, if they ever happen to have any guests.

Freydis has arranged for a few sleeping benches, in

case anyone should wish to spend the night. The walls are decorated with hangings bearing beautiful, lively images. A glacier breaking up, a pair of foxes on the ice in the moonlight, green light waves over the night sky, a colourful flower meadow at Brattalid, a white bear, swimming at dawn.

There is much talk about the woven pictures in the old house of sacrifice. At first from the guests from Tjodhild's church, who come over after their service.

In time, people start coming by just to see the massive tapestries of Greenland's landscape. They begin to take more pride in their land. Some of them want to buy the hangings, and they pay Freydis with food, tools and whatever else they have to offer. Now and again a trading boat calls in at Brattalid for the sole purpose of acquiring a woven hanging or two.

Soon, she has hardly time to do anything else but weave. And she needs to get wool from other farms. The wool produced by the Brattalid flock is insufficient for her needs. She is delighted that other people want to have her hangings in their own homes. Something of herself is being spread around in this country that she loves more and more, now that she knows she will spend the rest of her days here.

But there is one picture she will not sell. It is large, covering almost all of one of the short walls. The picture shows a thickset man standing tall. He is rough-looking and naked, covering himself only with a large drum held in front of him. He is odd-looking, too, many people think, with his narrow eyes that seem mere slits. His large, strange face. The broad hands. He looks unlike anybody they know. Many people ask who he is. Is he a skraeling, someone asks, someone who has heard descriptions of that people. Another thinks he looks like a man he saw on a glacier once.

But Freydis only shakes her head. She wants to keep Akku all to herself.

She notices that people have begun to drop their hostile attitude towards her. Almost all those she knew from the days of her youth are dead now. Most people have enough troubles in their daily life: getting hold of sufficient food, keeping sickness at bay, the vagaries of the climate. No good dragging things up. Besides, most people find Freydis friendly and generous. She serves food and drink to those who visit the house of sacrifice. She often sends a little dried meat out to poor families.

They work automatically now, her arms working the yard and the loom. And her thoughts run free.

Who is she really? Who is Freydis Eiriksdatter? Is that all she is, Eirik the Red's concubine's daughter, so like him in looks and temperament? That temperament that has got them into so many situations, both good and bad. The irascibility and violence that made them many enemies. The love of adventure that led them on voyages of exploration. Their strength in adversity. Their passionate need for love.

Freydis admits she would not want to be without this legacy from her father. If she had not had his drive, she would not have achieved anything at all. But now she wants to use her inner fire for good, like weaving pictures.

She still wants to confront the bad sides of her legacy from her father. She lists three of them;

All her life she has sought to win honour and she is tired of it.

The longing for honour is like the sea. So easy at the height of summer, when the warm sun is shining, when the waves sparkle invitingly on the water, when the birds are singing, and the flowers are blooming brightly. At times like this, you can stand in the bows of the ship, straight-backed, and imagine you are in command, you are a queen.

But when the winter storms howl and spread cold and fear, and the sea with its braying laughter smashes over the ship. When terror freezes the marrow of your bones, when you meet the stare of the sea troll. Then you wish you had not been so bold as to challenge the forces of nature.

And what does she actually need all these things she has collected for?

The pursuit of treasure is like the mountains. On a fine day they are tempting, towering high, enveloped in a halo of light. And inside them is the promise of gold and precious metals, riches you adorn yourself with in the flower of your youth, for feasts and pleasure. A new feast, a new ornament – a true delight!

But when the wolves stand between the cliffs howling in the bitter icy snowstorm. When the gleaming gold lies cold and hard in the bottom of the chest, when you are old and no longer bidden to feasts, when the larder is almost empty, and the winter has no intention of relinquishing its grip for a long time to come. Then you wish you had spent your time doing something other than always grabbing more and more, more of everything.

Then, the characteristic that has cost her the most.

Wrath is like fire. It flares up without warning. As the wind fans the flames, swift anger fuels the hot blood and makes the heart pound. The burning glow spreads, that which kindled the fire must fall prey to the flames. The fire leaps on it like a ravenous predator, its hunger must be stayed, without delay.

But when the fire is extinguished, when what you loved lies burnt and destroyed. When remorse floods in, snuffing out every spark of fire, when all that is left is smoking charcoal. Then you wish you had never fanned the flames.

As Freydis weaves more and more pictures and her thoughts churn over her own qualities and shortcomings, the steps down to her favourite rock become shorter. It is no longer thirty-seven steps down, but forty-two. The forty-one steps back up become forty-eight.

Spring becomes summer, summer becomes autumn, autumn becomes winter, winter becomes spring. The months go by, the years do too.

Many things are more difficult now, and everything takes longer. Yet inside she feels lighter and lighter, so light that at times she wonders if she is still inhabiting her own body. Freydis is soaring.

Sometimes it is as though she is sitting between the wings of a proud white gyrfalcon looking down on Brattalid. Stina carrying her water tubs, the fishermen on the fjord, the cows and sheep grazing. In the winter, she soars over the eternal glacier. White, white, white. Just like herself. She is all white now, her skin, her hair, her clothes. Only her eyes are dark.

Now there are only five of them left at Brattalid. They are all old, much older than most people. Many people ask whether those who live at Brattalid have drunk from the spring of eternal life. The norns must have been off duty when they spun the life threads of the Brattalid folk.

Freydis is entering her ninetieth year. Torgils and Loke are both in their early seventies. So are Stina and her husband, Hallstein. They are both slaves, really, but Freydis has given them their freedom. They have chosen to stay on, anyway. Where else would they go?

Freydis has fought many a battle in her life. Against men, against women, against storms at sea, against hunger, against enmity. Fought for love, for freedom, for food, for survival.

Now her fight is with old age. Never has she met such a tough or indomitable opponent. And she knows she will lose in the end. Old age defeats everyone. No matter how strong a man or woman might be, there is none who will not be defeated by old age in the end, struck by the final blow.

It executes a new assault each day. Every day it is as though a grain of sand settles on her neck. One more. So tiny that she does not notice them individually. But gradually they accumulate, forming a rock that presses her down. An insidious, unpredictable adversary. A new wrinkle, a little pain in the back that was not there yesterday, another thing she does not see, does not hear. Morning walks she no longer has the energy to take, food she cannot eat, fingers that refuse to obey her, all the things she forgets.

She has put her life in order, forgiven, asked for forgiveness, she has confronted her defects and her deeds. In her ninetieth year she is all done with practising atonement.

Can she have peace now?

IDUNN'S QUEST

BRATTALID, THE YEAR 1073

LET ME GO! I have made amends. Thirty years of loneliness. She screams out the words. Hoping her goddess will hear and understand. Enough, now.

Freydis does not see her so clearly anymore, the mysterious dark-haired woman, but as she sits on her rock by the beach, she feels the woman's presence. A flickering power, a tremor, a magic song in the splashing waves.

'You are not yet ready. You have more to do.'

Freydis had thought herself finished with all the men she had known, but there is one with whom she has not made her peace. The boy, the man she would have been so happy to love but was never able to. Her son, Einar.

There is news from Gardar that he is on his deathbed. Freydis's bones go cold when she hears this.

Is she about to lose another son? At least Einar is over seventy now. He has had a long life.

Hallstein the slave and a couple of lads from neighbouring farms transport her to Gardar by boat. She can no longer manage the long trek over the mountain, so first they have to sail out of Eiriksfjord and then in again. On the way she ponders what she should say to him. Is there anything to be said? After all this time?

All she can do is tell it like it is. Not try to hide anything. He will have to make of it what he will. She has nothing more to give, nothing more to lose.

It has been a long while since she last visited Gardar. There has been little communication between them since Birka went to Iceland. She hardly knows how many grandchildren, great-grandchildren or great-great-grandchildren she has thorough Einar. He has a great number of descendants, her son.

She peers towards land. The houses, the church, the animals out in the pasture, children playing in the yard, the mist hanging over the mountains. A lot of it is as it always was, yet it is different somehow.

On the beach she is greeted by Einar's eldest son, who now runs the farm. A rather sombre but friendly man with grey hair. He explains that Einar is so ill he can hardly eat, but his mind is sound. Einar's son takes her arm and helps her into the longhouse where she and Torvard lived when they ran the farm.

She is shown in by a peevish rough-built woman, Einar's last wife. He married again after Bjornhild's death some twenty years since. The house has lost the fresh, newly built air it had when Freydis moved in. A gloomy ambience fills the room with a heavy odour of cod liver oil and urine.

Where her loom once stood, her son is lying on a bench on a pelt, with a blanket covering him. He is unrecognisable. He has grown so emaciated.

Einar, who was always so well-nourished and stout. Now his face is hollow and deeply lined, his eyes have acquired a grey film, and his hair is like her own, as white as snow. He has been bedridden for several weeks. But his voice is loud and clear, although it quavers a little when he speaks to her.

'Well, if it isn't Freydis Eiriksdatter herself who comes visiting?'

Freydis ignores the mildly mocking tone. It carries no strength.

'I wish I were here under different circumstances, my son. It should be you visiting me on my deathbed. It is not natural for a child to die before his mother.'

Freydis falls silent and glances around the room. She fixes her gaze on the steam rising from the cauldron hanging over the hearth. It is about to boil. She turns back to Einar.

'But I have been through this before. Losing a child.'

He looks at her in surprise. He must not have heard about the son who fell into the sea off Vinland. Storm, as she always called him.

So, she tells him about it, and then pours out her whole life story, keeping nothing back. How she tried to love him as a mother should, but that when at last she did, it was too late. By then it was he who did not want her love.

'And I completely understand. Well, it's too late to make amends for that now. I hope you do not only think ill of me, even though I've done lot of bad things. But if there is anything I can do for you now, just let me know.'

Einar kept silent the whole time while she spoke. He does not say anything now, either, he seems half-asleep. He is worn out, Freydis thinks. But suddenly he sits up and looks at her with a piercing yet friendly expression.

'There is something you can do for me. As you know, I married Gerd after Bjornhild died. I also had a concubine, Halldis, who bore me a daughter, Idunn. Gerd threw Halldis out, and I am afraid of what may become of Idunn when I die.'

He stops, breathes deeply and looks at her.

'Could you take her in? If you do, everything between us is resolved.'

Freydis does not hesitate. After all, the girl is her grandchild.

'Idunn will come back to Brattalid with me. I know all about what it is to be a concubine's daughter.'

Einar also gives her two slaves, a man and a woman, both around thirty years old – Vilde and Vetle.

'You old folk and a young girl can't go on running Brattalid on your own. I've heard it's falling to pieces. That wouldn't have pleased Eirik the Red,' says Einar.

And he's right, too, Freydis thinks to herself. Stina can hardly manage to carry the water buckets from the stream anymore, and it is even heavier work in the winter when we have to melt snow. It will be good to have some young, strong slaves. We should have obtained a few long ago.

Idunn is a tall, slender girl of eleven with shining brown hair and blue eyes. Her features remind Freydis of Birka at the same age. The girl does not say much when she is told to pack up her few possessions for the journey to Brattalid. She merely nods briefly. But first, she spends a long time sitting by her father to bid him farewell.

Afterwards she goes about in a friendly way saying good-bye to the master, his family, the slaves and the animals. She avoids her father's wife. Obediently she gets into the boat.

Freydis tries to talk to her, but she is silent and prefers to be left alone. But just as they turn out of Einarsfjord over into Eiriksfjord, the young girl begins to weep. And when Freydis sits down beside her and puts her arm round her, she sobs into her shoulder.

'Father is dying. It's so awful,' she sniffs.

'Yes, I think it's sad, too. He's my son, you know.'

'And my mother's gone, I don't know where she is. Gerd is a wicked woman.'

'Yes, it was wicked to drive your mother away. But she is alive, and one day we'll find her. But now I'm happy because you're going to stay with me. I live all alone in a big house. It's lonely and I am so happy that you're coming to live with me.'

'Yes, it'll be great,' says Idunn laconically.

In the days and weeks that follow, Freydis tries to

discover what has become of Idunn's mother. There is no sign of her. But a farmer thinks he has heard she went to Iceland on a trading ship.

Idunn soon settles in well at Brattalid, where she immediately becomes the centre of attention. She is like a longed-for daughter to them all.

She loves weaving as much as Freydis, and she has inherited the talent. Soon she is doing most of the weaving. Humming to herself, she manoeuvres the weaving pins at break-neck speed.

Freydis works more slowly. Her hands are cold and stiff and her back hurts when she sits at the loom. Her eyesight is not the best, either. The colours grow blurred. Nor does her inspiration come so easily these days. Idunn's work is finer than hers. Now these are the most highly coveted. Most of them have a childlike cheerfulness about them.

Idunn has a more fiery temperament than Birka. Sometimes she flies into rages almost like her grandmother used to. Freydis often catches her kicking a rock in a fury, or bawling out a cow or a slave. Freydis encourages her granddaughter to use her energy on something more worthwhile.

Unlike Freydis, Idunn has a talent for farming. As she grows older, she takes over more and more of the duties on the farm. She seems to enjoy milking cows, doing laundry, cooking, gathering firewood and all the other daily tasks needed to run a farm.

Freydis has got hold of some red dye and the whole house is full of wool. All the sheep are now trotting about shorn and pale. She wants to weave her last batch of yarn. For days she has sat at the spinning-wheel spinning it. The yarn gleams, it is red as the morning sun, red as blood.

'I will weave, and I will sew dresses – red dresses, one for you and one for me. They will be good and warm.'

'That's great, grandmother. I look forward to seeing them finished. Then we'll have a feast, and we'll wear our dresses!' Idunn says dreamily.

'That's a nice thought. It's been a long time since we held a feast here. But in your great-grandfather's day things were very different,' Freydis says, and begins to tell her about Eirik the Red.

Working on the dresses has a reinvigorating effect on Freydis. It is as though she burns when she lets the red wool slide through her fingers. The old embers are kindled, warmth spreads through all her body, soothing her stiff, painful back. Something of the young Freydis is reborn. In flashes. But she knows it cannot last. She will never again be what she was.

Increasingly rarely, she takes out the mirror she exchanged for an ornament one time back in her youth. In those days she used to study her reflection daily, enjoying the sight of herself. Her long thick red hair, her round, fresh, soft cheeks, her white teeth, her big eyes, her haughty, rather aquiline nose, her voluptuous figure.

Not much to gladden the heart these days. Breasts as flaccid as flaps of leather pouches, her ribs visible. Empty folds of skin hang from under arms and chin. And the bits that do not hang are white and wrinkled. Her good features have disappeared, and her bad ones are all the more prominent.

Sitting down is painful, she no longer has a protective layer of fat on her rump. Now she has to place blankets on the seat before she sits down.

She has less of an appetite these days. Soup is about the only thing she ingests. She can barely chew. Her few remaining teeth ache. They are yellow, lined with brown. Her cheeks are now hollow, and deep lines and wrinkles criss-cross her face. She looks like a rotten tree stump, she thinks. But she cannot really tell. She no longer sees well, even though her eyes are still large and seem clear and alert.

No, she has no wish to contemplate this decay. She sets the mirror aside in the chest where she keeps the things that are to be Idunn's when she embarks on her life as a grown woman.

Age will soon win out. Even over her. But before it does, there is more to settle, decisions she has postponed. One of them concerns choosing an heir for Brattalid.

Leif was the only one of her brothers who had a child, but his son Torgils has no heirs. Now, since his slave Loke died, he has taken to his bed. He does not appear to care about the farm or what happens to it.

She will have to take charge. She has plenty of heirs, as do both her children, Einar and Birka.

The descendants of the concubine's daughter are going to run the two biggest and most important farms in Greenland, Brattalid and Gardar. The thought warms Freydis's heart. She straightens her bent back a little at the thought. If they only knew, those wretches who despised her so many years ago!

She would prefer Idunn to take over Brattalid. She

has all the necessary qualities, but she needs a husband. Freydis tries to introduce her to enterprising men of suitable age, men she could run the farm with. They are invited to Brattalid one after the other, but not one of them finds favour with Idunn.

'It is not my destiny to live in Greenland,' she says after she has refused the young man from Herjolvsnes, whom Freydis thought so highly of.

'Then what is your destiny, and where?' her grandmother asks in surprise.

'I don't know,' Idunn says curtly.

The person Freydis selects to take over Brattalid is one of Einar's grandchildren, named after his great-great grandfather. A cheerful, strong fellow. Freydis thinks he is capable of putting the proud farm in order again.

For the present, he and his family move into the house of sacrifice. The young Eirik has to wait until Torgils is dead before taking over the longhouse and making all the changes he wants to make at Brattalid. Eirik's presence seems to reinvigorate Torgils a little.

But what can she do about Idunn? She needs to get away from Brattalid, especially since the youngest of the slaves Eirik has brought with him seems to have become infatuated with her. Idunn is now an attractive young woman of eighteen. So far, the slave has kept his distance, especially after being put sharply in his place by Freydis. The slaves still have respect for the daughter of the celebrated Eirik the Red. But what will happen when she is not around anymore?

Another thing is tormenting her. Whatever is she going to do about that golden serpent that she promised Torbjorg she would look after? The family legacy. She must make sure it is passed on to a relative, preferably a woman, the goddess said. It cannot be put off any longer.

Her thoughts churn, then freeze like the inland ice. She has nightmares. Wakes up imagining the serpent is coiled about her neck.

Her salvation comes from the sea. A trading ship from Iceland calls in to Gardar. Freydis is told it comes from Snaefellsnes on the west coast of Iceland, not far from where Birka lives. She senses with all her being that this is a sign.

She sends for the trader, Steinar Torvaldsson, owner of the vessel, and entertains him with the best fare she has to offer.

'Do you know my daughter Birka Torvardsdatter? She married Sigurd Sveinsson and lives at Snaefellsnes,' she asks the personable Icelander, who is tucking into the newly-roasted reindeer meat she has set before him.

'Yes, indeed, I know Birka. She's been a widow now for some years. She runs the farm with two slaves,' the trader says, and then turns to Eirik to discuss trade negotiations.

Oh, poor Birka! She must be lonely, Freydis thinks. After some reflection, she speaks again:

'Could you take Idunn to Iceland on your ship, and

leave her with Birka? I can pay you with gold jewellery.'

'Yes, that could be arranged. I'll pick her up in seven days' time.'

Idunn beams with delight when she learns what her grandmother has planned. She has heard so many good things about Iceland, and she has inherited Freydis's love of adventure. And perhaps her mother will be there.

Seven days. Now Freydis has her work cut out for her. Her granddaughter will not be going empty-handed. In addition to the chest filled with clothes, she packs tablecloths and odds and ends. She locates the remainder of her jewellery, including Torbjorg's ring with the great green stone and Akku's magic walrus tooth.

Lastly, she takes out Sverre's precious scabbard with its colourful stones and drawings. When she sees it, she cannot suppress a choking, rare burst of laughter. But the most important thing of all she will send Idunn with is the story of her life. Her saga. A saga she hopes Idunn and Birka will pass on to their descendants.

Freydis has a lot to say. Now it is all going to be out in the open.

'Come here and sit by me. I have to tell you a story,' she says to Idunn as she walks in carrying the water buckets that evening.

The girl stares at her grandmother in surprise; She looks so serious. But she complies.

'You must listen carefully. For I want you to tell all this to Birka when you see her. My daughter needs to know what my life has been. And not only my daughter. I want the whole of Iceland to hear my story. You will find there are many stories about our family. My father, my brother and myself, we are all well-known. But much of what people say is false. You will see to it that the truth is told.'

Idunn nods. The stories are not just about her great-grandfather. Freydis tells her about Tjodhild, her brothers, and in particular Leif Eiriksson, the great discoverer of Vinland. About Torbjorg and Ragni, about the men she has known, her children, the voyages to Vinland. Every afternoon and evening they sit by the hearth in the house till late at night.

Idunn drinks in every single word. She knows she will need it all later. It is she who must spread the family's history to the world.

It is only two days before Idunn leaves. Freydis can postpone it no longer. The damned golden serpent. What in the world is she to do with it? She cannot send it to Iceland with Idunn, she does not dare to. What if the World Serpent, who dwells in the depths of the sea, should discover it and attack? What if it makes Idunn and the crew ill and they are ship-wrecked? What if the Christians discover it? The Christians are afraid of serpents, too. Indeed, a serpent was accused of being responsible for the Fall and the expulsion from Eden, when it cunningly convinced Eve to get Adam to eat the fruit of the tree of knowledge in the garden of Eden.

This story is one of the few she recalls from her lesson with Oddmund the Priest in her youth. At that time, she had thought less about the serpent than about the tree of knowledge. The same concept exists in the world of the Norse gods: Yggdrasil. She had wondered if the tree was one and the same, and where it was located.

Now she comes to the conclusion that she is unwilling to expose Idunn and Birka to the potential curse of the serpent. At the same time, she cannot oppose Torbjorg, fail her family inheritance or disobey the command of the goddess.

She can see no alternative but to conceal the serpent somewhere in Greenland and tell Idunn where it is. Then she can pass it on to the next generation. Whatever happens later is beyond Freydis's control.

But where should she bury the casket containing the serpent?

The answer comes to her as she sits, eyes closed, on the stone by the beach where she sits to reflect. She counts the waves and lets the familiar salty tang of the ocean embrace her. And it all falls into place, everything is clear. She will bury it in Eirik the Red's grave, where her mother, Ragni, and her sister also lie. There could be no more powerful custodians than these.

She strolls over to the pagan grave mound where they lie, a peaceful spot with a good view of the fjord. The grass has grown back years since. No-one could see that this is the grave of a mighty chieftain and explorer, but for the raised stones.

Freydis sits down beside the grave and the tears well up. She thought she had no more tears to shed. Now she is convinced that this is the right place to bury the golden serpent. It is a safe place. Nobody will desecrate the grave of a chieftain. The people of

Greenland honour Eirik the Red and respect his gods, even though by now Greenland is mainly Christian.

She takes her horse to the cave where she concealed the serpent. As fast as she can, she packs the casket into the bag she has brought along and places it on the horse. Nausea surges through her body. The horse, too, seems upset by his burden. He snorts and neighs and tries to throw the bag off, but Freydis holds him firmly.

At last they reach the farm. She sneaks the bag in under a bench in the longhouse, while the horse, exhausted, lies down in the grass.

When everyone else on the farm has gone to bed, she steals out. She fetches the casket from its hiding place. As she expected, she feels nauseous again, and she quickly drops it in a bucket and throws a blanket over the top.

Fortunately, there is still a breath of summer in the air, and outside it is only twilight, so she finds her way easily. The power of the serpent is tangible as she creeps along to the burial site. She senses evil surge through her, and she feels an urge to vomit, but she resists it.

She must carry out the task she has been charged with.

She can hardly walk. She shoves the bucket ahead of her and crawls after it. Several times she is forced to lie down in order to summon up the last of her strength. The bucket stands a way off, as she begins to dig with the iron spade she has brought with her.

It takes a while. Her hands are stiff, cold and painful. They no longer do her bidding like in the old days. But she forces them to do their best. At last, the hole is big enough and deep enough. She has to cling to a rock in order to get to her feet again.

She bravely fights the waves of nausea as she settles the iron box in the hole. Then she shovels earth over it and finally tufts of grass, so there will be no sign that anyone has been digging there.

The rest of the night she sleeps heavily. When she is woken in the grey dawn by Idunn, she is a little confused. She has felt this way quite often recently. Sometimes she has fancied she was waking up in the Gardar longhouse, or in Leif's longhouse in Vinland, or in Akku's cave.

It takes her a moment before she recognises her own house at Brattalid, Tjodhild's old home. Her blood runs cold. Has she slept and not fulfilled her mission? Has she not buried the golden serpent? Did she just dream that?

She needs to be sure. The casket is not where she hid it, but she needs to go out and scramble up to Eirik the Red's grave. Clearly, someone has been digging here. Her attempts at disguising her efforts have not been as successful as she thought.

She must have buried the golden serpent. Of course she has! Now you are really losing your wits, Freydis, she scolds herself.

After breakfast, she takes Idunn to the grave.

'This is the grave of Eirik the Red. Ragni and Torbjorg lie here, too. Last night I buried the golden serpent, the legacy I received from Torbjorg Lillevolven. You must tell this to Birka. You must select a woman from the next generation to be the next custodian of the inheritance.'

Idunn sits quite still with clear, wide-open eyes, daunted by the duty being imposed upon her. Her eyes shine too at the important and honourable mission being entrusted to her, to carry on the inheritance: The knowledge of the serpent.

'You understand what I am saying to you,' Freydis says, her eyes boring into the young girl.

'Yes, grandmother. I will do as you say,' she pronounces firmly.

'Good.'

That is the last story Idunn gets to take with her.

The next day, a tall young girl in a fine blue dress with a thin brown plait down her back embarks on an Icelandic trading ship. She takes with her two chests and a slaughtered sheep to be shared with the ship's company.

In the larger of the two chests she has equipment and clothing, including a new red dress. In the smaller chest she has collected her valuables. She will need to take good care of it and of herself while on board the ship. Although Freydis trusts the ship-owner, there are others who appear less reliable. There are only three women on board, and the other two are slaves.

For this reason, Idunn has a knife attached to her

belt. It can be used both to cut up meat and to defend herself with, should that prove necessary.

And so Idunn sails out of Eiriksfjord for the last time. The sun highlights the soft hairs that have escaped from her plait. A day full of promise. The end of her life in Greenland, the beginning of a new life.

On the beach at Brattalid stands an emaciated woman with flowing long white hair and huge deep eyes. She is leaning on a staff. She grows smaller and smaller until she disappears and is seen no longer.

EPILOGUE

Greenland, the mouth of Eiriksfjord, the year 1080

The Greenlandic smallholders Bjarte and Einar are out fishing. The catch has been good, and their boat is almost full. But Bjarte glances towards the horizon. He looks worried. A huge menacing dark cloud is looming. Already the sea is splashing hard against the boat's sides. It's time to go back to land, he thinks.

He glances to the side. A cold shudder seizes his body when he sees a massive ice floe rushing towards him at full speed. He fears it will crash into his boat, but at the last minute it veers off and changes direction. He breathes a sigh of relief.

But just as the ice floe drifts past something catches his eye. Is there something lying there on the ice floe? Something red, shaped almost like a cross. A human being, a woman, lying on the ice with her arms stretched out? Incredulous, he shakes his head. He must have been mistaken. Quickly he turns to Einar to ask him. But before the two fishermen can study the ice floe again it has floated far out to sea.

They do not see that the ice floe with the woman on it circles around and around, with a steady course towards the merciless open sea. Nor do they see the dancing wavelets that follow in the wake of the ice floe, nor hear their song, almost rejoicing.

All at once it is silent on the sea. The lull before the storm. Bjarte and Einar turn the boat about and row as fast they can, heading towards land before the storm sets in.

They have just made it into coastal waters when a great flash of lightning lights up the dark-blue sky, quickly followed by a deafening clap of thunder. Then all the floodgates open and the rain pours down. Thor, blowing with all his might. The gods and nature in fierce competition, showing off their finest moves.

But suddenly, all is still again, the battle is over. The endless black sea lies there, glassy, deep, mysterious. Far in the distance the sea meets the light-grey sky.

The line. The edge of the world. Ginnungagap.

HISTORICAL NOTES

(The dates are estimated according to the sagas and my own imagination, Wikipedia, snl.no)

950: Eirik Torvaldsson The Red is born in Jaeren, Norway.

964: Eirik's father, Torvald Asvaldsson, kills people and moves to Iceland. Eirik accompanies him.

970: Eirik marries Tjodhild. They have three sons: Leif, Torvald and Torstein.

982: Eirik the Red is found guilty of murder. He is sentenced to stay away from Iceland for three years. He searches for a land to the West, allegedly seen by Gunnbjorn Ulvsson. He discovers Greenland, explores the country and builds a house up Eiriksfjord. The farmstead is called Brattalid.

983: Freydis is born in Greenland.

985: Eirik the Red returns to Iceland.

986: Twenty-five ships and three hundred people set sail for Greenland. Fourteen ships arrive.

998–1000: Leif Eiriksson sails to Norway and later discovers Vinland, where he builds a house and spends the winter.

1001: Freydis marries Torvard Einarsson and moves to Gardar. Gudrid marries Torstein Eiriksson (who dies young).

1002: Freydis's son Einar is born.

1003: New expedition to Vinland. Three ships set sail. One is commanded by Freydis and Torvard and her brother, Torvald. Eirik the Red dies.

1005: The Vinland explorers return. Torvald Eiriksson dies. Freydis loses a son.

1010: New expedition to Vinland.

1020: Leif Eiriksson dies.

1022: Torbjorg Lillevolven dies.

1024: Freydis's daughter Birka is born.

1031: Torvard Einarsson dies. Einar takes over Gardar, and Freydis moves back to Brattalid.

1041: Birka marries Sigurd and moves to Iceland.

1073: Einar dies. Idunn, his daughter by his concubine, remains with Freydis at Brattalid.

1080: Idunn sets sail for Iceland

POSTSCRIPTUM

We think we know a lot about the Viking age. But we don't. As Jón Vidar Sigurdsson writes in his book "Det norrøne samfunnet" (The Norse Society): 'The thing is that most of the history of the Viking community has become sediment in the sea of oblivion. Unfortunately.'

But it must be assumed that it was an era packed with incident. Ships of a revolutionary new design took the Norsemen all over the world, inspired by a spirit of discovery and the dream of a better life. But the Viking voyages also brought brutality and war in their wake.

Two of these expeditions culminated in the discovery and settlement of Greenland and later Vinland/America. These voyages are mentioned in Eirik the Red's saga and the Greenlanders' saga, where we meet Eirik the Red, the discoverer of Greenland, and his son Leif Eiriksson, the discoverer of Vinland.

There are ruins and other traces of Vikings in

several locations in Greenland. I myself have seen the stones that remain of what we assume was Brattalid, Eirik the Red's farm. Today, the place bears the name Qassiarsuk.

For a long time, nobody knew where Vinland was. Not until the Norwegian explorer Helge Ingstad followed the sagas and Leif Eiriksson's descriptions of the course he followed on his journey to Vinland. He sailed north along the coast of Greenland, then set a westerly course and came to a land, whose coast he followed in a southerly direction. He found places which recalled Leif Eiriksson's Helluland and Markland – Baffin Island and Labrador in Canada.

Then he reached Newfoundland's most northerly point, L'Anse aux Meadows. He thought the landscape resembled the place where the Vinland explorers settled, according to the descriptions that were known. Here he found some ramparts reminiscent of those he had seen in Greenland.

Encouraged by the archaeologist Anne Stine Ingstad, his wife, he began to undertake archaeological excavations. These were conducted over a number of years and revealed much evidence of the presence of Vikings. During the last week of the last summer in which excavations were conducted, the proof was found – a bronze ring pin from the Viking Age.

What we think we now about the Viking Age relies heavily on sagas which were often composed two or three centuries after the events. The stories have been passed down orally from generation to generation.

The sagas were usually written by priests. There is every reason to believe that they did not always describe those who swore allegiance to the Norse gods in the most favourable way.

How historically accurate the sagas are is debatable. And yet they are a cornucopia of thrilling tales which have inspired many writers, including myself, to develop them further.

The central characters in my novel, Eirik the Red, Tjodhild and their three sons Leif, Torvald and Torstein, are mentioned in the sagas, as is Freydis. Those also mentioned include Gudrid Torbjornsdatter, Torfinn Karlsevne, Bjarne Grimolvsson, Torvard Einarsson, Torgils Leifsson, Torgunna, Torbjorg Lillevolven, and the brothers Helge and Finboge.

Freydis's other lovers, her children and grandchildren, the slaves and other main characters are the product of my imagination.

As well as the two sagas, I found inspiration in the work of newer writers, especially Vera Henriksen's books about the life of women in the Viking Age.

Some stories were borrowed from other sagas. These include the story of the theft of Odin's sword. A similar tale is found in the saga which recounts the dramatic love story of Kjartan and Gudrun Osvivsdatter, who lived in Iceland around Freydis's time.

It is assumed that women enjoyed greater freedom under the rule of the Norse gods that they did after the introduction of Christianity. Yet the sagas are mainly concerned with men. They were also written by men and interpreted by men. Very few sagas have a female principal protagonist.

The presentation of women is also stereotypical, as for example the two most prominent women in the sagas about the Vikings in Greenland, Gudrid and Freydis. Gudrid sings magical incantations which conjure up pagan spirits, she is married three times and possibly has a relationship with a fourth man before her second husband is in his grave. Nonetheless, Gudrid is presented as a devout woman according to Christian precepts. Could this possibly be because she was the ancestress of several Icelandic bishops?

Freydis is the personification of evil. She encourages battle, she slays people, she marries Torvard for his wealth, and so on. But in one scene she is depicted as a heroine, when she bares her breasts and rubs them with a sword, a sight which strikes fear into the hearts of the attacking skraelings and scares them off.

My curiosity was piqued by Freydis, Leif Eiriksson's sister, who reputedly led two expeditions to Vinland. Who was she? We shall never know. Regardless, I felt that Freydis deserved a saga of her own.

ACKNOWLEDGMENTS

A book never comes into being without the help and inspiration of others. Thank you to my closest family and good friends, who have put up with the fact that at times I have lived more in the world of books than in the real world. Thanks to my friends Tone and Siw and my husband Brynjar, who have read the work in progress and made helpful comments.

Thanks to my professional advisers, especially Jón Vidar Sigurdsson, Professor of History, whose knowledge of the historical situation and life in Greenland a thousand years ago was invaluable.

Thanks to my Norwegian editor, Anne-Kristin Strøm, from former publishing house Juritzen for excellent co-operation and for her determined efforts to ensure that the manuscript appeared in the best possible shape.

A lot of people have helped me giving birth to the English edition of the saga about Freydis Eiriksdatter.

Thanks to all of you, not least the very experienced and inspirational translator Jennifer Kewley Draskau. Thanks also to talented and enthusiastic Alexandra Lyngstad for thorough proofreading and editing. Linn Tesli has made a fantastic cover, which I am very pleased with, and she has also contributed a lot of good advice. You are the best helpers I could get.

Thanks also to a large number of others who have helped me with small and large bringing the English edition to life, not least several active members in the "Indieforfatterforum" on Facebook.

I received many delightful responses to my novels in Norwegian, from bloggers, the media, other authors and especially from ordinary readers. This meant a great deal to me. It inspired me to continue writing, to continue to indulge my delight in storytelling. I owe you everything.

Gunhild Haugnes, the author
Norway, 2019

Made in United States
North Haven, CT
23 October 2025